Books, Pens & Larceny

By
J. F. NODAR

ISBN 978-0-6453014-0-3 (print)

ISBN 978-0-6453014-1-0 (large print)

ISBN 978-0-6453014-2-7 (Kindle)

ISBN 978-0-6453014-3-4 (E-pub)

ISBN 978-0-6453014-4-1 (audiobook)

About This Book

I started writing this book on a lark after writing a short story that is included in 'Stories to Share with My Partner – Book 1' and before I knew it another chapter brood in my mind and then another.

My goal in retirement was to travel as much as possible with the small funds I had been able to save prior to my retirement when several life changing events occurred which threw a spanner in the works as the cliché goes and it put a quick damper on the travel goals.

Confined to a hospital bed for over 120 days in 2020-2021 and then COVID-19 lockdowns in Sydney further confined me and my wife to walking around the neighbourhood and waving at the many neighbours we found in our daily walks.

With my energy building up daily and my mind wondering about the short story mentioned above other short stories sprung up and before I knew it, I was writing this small novel.

During all these events mentioned I had one vision in mind – to be with my wife – who had also gone through a perilous moment in her life months before me as well – in some paradise beach. It is her love that made everything worthwhile and keep me going so this small effort is totally dedicated to her – my Red!

I hope you enjoy this book and if you have any comments, please email me at info@jfnodar.com.au and I will respond in 24 hours. Promise.

Thank you for your support and once again, enjoy!

Contents

INTRODUCTION

I have been told that stories should start with a quick explanation of who is telling the story, a quick view of their life and how they got where they are today. I have also been told that I should detail who is their antagonist, what they are trying to achieve, their love interests, their friends and, of course, a fantastic opening.

In my case, I can say that my life was very pleasant growing up in Northport, a small village in New South Wales, (NSW) Australia. Northport is about 80 kilometres southwest of Sydney and has a small population of around 7,300, according to the last census. My family was a middle-class family. My father worked in the local hardware store *Williamson's* and my mother worked as a librarian at the Northport Library on Mavis Street. I led the idyllic life in rural NSW and had a mostly uneventful childhood. After finishing high school, I started university with the initial career thought of architecture. However, while I did okay in high school and university, I knew after taking the first course that I was not an architect at heart. Instead, I found out that I enjoyed the retail world.

To help with the expenses of going to the university, my mum got me in touch with Mr Hebert McCullum, owner of the *McCullum Booksellers* who hired me as a part-time retail salesperson, shelf stocker and general all-rounder. This part-time job, being around books, made my career choice a str aightforward one and so I changed my degree to a Bachelor's in Fine Arts from Architecture.

During all this time, my mum continued to work at the library while my father continued working at the hardware store and both kept asking me when I was going to 'settle down.' I dated in high school and while at university, but the 'true love of my life' has not popped into my biography. So, I kept my nose to the books and my job with Mr McCullum before finally making my most ambitious move, going into business.

Working at the *McCullum Booksellers* was a great daily experience, as I found out from day one. Mr McCullum decided that the primary service of the store was the retail sale of stationery, such as office supply paper and paper products, and paper novelties. This was a successful business in the early days for Mr McCullum. As the internet took off and the old status quo of retail changed, Mr McCullum decided not to combat the electronic warriors and instead put the business up for sale.

Thus, my entry into the full retail business world as a store owner took place. Taking a little of the inheritance that I had received from my parents from the sale of their home when they passed, I plunged right in, unaware of the many pitfalls in the retail world. Previously in my part-time position with Mr McCullum, I only worried about stocking the shelves, dusting a bit, making sure the place looked tidy before opening the store, serving the customers, and then helping him close the store. Now I had to worry not only about what I have already mentioned and add to this everything else, which was quite an eye-opening experience. All of which also had long hours associated with it.

To accomplish my aspiration in retail, I wrote a decent business plan that integrated an online business part and sold both bestsellers and antiquarian books. The best sellers came directly from several publishing houses and some distributors, my favourite being the *Northport Booksellers*, where I get excellent books from local Northport authors. The antiquarian books came from my parent's home library, which I had kept after realising that there was a small fortune in the collection of books they had acquired over many years.

Borrowing money from the local bank branch was difficult because bankers loved to lend millions and I did not ask for much. However, taking pity on me and realising they had nothing to lose since the loan collateral was enough to cover the loan, the bankers approved it, and I launched my new business owner's career.

I decided that keeping Mr McCullum's stationary stock would be an asset since folks always needed a quick pen or ream of paper when the deliveries from the large box store arrived late.

So, on the most massive rear wall of the store, I display, in several beautiful mahogany bookcases, my parent's extensive collection of unique and antique books of all genres and the ones I continue to add from deceased estates as soon as I find them. On the left side of the store, I carry all the latest paperback and hardback best sellers and a good mixture of other genres. I left the right side of the store to carry Mr McCullum's legacy of all the small office supply necessities, such as pens, and paper reams of various sizes and an excellent selection of postcards and birthday cards.

The centre of the store was bland when Mr McCullum owned it, but that changed when I bought the business. It now has several lounges and large comfortable chairs where customers can sit and grab a book and flip through it, thus helping in their decision to purchase the said book. I never rush them. At the front of the store is my counter where I have a small cash register and my store software tablet using the latest version of *Shopkeep* which is a blessing for keeping up with inventory and prices and ensuring that all online purchases go out the very next day to my customers. This counter is about three metres long and here is where I sit and purvey my little kingdom. My throne is my advantage point in the entire store since I can visually watch the store using the six cameras I had installed or the old peepers that I inherited from my mother.

The final decision was to either keep or change the name of the store. My two options were to either keep Mr McCullum's name on the store or start with a fresh new name. I chose the latter and thus, *Village Books & Stuff* was born.

Most knew me as Mr Monk, but my friends called me Danny. Okay, I am not a Brad Pitt type, but I thought of myself as a 'good plain' type of man. Carrying a fairly solid body of seventy-seven kilos and standing at 184cm I think I look physically OK. Bearing a well-manicured face that highlights my twice a day shaving hard beard that I inherited from my father with brown eyes, mahogany brown hair with exceedingly preliminary stages of grey but overall, not too bad.

I have been in business now for a little over three years and have seen how hard it is to make a living in the retail world. With no employees (both a blessing and a curse), the store demands a lot of my life, leaving only the evenings available for relaxation. I have even considered taking up a part-time occupation of some sort to make ends meet, but I have not stumbled upon that perfect occupation since the hours I keep do not fit into anything I have found.

My store is nestled between the local optometrist, *For Your Eyes Only Optical*, owned and operated by Dr. Frank Freeman and *Northport Dental Smiles*, part of a large Australia wide franchise and operated as a company store, I find their proximity to my store fantastic since many of their clients wander in sometimes to browse before or after their treatments. A few doors down from my little store is the premier hair salon in Northport, *Cut Me Crazy*, owned and operated by Albert Matthew Guzman, going on his sixteenth anniversary.

Albert is an institution in the whole of Sydney. He has established a reputation for offering the best hairstyles through the hard work of his eighteen-person crew, all individually trained by Albert. This eye for perfection has made *Cut Me Crazy* the envy of all hair salons in Sydney. His ten chairs are always full of prominent citizens from Sydney, the local area, local and national politicos, and celebrities, all of them wanting to be pampered by Albert's staff.

Standing at 173 cm tall, Albert is slender, with a weight of just 69 kilos, perfectly coiffed blond hair, and the most beautifully manicured hands to rival Cleopatra. His blue eyes resemble the ocean and what truly marks him as unique is, of course, his outfits.

Albert was the first to welcome me to Mr McCullum's employment and even tried to recruit me as an apprentice. While his recruitment failed, our friendship blossomed over the years and when I bought the business even more with words of encouragement and financial advice.

So, my days are pretty normal, mostly. Customers come, browse, some buy, some do not and repeat for six days a week. Monday through Friday, my store is open from 10 AM until 6 PM. On Thursday, I do a late-night trading hour until 7:30 PM while on Saturday my schedule is shorter. I open at the same time, 10:00 AM but close a little earlier at 3:00 PM. Nothing really exciting but now this is where my story goes a little wild for it was the day, I received extra special financial advice from Albert which I will never forget.

The story goes that on that special day (it was a Tuesday by the way at 8:30 AM to be exact) a local politico was raving to Albert that in the back of his car he had this little square slab of white marble only 63.5 cm X 57 cm from the late Roman-Byzantine Era, circa 300-830 CE and inscribed with 20 lines of Paleo-Hebrew characters rendered in the Samaritan dialect. He tells Albert; 'Albert, today I acquired a wonderful object d'art and I have it neatly wrapped in the boot of my car. Do you have any idea what the slab containing the Mosaic Ten Commandments in the form used by the Samaritans is worth?'

Albert smiled and responded; 'You make it sound valuable. How much do you think it is worth?' 'To the right buyer,' spoke the politician, 'At least $4,800,000,' 'So, I am celebrating before I deliver this gem to my buyer. I want the complete deluxe treatment today, starting with the finest hair shampoo, some colouring to get rid of these pesky grey hairs, both a manicure and a pedicure, and the best cut Felicia or Miguel can do for me.'

'That should take only four to five hours. How are you for time?' asks Albert. 'No problem, my dear boy. Today I have all the time in the world!' quips the politician.

Knowing that the politico will be 'out-of-pocket' for at least that time and armed with this bit of information, Albert goes into his office, gently closes his door, and dials the phone. After twenty minutes, Albert comes up with a plan but needs someone to execute it and who do you think he thought would be interested in an 'acquisition opportunity.' Yes, you guessed right.

Albert walks into my store at 10:04 AM (yes, I remember the exact moment) because my security system, my little doorbell always rings and tells me when someone has entered or departed the store, tingles and I glanced at the wall clock: 10:04 AM. Albert waltzes in, turns my little 'We Are Open' sign to the 'We Are Closed' position and says, 'Danny dear, you always wanted to buy this building and pay off that nasty business loan of yours, correct?'

The first thing I notice is today's outfit. The outfit is a dawn shade tuxedo looking suit that has a slim fit metallic floral suit jacket, white shirt, and black bow tie and, do not ask me why, leather flats Latin ballroom swing dance shoes. Only Albert can get away with such a combobulate ensemble.

'That is correct, Albert. All I have to do is win the Lotto, and I will buy the building!'

'What if you could buy the building, have a little money left over and not have to win the Lotto? How would you like to earn $1,250,000 in a matter of minutes? Buy your building, have a little money left over and start a new career in the arena of 'acquisitions?' What do you say to that?'

My mind spun in a million ways upon hearing Albert's question. 'What do you mean, Albert?'

Albert leaned a little closer to me, even though there was no one in my store and he had already locked the front door. Albert continued: 'My darling boy, you know that I have been watching you struggle these past few years trying to make a success of this cute little business endeavour you got yourself into and I admire the persistent effort that you employ. However, retail is hard, I know, and in my younger years, such a long time ago, I had to source other avenues of revenues to ensure that my passion, *Cut Me Crazy*, would stand for many years.'

I listen to Albert with intense attention. We had previous conversations before about our businesses and the different struggles we both had, but never had Albert mentioned he had looked for other sources of revenue.

'Albert, tell me,' I said, 'How are you going to get me $1,250,000?'

'Easy, my sweet. You and I are going into the 'acquisitions business' starting immediately!'

'Acquisitions, what do you mean?' I asked Albert.

'Oh, grasshopper, you have so much to learn,' chuckles Albert. He then takes me through the stockroom towards the back door of my store, opens it and points to a silver CLS Mercedes in the rear parking lot and slowly closes the door and we retreat to my stockroom.

'Danny, sweetness, when we went outside, you might have noticed that there are no cameras in any of the buildings surrounding the parking lot. You may or may not have noticed that the Mercedes CLS had an onboard camera that is most likely sensor sensitive, so if anyone goes within one metre of the vehicle the alarm will start unless you have turned it off first. Did you notice those points?' Albert asks me, profoundly serious.

'Well, no, I did not notice any of those points, but what does that have to do with me?'

'Oh, Danny boy.' Albert sings in a low pitch voice imitating an Irishman and stops abruptly and says: 'OK, Danny boy; you are going to break into that car's boot and acquire a little slab of marble that lies there.'

My mind raced at the words that Albert spoke out. I now realise what the 'acquisition business' that Albert infers is. Plain thievery, burglary or whatever the NSW police call it, that was the new 'opportunity' that Albert was offering.

'Danny boy; you are much younger than I am and able to handle the stress that comes with this line of business, whereas I have a lot of connections and knowledge that can benefit both of us. Are you able to join me in this venture?'

My thought process arrives at two points; first, $1,2500,000 coming into my hands is a temptation that I cannot resist and second; I can do this, so I answer Albert's question: 'Yes, I am. How much time do I have?'

'Wonderful darling. Let's see, first, the client started on a manicure and pedicure so that is about two hours almost spent, leaving us about another one hundred and thirty-eight minutes before the owner of the car drives away with our money.'

Albert reaches into his suit pocket for a large plastic bag: 'Here, take this fake beard and moustache, you might need them.' Says Albert as he walks to my front door, unlocks it, and leaves my little sign in the 'We Are Closed' position and leaves my store. I go over and lock the front door and looked at my watch; 10:18 AM. Time left, according to Albert: one hundred and thirty-eight minutes.

Remembering the title of a book in the mahogany bookcase, I walked over to the bookshelf and extracted *Terahertz Frequency Detection and Identification of Materials and Objects'* by R. E. Miles, which, by the way, you may purchase for $189.50 and I head to the stockroom out of sight from the store window. A detailed, but quick, research of frequency detection told me enough to know what I needed to do to avert the alarm system on the Mercedes CLS.

Taking out my own car keyless entry key, I open the back of it, find the appropriate wires and fiddle with it, hoping that my reading of the book's information is correct and when I walk to the car, I hope all hell does not break loose.

Time 12:08 PM. Time left: twenty-two minutes.

Quickly, I returned to my counter. I took out the bag from the rubbish bin and went to the back of the store, where I found a couple smaller rubbish bins and empty the contents into the bag. As Albert suggested, I put on the fake beard and moustache and opened the rear door.

There is no one around, so I walk over to the rubbish dumpster, lift the lid, and place the bag inside as I watch for anyone who might be out and about, knowing that it is now or never. I walk as close to the car as I can, so the camera does not detect me, and push my car's key entry button.

That little 'beep, beep' that you hear when your car welcomes you comes out of the Mercedes, and I push the boot button and as if by magic, the boot pops open. I glance at my watch; 12:24 PM, cutting it close. I look inside the boot and see what appears to be the slab of marble wrapped in a cloth. I grabbed it. Close the boot softly, then I press the button to lock the car, hurry back to my back door and close it. I take the wrapped small parcel and place it under my counter.

My heart was pounding. It felt like it was about to come out of my chest. I felt like fainting. 'What a rush!' I think aloud to myself.

Later that afternoon Albert told me that at precisely 12:46 PM a well-groomed gentleman walked out of the *Cut Me Crazy* hair salon turned left, stopped, and looked at my display of stationery and books on display while admiring himself in my window and after a minute or two, continues his walk to the end of the block and turned into the back parking lot and drove off. So, I even had time to spare, I thought.

Close to 1 PM I see Albert walking by, stopping in front of my display window, running his hand through his hair, and looking at me. I give him what had to be a stupid grin and a thumbs up. Albert smiles and does the funny hand sign that he will call me and reverses his course back to his shop, as if he did not have a care in the world.

As if on schedule, Albert rings me telling me to be at my shop at 6 PM (hey, I close at 6 PM, so where would I be?), I thought to myself. A few minutes after 6 PM I see Albert, who somehow finds time to change his outfit, with an elderly gentleman wearing a yarmulke holding a large briefcase and a satchel over his shoulder at my door to which I quickly unlock.

Locking the front door without saying a word, Albert gestures to me to bring out our 'acquisition' to the rear stock room, which I lay gently on a stack of boxes containing best sellers yet to be placed on the shelves. The man gingerly picks up the slab, looks over the piece, reads and mumbles at the Paleo-Hebrew characters, nods to Albert. The man then hands the briefcase to Albert, takes the small tile, places it in the satchel, shakes our hands and walks to the front of the store where I promptly open the door for him, and I watch the man wearing the yarmulke as he walks out of my life.

Not a word is spoken.

Locking the door again, I walked back to the stock room and find Albert with a grin that would make the Cheshire cat envious. Albert has the briefcase open, showing it full of stacks of neatly bundled $100 bills. A quick count and we have $2,500,000 as agreed, which Albert has separated into two neat and equal piles.

'My dear Danny, as promised, your share!'

I will say to the reader that becoming a thief/burglar or whatever the right terminology used by the NSW police was never my goal in life. I just wanted to make a reasonable living in my little store, save a little of money and eventually retire with a few funds for the occasional holiday. My new 'partnership' with Albert

Matthew Guzman proved to me two things; one, it was a lot easier to steal than I thought, and two; it was fun.

If my mother could see what I did, she would roll in her grave, God rest her soul, while my dad would be so proud, the wonderful bastard.

'Danny darling, I am sure you will now be able to buy the building and have a little left over, not much, but enough to be a bit more comfortable. Do you feel we could work together in these types of activities in the future?' questions Albert.

I glanced at Albert as he stood there in what I can only describe as a confetti suit: yellow background, polka dots, a jacket with padded shoulders and notch lapels. Top this with matching pants and a dark navy shirt, matching polka-dot tie, and Albert was ready to be the life of any party.

'Albert, I genuinely believe this will be the start of a wonderful relationship. I am so grateful for the introduction.'

A JOYFUL CAREER

We can make a bit more money', quip Albert, as he drinks his Evian bottle of water while leaning on the counter of my little store, the *Village Books & Stuff*.

Today Albert walks into my store wearing a notch lapel collar blazer in a floral blue with an open collar black shirt and pants and sandals. Quite spiffy, I thought.

'Danny, I did some research, and these baseball cards are worth $8,500,000.'

'You have got to be kidding!' I responded.

'Darling, you know so little about baseball cards, do you not? For example, the Honus Wagner 1909-1911 ATC T206 is valued at $2,820,000 alone. We grab just this one, and we are in the black for the year. We might be able to retire.' A smiling Albert states.

'Albert, I know little of baseball, so cards would be out of the question,' slight aback at Albert's saying 'we.'

A short while back, Albert introduced me to a whole new world outside the retail one in which we both live every day. A small trip to the back-car park of our stores and in a matter of minutes, we had hit the mother lode of 'acquisitions', as Albert loves to call them. Yes, Albert says we are by day humble retailers, Albert with his hair salon and I with my bookstore and by night, as distasteful as it is when you say aloud, we are burglars, well at least I am.

You see, Albert is the one that seems to find new opportunities for our acquisitions and now it seems it is going to be baseball cards, but it is I who puts his neck on the line, and if caught, I get to spend some time at the Emu Plains Correctional Facility courtesy of the State of NSW. This prospect, however, does not deter me from continuing the conversation.

'OK, Albert, tell me a bit more. I am intrigued.'

Sipping a mouthful of water and making sure we were alone in the store, Albert continued his story; 'Danny, thirty of the most valuable baseball cards are now in one hardwood display case and simply hanging on a wall. And this case is hanging inside the home of Mr and Mrs Michael Addington, the owners of Kusto Coal and Mining, who live right here in our fair city in the little suburb of Leichhardt. You are following me so far, Danny?'

I nodded, still waiting for the 'opportunity,' to come up in the conversation and then Albert lets me in his surprise; 'My sweet Danny, how this Australian couple came to gain this fantastic baseball card collection. I am not informed. I am aware, however, that a certain millionaire from Alabama is keen to have them all, and he has put out the word that he is offering a kingly sum of AU$4 million for it. No questions asked?'

'How do you know this, Albert?'

'Sources, sweetie, I have lots and lots of sources,' smiling he says. I asked a few more questions and Albert informs me that Felicia, who does hair styling at his salon, is well 'acquainted' with Mrs Hermione Addington and knows that the Addington's will be out of their home this weekend.

This fact and the subsequent knowledge acquired later through research told me I did not need to walk out with the display case since the cards were all graded, I found out that 'graded' meant the cards were in small individual casings generally called a mini snap card holder which is made of high impact, crystal clear polystyrene and feature a precision fit, two-piece snap design, hence the name–snap card. Most collectors use this product to protect, store and display collectible trading cards like baseball cards, NRL rugby cards, basketball cards, and others, which made it a cinch of an opportunity. Again, the prospect of a long-term residential tenure at the Emu Plains Correctional Facility did not phase me.

Upon closing my store with a simple twist of the wrist I flip the 'We Are Open' sign to the 'We Are Closed' position, lock the front door and I do a quick perusal of the store noting that all is in place for the next Monday morning. I head to the back of the store, turn off the store's lights, leaving just the two display windows lit, and I turn on the alarm system and walk upstairs to prepare.

A quick nap to rest up for the evening's activity and, upon awakening, a shower, followed by preparing my evening outfit. A black pair of jeans with a black turtle long sleeve t-shirt, black socks, and black moccasins. Yes, I still call them moccasins. Cannot help myself. I then go to the kitchen, where I fix up a light evening meal consisting of pastrami with Dijon mustard with a kosher pickle. I bought the pickles from one of the membership large box stores that decided that Northport would be a fantastic place to launch their invasion of Australia. I add a bottle of Evian water. Albert has me hooked now, some potato chips, and this would be the extent of my evening meal tonight. I tune in to the television to catch up on the world news and casually eat my sandwich while I wait for the appointed hour of eleven PM for Albert to call me from the car park out back.

At exactly 11:10 PM, Albert calls my mobile (he is always late); 'Darling, I am waiting in the car park. Come on. Chop, chop. Fun awaits.'

So, I place the plate in the kitchen sink, the bottle in the recycle bin, leave the lights and the TV on, pick up my laptop bag and place my small bum bag around my waist in which I will place the baseball cards in, and I go out my back door, down the steps into Albert's car.

Driving to Leichhardt after 11 PM should not take longer than one hour, since traffic should be modest at this time of the evening along the M5. Albert is not your usual partner in crime. Compared to my quite dark clothing, Albert has decided that he should be dressed like a Ninja warrior meets a cat burglar. He had a tight black outfit that one of the action Ninja warriors would wear in a Jackie Chan movie, but it also included a mask that made him look more like a Halloween partygoer than a criminal. I guess if the police stopped us on the way to Leichhardt, we could have said that we were going to a costume party and would most likely they would have believed us. At least he was not wearing the mask while driving.

'By the way, Albert, where did you get this car?'

'This old thing? Long story short. Felicia's cousin knows a guy who knows a guy that was trying to get rid of it and was willing to part from it for a little money. I paid $3,000 cash for it and I figure we can get rid of it once we accomplish our activity at the Addington's.'

'Makes sense, Albert. You know how to get rid of a car?'

'Yes,' was his one paragraph answer. Then he went silent, which suited me fine, for I needed to think what information Albert had gleam from Felicia since she had been to the Addington's mansion before.

So, I visualise the house and think back to Albert's description. 'Danny, sweetness, let me tell you about the house. This is a period double storey and double-fronted house. They are now the hottest residential property category in Sydney's inner city at the moment. These large and wide homes are on track to achieve extremely soaring prices for their owners if they decide to sell because of their scarcity and the strong interest they attract from competing buyer groups. In the current market, newly renovated double-fronted houses in excellent locations are almost always listed with $2 million-plus expectations. Some, especially free-standing double-fronters and semi-detached houses on large blocks, are commanding considerably more money than this. The new money coming into the inner city is offering $2 million to $3 million for these high-quality inner-city houses, sweetie, and buyers pay even more if the house goes to auction, which many do,' said Albert.

I remember asking Albert if he had given up the hair business and gone into the real estate business. He laughed and said, 'Precious, I need to know a lot about everything with my class of clientele.'

At 11:48 PM we arrive at the Addington's and park about ten houses away.

The house was exactly like Albert had described it to me. Before I open the passenger door, Albert asks; 'Danny, will you be able to get into the place? As I mentioned before, the house is a double-storey double-fronted house with the main entrance is in the middle of the house, well-lit with windows on both sides, in a beautiful symmetrical arrangement around the entrance. The Addington's always leave the house well-lit and turn on their alarm system when they leave on holiday. This weekend they gave both the house cleaner and the butler the weekend off. I hope Felicia is right with her intel.'

'Well Albert, if the intel you received from Felicia about their Adecco Link Cyber system model 4528 is correct, it means the system has a main control console containing a keypad, sounder, circuit board and backup battery. Doors, windows, CCTV, and motion sensors connect wirelessly to the main console. All I have to do is hack into the wireless network and disable the system. To do this, I need to be near the house.'

'Have you figured out how to get in, Danny?'

'Yes, I have. I believe so. I will use an online search engine called veryangryip.org to see if I can access the default manufacturer's password and disable the system and the CCTV cameras. If this does not work, I will then try another system called shadowsys.io and that should be it. One of these two will work and I should be able to disable the security system. We just need to get close, but not too close to be seen by the CCTV cameras and I can use the cracking software. Let us get started.'

So, like two dark shadows, we walk toward the Addington's' house and cut through the neighbour's side gate, as Felicia suggested. The neighbour made our life so easy in two ways: first no dogs and second with a low height fence which we, well, I, climbed easily and had to give Albert some help. Once on the grounds of the Addington's we got as close to the house as possible, hiding behind some very tall juniper skyrocket bushes. We waited a few minutes before I took my laptop out and with the screen light dim as much as possible, I started accessing the first search engine. What seemed like an eternity but actually was fourteen minutes and a lot of algorithms formulations. I hit on the default password for the Adecco Link Cyber system and disable the system.

Time 12:23 AM.

Now to pick the back patio door, which should be easier. I put on my gloves when I glance at Albert.

'Albert, you really do not need the mask, you know. You are staying here in the bushes while I go in. The security cameras are offline but only until the security company sends someone. So, hang tight and I will be back shortly.' As I hand him my laptop; 'Albert, as soon as I get out and join you, push this button on the laptop. Just wait until I join you in the bushes, OK?'

A serious Albert simply nods and I start running towards the patio door, I take less than a minute to pick the lock. Then I hurry to Mr Addington's master bedroom (yes, they have separate bedrooms and I do not need to know why), and I find the baseball cards hanging on the wall in the glass display case, just like Felicia had told Albert. Taking the glass case down, I open the case from the back, quickly stuff the mini snap card holders into my bum bag and place the now-empty case back on the wall. I check my watch; 12:31 AM, time to go.

I run downstairs and go out the same way I entered, lock the door, and rush over to Albert. As soon as I reach the bushes, Albert, as instructed, pushes the laptop button and the security system is activated. We wait in silence and at 12:33 AM, we notice the arrival of the security car. The car stops and the security guard comes toward the house. Ten minutes is not a bad response time, not as good as the police, but it will do for a security company. Mr and Mrs Addington will probably review their security company services after this weekend.

A quick walk around the house by the guard, who does not even venture a look at the back yard, then I notice he uses a walkie-talkie and reports the 'all clear' back to his office and climbs into his car and departs. We wait for another ten minutes and then we exfiltrate back to our car the same way we got there, and it is like we were not even there.

My second acquisition, pardon, our second acquisition, was a success from my point of view.

Albert set a meeting up for later in the week with the buyers' representative. A quick exchange of the cards for a leather case filled with $100 bills completed the transaction.

Later Albert, contacts his 'friendly distributor' who contacts our 'new banker' and somehow our $4 million has been reduced to $3 million (Albert calls them a 'finder's fee for Felicia and transaction and setup fees by the distributor) but when you think of it, we each walk away with $1,500,000 tax-free into our respective Nives bank accounts where our retirement funds are now held, so I am not complaining.

Maybe this is all the incentive we need to retire?

Perhaps it all stops here?

Maybe we will retire today, but somehow, I do not think so. After all, I am having too much fun.

Why would I quit a career that brings me joy?

Would you!

WE'VE BEEN HAD

I am sitting behind my sales counter reading a book on a branch of pathology, *'Canine and Feline Cytology; A Colour Atlas and Interpretation Guide'* by Rose Rankin available for sale for $197 and the door opens and in walks for the first time this young woman that I can only describe as striking. She walks in wearing a dress shirt and it is tucked into a high-waisted pants, a long chain dangling with her sunglasses in her hands. Not stunning because of her beauty, which she is, but in her presence. She is about 165 cm, with silky, confident auburn hair. Her face does not show one blemish, and it immediately draws you to her almond-shaped wet stone eyes. Her inviting, wonderfully sultry moist lips just seem to beckon you and with a wonderful shape that shows that she enjoys mild exercise to help herself tone up.

'Good morning,' I say. 'How may I help you?'

'Hi. I was wondering if you by chance have *The Motorcycle Diaries'* by Ernesto 'Che' Guevara?'

'One moment let me look it up on my computer,' as I type in the title and find that I do have the title for a price of $660.

'Why yes, I do. It is in the first edition section at the back of the store. Let me walk you there.'

As I lead her to the rear of the store, I can smell a flowery sense emitting from her as if I am in a misty field of green. Goodness. Concentrate, Danny - you got a book to sell. You are not here to meet women, although I cannot help but notice she has no ring.

'Here is the book,' I said, opening the secure case. I handed her the book to inspect. 'It is a hardcover first edition published by Verso in the United Kingdom in 1995 in an exceptionally excellent condition, as you can see.'

'Oh, it looks wonderful. How much did you say are you selling it for?'

'I priced it at $660.' I answer.

'Oh, a bit more than I wanted to pay. Can you move a bit on the price?' the beauty asks.

No, I am sorry that is the going price. I cannot go any lower, I thought to myself. What type of businessperson I would be if every time a beautiful woman walks in and asks for a better price and I give it to her? My mother did not raise a dummy.

'I tell you what. I will let you have it for $500.'

Oh my, I raised a dummy, my mother would say.

'Excellent. I will take it. Thank you for the great reduction in price.'

'Not a problem. Please let me take the book and put it in a bag for you.' As I walked back to the front counter, I heard the front doorbell system tinkle, notifying me of another client and when I looked, I saw it was only Albert.

'Good morning, Danny, how is it going in the book sales business?'

'Be right with you, Albert. One second, please.'

I quickly place the book in a bag and ask the young lady how she would like to pay. She hands me a VISA card. I cannot fail to notice her name, Alessia Vassallo.

'Would that be debit or credit, Miss Vassallo?'

'Credit, please,'

I run the card through the machine. I wait one second and then see 'approved' on the screen and hand her the card and hand her the bag along with her receipt.

'Thank you for your purchase, Miss Vassallo. Please do return. You are always welcome here.' Damn, what a stupid thing to say. Thank you for your purchase, Miss Vassallo would have been enough—not all the rest—what a jerk.

'Oh, you read my name on the card. You now have me at a disadvantage Mr…'

'Monk. Daniel Monk, but my customers call me Danny.'

'In that case, so will I. Thank you, Danny, and please call me Alessia. Here is my personal card. Bye.'

Alessia Vassallo.

Head Librarian

Northport Library

Northport, NSW. Australia 2570.

+610246345555.

And with that, I watch her go out the front door and I place the card in my top drawer.

Albert has stood there watching the entire scene and finally says; 'Oh my, someone has been bitten!'

Albert, as always, is in his splendour. Today, Albert is wearing a white button-down shirt emblazoned with parrots and pineapples. Maintaining this South Pacific theme he has a bright blue matching jacket, trousers, and a tie. This outfit is perfect for, let us say, Melbourne Cup Day and is something not too many men could pull off, but Albert can and does, down to the matching tie.

A successful salon owner staffed by an ensemble of talented hairdressers, Albert's job has been to ensure his clientele is treated like the kings and queens they believe they are. Thus, he is kept busy but still comes into my small store for our daily morning tête-à-tête, as he calls it.

'My selling is going as your hair clippings go; down. That was the first sale of the day' I said to answer his first quip when he walked in and to avoid saying anything about Miss Vassallo.

'Oh, so you do not want to talk about her. I understand. Maybe later. Besides, I have something to share with you that can help you,' said Albert.

'How's that?' I answer quickly.

'Well, Danny, you know Felicia who works for me? It seems she knows someone who has an excellent stamp collection set, ready for the taking.'

'And how much does Felicia think this collection is worth?' I ask.

'Darling boy, Felicia does not know, but I do. The British Guiana One-Cent Magenta valued at $4,480,000 by Sotheby's and is now residing in the home of Mr and Mrs Franklin Carmichael.'

'And why the interest?' I am querying.

Albert explains Felicia met Mr Carmichael once while doing his hair and somehow or other she ended up in his company's apartment with him in the Quay West in Sydney's CBD. And after a few nights of 'entertainment,' he abruptly dumps her for a server from a nearby restaurant, but not before Felicia had a glimpse of the stamp.

'So why is Felicia sharing this with you, Albert?'

'Why? Why does a scorned woman do so many things? Revenge darling, and a little money.'

'And you think, Albert, this is an opportunity for us to acquire such an item? Where would we fence it?' I ask.

'I know a Russian oligarch that would be willing to pay $1,500,000 for it; no questions asked,' responded Albert. 'But of course, a small 10% referral fee would go to Felicia so we would get to split the difference, $675,000 each, after any 'distributor's fees' we would end up with about $500,000 each. So, what do you think?' A smiling Albert says.

As my mind whirls with excitement, the Quay West slowly comes into my vision, and I realise that the building itself is not impregnable unless Mr Carmichael has some particular door lock and a distinct safe, but nothing comes to mind. I feel that because of the skills I have acquired over the past few months during our extracurricular activities, this will not be difficult.

'I am in, let's do it.'

The next day, Felicia, Albert and I meet in the backroom of my little store and plan our strategy and approach. Using my skills and Felicia's knowledge of the building, door attendant's schedule, concierge location, and other workers and all the appropriate entrances, we decided we go in through the back-service entrance.

The night in question Felicia makes a couple of phone calls to Carmichael's home and, after numerous times, there is no answer. That is our cue. Arriving at the building, Albert and I go into the building unnoticed (thank goodness someone forgot to place any security cameras on this door), and up to Carmichael's apartment, we enter without an issue. Albert and I turn on our penlight torches to look for the stamp in the study where Felicia said she saw the prize, but we have no luck.

We spent almost twenty minutes (a lifetime in this business) when we hear the front door unlocking, so both Albert and I dash in a different direction, Albert into the hall powder room and me into a bedroom. We hear someone walking in, rummaging through the dark in the study, and then in less than five minutes, the front door opens and locks.

As I inch my way back to the study, I see Albert standing by the powder room door, white as a sheet, motioning me over and pointing into the powder room. A quick look and I find what we believe is Mr Carmichael, still on the throne.

'Danny, do you think he is dead?' asked Albert.

'Well, if he is not, he is a wonderful actor.'

'What do we do?' quipped Albert.

Not only we do not have the stamp, but we have a chance to be charged with murder (unless the old guy died of natural causes). A quick call on my mobile to Felicia goes unanswered, so we decide to have Albert find us a wheelchair.

Forty-five minutes later, Albert shows up with the wheelchair (no idea where he got it from and I did not ask), and we bring Mr Carmichael out of the same service door.

'Danny, did you find the stamp while I went looking for the wheelchair?'

'No such luck,' I said. 'By the way, anything on Felicia?'

'No, she vanished,' answered Albert.

As we exit the building, I roll Mr Carmichael down a steep hill, and I lose my handle on the wheelchair, and it takes off at top speed, straight into George Street, where one of the new trams runs over Mr Carmichael.

We disappear.

The next morning, the Sydney Morning Herald reports that Mr Franklin Carmichael died of a heart attack while he pushed himself in a wheelchair and traversed into a light rail tram.

A month later, Albert walks into my store and hands me a letter and says, 'Get a load of this.'

The letter contains a simple note which says, 'Wish you were here.' It also has a photo of Felicia and Mrs Carmichael on a beach in sunny Salinas Ecuador, looking at each other very intimately. Albert and I look at each other. We've been had.

SOMETHING NICE FOR A CHANGE

The Quimbaya inhabited the areas corresponding to the modern departments of Quindío, Caldas and Risaralda in Colombia, around the valley of the Cauca River. There is no clear data about when they were initially established; the current best guess is around the 1st century BCE. Around the tenth century, the Quimbaya culture disappeared entirely because of unknown circumstances. One thing they left behind is an excellent art form using gold, a symbol of the afterlife, for current and future civilisations to enjoy,' said Albert slowly, catching his breath.

'Eight weeks ago, during a visit to the Maximillian Museum, I spotted a sign saying that a pre-Columbian artefact exhibition will be held at the end of the month. The display showed several pictures of some of the artefacts the museum will put on display,' Albert again, pausing for effect.

'The exhibition will have a fascinating artefact. It is a standing figure of a shaman 16 ½ cm high, CE 550-1000 comprising 287.4 grams of gold which will be donated to the museum by the Gordon Wallace Foundation and appraised at $223,000,' said Albert concluding his dissertation.

I waited. Albert is privy to a lot of different avenues of possibilities, or 'opportunities,' as he loves to call them. I remain quiet and let Albert continue.

'Danny darling, I am not boring you, am I?' I swung my head left and right to which Albert continued his dissertation in my little shop.

I looked around my store and stand proud knowing that as the owner of *Village Books & Stuff* I can afford to listen to Albert all day long for thanks to him all of this pot-pourri of cards, stationery, an entire wall dedicated to the latest paperback bestsellers and a massive rear wall that includes antiquarian and unusual books which are all available for sale are 100% debt-free thanks to his 'opportunities.'

Albert and I have partnered in the past year or so in some extracurricular activities that the Robbery and Serious Crime Squad of NSW might find interesting if they get wind of what we have done in the past and might do in the future. Luckily, we have been cautious.

'Well, it seems that Miquel, you know Miquel, don't you Danny?' I nodded yes, acknowledging that Miguel is one of Danny's employees. 'Well, Miquel did Mr Gordon Wallace shampoo and cut the other day, and I overheard Mr Gordon telling Miguel about the upcoming exhibition at the museum.' 'Mr Wallace told Miquel that the small statue is still in his possession in his home in Mosman and will be there until the museum sends a courier to his home to pick it up and deliver it in time for the exhibition.'

'Danny, sweetness, you know how proud I am of my heritage, and I know that a lot of artefacts have somehow wound up in people's collections in an unsavoury manner and that, in my opinion, they should be in the local museum of their country.'

'Yes, Albert, my friend, you have mentioned your passion for this aspect of art. What does this small statue have to do with you and me?' I ask.

'Precious Danny, I am getting to my point. My cousin Silvio Fernandez is a curator of the Museo Nacional in Bogotá, and he is adamant that this little shaman was stolen from his country in the early 1900s by unscrupulous individuals who sold the artefact over the following years, finally resting in the hands of the Gordon Wallace foundation.'

'So?' I ask.

'In a very delicate conversation, my cousin would like to see if we could acquire said little statue for him for a small sum, say $100,000?'

I knew Albert had an ulterior motive. Ever since our second escapade in which we also 'acquired' ourselves some baseball cards and later sold for a tidy profit we have continued adding to what Albert loves to define as our 'shadow super,' in the Nives and since then he has been keen to add to the said fund as much and as often as possible.

'You know Albert; the risk does not warrant the potential reward here. The reward comes down to $50,000 each, and if I get caught, my visit to the Emu Plains Correctional Facility could be for a maximum of 25 years if the judge is in a foul mood. I am not sure, Albert, if it is worth it.'

Albert looked solemn when I said that which is nothing like him.

Albert dresses the part of the successful hair salon owner, always wearing something that I would not be caught in ever. For example, today, the old solemn face is wearing a relaxed turquoise fit, flowing shirt with a lapel collar, long sleeves with buttoned cuffs, and a button up front. I could not wear this shirt, yet Albert is natural in it. And he is wearing carrot top pants and sandals, to boot!

I could not handle Albert's sad face, and I relented and said 'OK.' To which Albert beams a smile that seems to radiate over the entire room.

Albert has the share in our partnership that obtains all the information on the 'acquisition' we are going after. Old Danny boy takes all the risks (I mentioned this before, I am sure) but it seems a fair trade-off since I find my part of the partnership; the fun part, while Albert has; the boring part.

Mosman is a suburb in Sydney where the median house price is $3,760,646 (yes, I did some research) and privacy and security are basic requirements when purchasing a home. So, at the end of the business day, Albert and I met in the back room of my store and planned our strategy.

Our strategy was simple. Avoid any entanglement. Thus, there seemed to be only one solution. Become a courier service.

Crafty Albert recalled that Mr Wallace told Miquel that the museum would send a courier to retrieve the statue. Said courier would then deliver the sculpture for the exhibition, so Albert, through his sources (I do not know how he gets all this information. Really, I don't), so somehow Albert was able to obtain the schedule, the security code, official letterhead from the museum and the time of the pickup. Albert takes part once in a while in our 'acquisitions', seldom doing the grunt work I do but since this time my skills in opening doors, openings safes would not be needed. I had him take part. His simple job was to delay the courier in his arrival at the home of Mr Wallace. Again simple.

My job was to disable the camera in the front of the house (a simple hack) to show up at the appointed time, all clean and proper with my disguise (Albert does unusual disguises with all the hair from his salon) and the letterhead from the museum. Pick up the statue and meander off into the sunset.

Cutting this story short. All went as planned. Not a hitch. All on schedule and I will share with the reader what I later read in the Sydney newspaper that there was a lot of excitement at the Wallace home when the real courier showed up, then the police showing up; asking for the security CCTV film (none to be seen) and what was given as a description of a chubby man with an overgrown beard with grey in it, glasses and a 'Rapid Courier jacket and hat.'

So, Albert made his cousin happy by reuniting the Quimbaya shaman statue with the Columbian people. His 'shadow super' (as well as mine) expanded a little bit, and we did something nice for a change.

FUNNY CARS

U sually, summers are a bust to retailers in Northport. Summers mean most folks head to the beach and, along with their swimmers, thongs, beach towels and suntan lotion, the furthest thing on their mind is carrying a delightful book to read. All that water, sun and wind give the crowds a chance to reflect on their lives and they realise how nice they have it. I hate it.

Presently, I am glancing at *'Miller's Anatomy of the Dog'* by Evans and De Lashanda. The book is a first edition and for a miserly $185, it can be yours.

My little doorbell tingles and I see my dear friend Albert waltzing in a coquelicot orange-red colour suit that I would not even wear at Halloween; he looks smashing in it.

'Danny, cariño, I have an interesting proposition for you today,' Albert quips.

This time Albert's salutation tells me that he has something splendid to share with me. I have learned that much as to the tones of his greetings and this one sounded promising. As I mentioned, Albert walks in wearing a suit that just wows! A soft background of palm trees and flamingos with a white shirt and a palm tree and flamingo tie and loafers made of Nappa leather with a metallic toe.

'What is up with you Albert, a lot of wet hair today?'

'The same as you collect dust here, darling.'

'So, what is this proposition?'

'The other day, a client of Felicia came in asking for her. You remember Felicia?'

Oh, yes, I remember Felicia pulling a double con on us a while back and she is now sipping many piña colada de Avena with naranjilla in Salinas Ecuador with the former Mrs Franklin Carmichael.

'Yes, I do. Why do you ask?'

'Well, as you know, she was one of the premier stylists in the city and many well-to-do clients always ask for her and today was not an exception with young Antanios Haddad doing the asking.' Albert continued: 'I responded Felicia had 'retired' and that Miquel would be more than happy to attend to his needs, and he appeared pleased with the change.'

'During young Antanios and Miquel's conversation, I overheard an intriguing piece of information. Lucky me.'

'I bet,' I thought. 'Please share.' I ask Albert to continue.

'It seems young Haddad has a scale model collection of 33 cars that together are worth in the vicinity of $575,000.' My heart palpitated, might have skipped a beat, at the sound of $575,000.

'My sweet Danny, do you know that Mr Habib Niram from Lebanon is in town for the die-cast model expo next week at the International Convention Centre and is looking to increase his current model collection of 38,707 model cars?'

A beaming Albert noted I did not know, so he continues: 'It seems that young Haddad been in contact with Mr Niram and Mr Haddad is willing to sell the collection to him for said $515,000 but

Mr Niram is only offering $400,000. I thought we could 'acquire' the collection and sell it to Mr Niram for, let's say the same $400,000, he is offering Mr Haddad. saving Mr Naram heaps of money, time and frustration and earning us additional funds to deposit into our 'shadow superannuation,' what do you think?'

I question Albert; 'What is this collection, anyway?'

Albert again smiled and lets me know he had all the details. How he arrived at them, I did not ask.

Albert set out to describe the collection of model cars:

- 1968 'Cheetah' Base Python (Hong Kong Base) - $48,000
- 1969 Pink Rear-Loading Volkswagen Beach Bomb - $72,000
- Mattel's 2008 Diamond-Encrusted 40th Anniversary Special Edition — $60,000
- 1969 Pink, Rear-Loading Beach Bomb—$175,000
- The rest, 29 model cars are worth $220,000 in total.

The last one Albert specifically mentions as priceless only because as of now, only two are believed to remain in the world. Albert winds down from his detailed verbal presentation. How can he remember all this minutia is amazing? I thought to myself. With a few seconds taken to resuscitate himself, Albert finishes: 'They are all in his company office safe in Auburn, what do you think?'

Remembering my last venture with Albert and Felicia, which was entirely unsuccessful thus leaving me with a bit of a low confidence level, I answered, 'Let's do it.' And in less than a week,

Albert gets the office floor plans for Mr Haddad's company and the location of the safe—a Chubb Oxley MKIII 5C.

Too large and heavy to carry out so that leaves one solution; I would have to break into the premises of Haddad Business Solutions Pty Ltd on the ground floor of Auburn Avenue in Auburn, use my trusted NNC Lock Set, my favourite, by the way, and all that is left is to open the safe.

Our plan is simple. We set out to have dinner on Saturday night after work. We headed to Parramatta to the MSW Restaurant for a nice and leisurely dinner. The MSW is famous in Sydney for its meats, seafood, and wine selection hence the name. Albert enjoys thier food immensely and we arrive without a booking, I will add, but the maître d' hôtel smiles and gives Albert an enormous hug.

'Albert, mon bon ami. Tellement content de te voir!'

'Hello, Francois. Content de te voir aussi.' Who knew Albert spoke French? He always surprises me.

'Francois darling, we do not have a booking. I am hoping you can accommodate us since we are starving!'

'For you, my friend I will always have a table. Please follow me.'

Francois walks us to our table and of course, we are not dressed for the establishment, I can tell by the looks we are getting. Both Albert and I are wearing jeans, Albert has a short sleeve black t-shirt with black pants and pink runners while I am wearing a long sleeve black button-down shirt and black jeans with my well-worn black moccasins. Oh well, I never thought you should be over dressed during one of our 'acquisitions' so let them stare. Our money is as good as theirs.

'Here Albert,' as Francois's hands point to the table and hands us the menu. 'Everything is excellent tonight. You cannot fail in your choosing. Enjoy. I will send your server in a moment to take your order,' and with that last statement, Francois shoots me a wink. A friendly chap, I thought.

Putting down the menu Albert is ready to order. 'I am starving, Danny. I am going to go with the Boerewors which is their premier entrée. It consists of South African beef sausages with coriander & cumin, chakalaka sauce, fresh coriander, maize pap & corn croquettes. I will follow that with the shorthorn 200 grams fillet, medium with a bit of creamy mushroom sauce on the side and a wedge salad. I am hoping I have room for dessert because they are wonderful here.'

'Obviously, you have no fears during an 'acquisition.' I for one will go for something lighter like the Portuguese Prawns which I see come marinated in tomato and Portuguese seasoned barley, tomato & coriander salsa. I will add a bit of bread to soak up all that juiciness.'

The server arrives to take our order and before I can order a beer Albert speaks up; 'We will have a bottle of your 'Wirra Wirra NSW 2017,' and continues ordering our meal for the both of us.

As the server leaves, I say, 'Albert, you know we are not on a date but a heist.'

'Ah, ma chérie, let me treat you tonight, for when we are successful the reward will more than cover this small expense.'

Our wine arrives shortly, and Albert does the customary sniff, swirl and taste and nods and the server pours to our glasses. Shortly afterwards our meals arrived and now I am hungry and both of us devoured the meals. Finishing the bottle, Albert is ready to motion to the server for another one when I stop his arm from going up and turn my head left and right indicating that we had enough. 'How about dessert?' he says. Again, I turn my head left and right so that Albert does the international sign to request our bill. It displeased Albert at not having dessert for he had a frown on his face as we drove to Auburn and parked in the back alley of the premises of the Haddad Business Solutions building.

As we got out of the car both Albert and I put on our two sets of cotton gloves each thus enhancing our chances of not leaving any 'glove prints.' The next thing I do is disable the Hikvision Iris network camera: an excellent piece of equipment described as 'vandal-proof' but not 'Danny-proof.' With a little magic, I make the camera 'look but not see,' (you do not expect me to describe my tricks here, do you?), and we enter the building.

Security cameras and safes give their owners the illusion of security and provide experts and yes, I consider myself by now an 'expert,' since I have added this type of entertainment into my life. I proceed to do a quick tumbling of several pins, apply pressure on some bolts, add a simple pick of its key/lock combination, and the safe is open and releases its treasures.

Inside we found a lot of paperwork, a large envelope with some cash ($13,200 to be exact, we counted later) and a little case containing the entire scale models collection.

Opening the case to ensure the model cars are there (the first rule of breaking in, make sure the stuff is there). We lock up the safe, go out the door, 'reassemble' the Hikvision Iris network camera to its original configuration, and we stroll back to our car knowing that this time, at least, we were successful, and this time, no dead bodies.

What a life, making a living from funny cars!

ARROGANT AND RICH

'It is a fake, I tell you.' Said Dr. Gabriel Frome. 'I looked at it this past Friday when I attended a meeting at the Maximillian Museum. I scrutinised it for a second time, and I am telling you it is a fake, the Vasily Kundansky's *Composition 19*, is a fake.' Wiping his sweaty brow with his lace handkerchief.

'Eight weeks ago, when Mr Charles Prudhomme III asked me to his penthouse, as curator of the Maximillian Museum, to appraise it for him and I valued it at $20 million, he then donated it to the Museum. Friday was the first time I saw it since the appraisal, and I tell you again, this one is not the one I appraised. This one is a fake,'

As I stood behind my counter in my little store, my friend and owner of *Cut Me Crazy*, Albert is wearing a complete purple outfit involving purple pants, a purple jacket, button-down black shirt and a matching purple tie and black shoes, and of course, purple socks and he is trying his best to comfort Dr. Frome and I knew Albert already had a plan developing in his little grey cells.

'It was so nice of you Danny to have Albert bring me over here after my haircut to calm my nerves. This is all so stressful. My reputation is in ruins if this comes out.'

'Do nothing is my best policy,' I said to Dr. Frome.

To which Dr. Frome thought that would be the most sensible thing to do. Playing dumb may not help him get out of this predicament, but he had his notes of the appraisal so that would be his fallback to strategy.

'How large is this masterpiece Dr. Frome?' I ask.

Still, a bit discombobulated, Dr. Frome answers me, 'The Vasily Kundansky's *Composition 19* is 40 cm x 60 cm without its frame. A delicate masterpiece emphasising the process of formation and the value of a natural painting, as opposed to the subject matter. Kundansky steadfastly believed colour and form possessed an emotional power to separate from an object. The man was ahead of his time in my opinion. Kundansky painted his compositions over thirty-five years and when you mount them on a wall all in chronological order, well, tears form in your eyes at the beauty in simplicity he brings to the art.'

'Dr. Frome, why is the appraisal of $20 million that high? Is there something special about this Kundansky piece, the *Composition 19*, that makes it so valuable?' Albert asks now, ensuring that Dr. Frome calms down a bit more by talking about the painting.

'Albert you are a man of culture. You must see that Kundansky extended beyond the territories of Cubism, Futurism, and the movements of his contemporaries. His motifs, over time, have evolved and transformed where he created a new world of colour and form not seen since. Kundansky's driving energy creates the unusual using simple forms and lines interlace with brilliant colour brought new definitions to the masses' visual thoughts, and Kundansky entwined all these factors, these emotions, into his works. Just seeing these compositions does that to you but seeing the last composition, the *Composition 19*, among these magnificent and fascinating works, we, the public, gain further insight into his epic process of creation.'

After an hour of more questions and more lamentations from Dr. Frome, Albert escorted him to his car and returned to my store.

'Darling, I am so glad that is over. That man can talk. Now cariño I could not help but see your face brighten up the moment the dear doctor mentioned the $20 million, and I knew you could see that I already had something up my sleeve.'

'Well, it seems to me Albert that Mr Charles Prudhomme III made sure that the good doctor had the original copy appraised, then Prudhomme III had a copy made, switched it, donated the fake one to the Maximillian Museum, took a nice deduction from the Australian Tax Office and has the original at home somewhere. So, what do you know that I do not?'

'You know dulzura, my sweet, that the Kundansky could fetch us about $10M to $12M. Something which I can arrange if you could manage to acquire it for us?'

'Albert my friend, do you know where Mr Prudhomme III lives so we may pay him a visit,'?

'Ah Danny cariño, I thought you would never ask, he lives alone at 64/910 George Street in the Sydney central business district, the penthouse. His office is right next door at 54/920 George Street. What is the plan?'

'The obvious Albert, I am to 'acquire' the original, and you are to find us a buyer.'

'It is done,' said Albert, clapping like a silly goose. 'Do you have an idea of how you are going to do this?'

'No. Not yet but you know me Albert I like to study. Studying the ins and outs of Mr Charles Prudhomme III will take a few weeks and many trips into the city and a few hours on the computer. You just find me the blueprints of both the office building where his office is and the building where his penthouse is. That should help us a lot.'

In less than a month, Albert had the blueprints of both buildings, had set up a buyer from overseas for $8 million (well, burglars cannot be choosers when it comes to how much people will pay for stolen masterpieces). Now it was up to me.

The blueprint shows that the penthouse building *'The Ovation'* at 910 George Street was built in 2012 to the highest standards of architecture with an appointed entrance, reception desk with security guard station, and separate lifts for use for its residents. You do not need an access card for the lifts. The building at 910 George Street was just as nicely built by the developer but it is more dedicated to residents and they dedicated only a few of the first levels to office space. This meant that while there was a security guard here as well the security would be laxer.

The sister building at 920 George Street is an A-grade office space building used by multiple ASX top 200 companies with most of these being in the fintech technology that is all avant garde these days. You need an access card to call the lifts and go up and down registering your every move. Most of the venture capital companies have their offices here. The reason you might ask. It is easier for them to share on a venture by simply walking from one company to another in case you need a few more dollars to seal a deal.

The best information that the blueprint showed was the lifts have communication with their respective security desks in case of an emergency but no video.

So, the best way to determine how to circumvent a building's reception and its security is to head right to it and your best weapon is pizza. Because the more residential units mean the more pizza deliveries. Simple!

Some venture capitalists like living close to their work and most are arrogant and rich. They work long, odd hours and what better way to celebrate to finishing work after making beaucoup money than to enjoy long and juicy munches of a pepperoni pizza with extra cheese.

I know because I watched this ritual take place over several evenings of painstaking observing the many late-night deliveries. Most of the deliveries seem to go to building 920 where there was always a beehive of activity into the late night since venture capitalist and their worker bees transact their business across the globe, which means, strange hours. The pizza deliveries also delivered to 910 but not as many so my chances were to wait around building 920 for my target.

So, the night of our 'acquisition' Albert works his magic on me. He provides me with a super nice beard and moustache from hair obtained from his hair salon. Adding a bit of spirit gum to the beard and magically I am now a new bearded pizza delivery person with a matching moustache. I now have more facial hair than I inherited from my father and only a face a mother would love.

Next came a reversible jacket that we had made. On one side it looks like a Fendi reversible windbreaker jacket with brown and yellow colours printed with the swirling FF Vertigo pattern and finished with a drawcord hood and pockets on both sides. The other side shows Giuseppe's Pizzeria on it and it looks like I have worn it over decades. The last touch is a baseball cap with a big 'GP' on it also looking worn to hell. Now I wait.

Standing close to both building 910 and 920 George Street to be seen as belonging to either building but out of reach of the view from both reception desks and its inhabitants I see my target arriving. Tonight, it is a young Asian boy getting out of his cycle delivering another fantastic pizza from Giuseppe's.

'Good evening my young man, I was out here partaking of a nice cigarette and waiting for my delivery of delicious pizza from your establishment.'

'You, Mr Cochrane from level 34, Unit 34-D at 910 George Street?' asks the young man.

'I am my dear boy. Here is $50. Please keep the change and thank you for such a prompt delivery service. I will commend you to your manager when I get back upstairs.'

'Whatever and thanks,' taking the note from me, probably saying to himself that tonight was a good night for tips as he gets on his cycle and departs.

Quickly reversing my jacket to show 'Giuseppe's Pizza' on the back I withdraw my 'GP' hat from my pocket and with the pizza at hand, I walk into the reception 910 building, sign in making sure that I keep my head low and scribbling a name that is not legible and without the security guard noticing I pocket the pen, avoiding leaving my fingerprints. You would expect some sense of security in the building with the high rents in the city but not tonight since the security guard is more involved with his phone and has assumed that I am just another of the many pizza delivery folks coming in to deliver tonight's delicacies to the powers that be upstairs. Without saying a word, I proceed to level 34 to deliver the pizza.

Mr Cochrane from 34-D turns out to be a tight-ass pulling out a $20 and a $10 for a $28-dollar pizza, including delivery. I smile and walk away toward the lift but instead of going down I go up and head to the penthouse. The lift stops at the penthouse entrance showing a wonderful marble floor and a few ornamental vases with fresh flowers scattered about and to each side of the penthouse door.

I first ring Mr Prudhomme III's doorbell, then his landline number which Albert had obtained, and as expected there is no answer. Tonight, we knew Mr Prudhomme III would be busy at one of the many exhibitions he attends. Prudhomme III entire social media is full of photos and events skewed toward the art world with constant selfies with local artists at their exhibitions and art shows.

One of the things, when you are about to acquire something that does not belong to you, is to know your target. This target loved making money and then spending an evening parlaying his knowledge of local artists and their works at many exhibitions that happen around the city. Tonight, was no different. Prudhomme III was out at some artsy-fartsy show showing off how much money he has made but tonight he was going to lose a lot as well. Lucky for Albert and me, he loves the arts!

The lock was no big issue, why bother with strong door locks when you have security downstairs. A quick search for the Kundansky *Composition 19* proves successful, and it is in my possession.

Removing my fake beard and moustache and flushing them down the toilet, one at a time, I reverse the jacket, pocket the hat, and roll *Composition 19* which is small enough that easily fits under my jacket. Reversing my entry route, I walk out of the building just looking like any venture capitalist who lives there does.

Arrogant and rich.

ONE OF THE USUAL SUSPECTS

This morning was typical of all my mornings. The sun came slightly through my front window washing the store with its warm rays. As I walked around the store, ensuring everything was in place, I thought to myself; 'Life is good!'

I am proud of the *Village Books & Stuff*. I changed its name from the old printing company building where my store is when I purchased the business and building from Mr McCullum over three years ago. The building was built in the early 1850s and is one of the earliest buildings in Northport and thus is deemed heritage on the outside, but I have managed in just three-and-half years to modernise the store with the latest technology, both crucial for my business and the building security. You see, I used to rent the store but a little while back, with the help of my friend, Albert Matthew Guzman, proprietor of the premier hair salon in Northport, *Cut Me Crazy*, I was able to 'acquire' the funds to purchase this beautiful building.

Albert and I partner in some activities that I am sure the police force of NSW would define illegal, but we have been fortunate as to not attract a bit of attention to ourselves, or so I thought until this beautiful morning I encountered a dark cloud by the name of Detective Malcolm Cassell.

A few minutes after 10 AM, I had just placed my little 'We Are Open' sign on my door, and Albert burst through the front door in one of his usual outlandish suits. This time he is wearing what I would call a 'Where is Wally' suit. A horizontal red and white striped jacket over a baby blue pant with a white shirt and the tie matches the jacket. White sneakers are the thing with this outfit and no socks. Albert makes my little bell tingle excessively, looks around and makes sure that there are no customers, locks the front door, turns my little sign from 'We Are Open' to 'We Are Closed' and blurts out: 'Danny dear, have you spoken with him yet?'

Taken aback I said: 'Spoken to whom?'

Just before Albert could start his conversation, the front doorbell rumbles a bit as if someone is trying to get in and pays no attention to my 'We Are Closed' sign and then bangs on the door requesting admittance.

Albert looks at me, makes a funny face and turns and goes to unlock the front door for me and leaves the little sign in the 'We Are Closed' position. As he unlocks the door, in walks a short, stocky fellow maybe in his early fifties, early balding but with some hair still, that can be strategically combed, reasonably good teeth and dressed in what Albert would describe as a medium charcoal hue suit that looks so-so good with a rumpled white dress shirt and a slim dark tie. However, he is not what I would describe as looking good in the suit, for the suit looks like it has not seen the inside of a dry cleaner's store in ages. On the redeeming side, he had black lace shoes well shined that the sun's rays could reflect from if the sun could reach the shoes because of his rotundness.

'Well, good morning gentlemen, beautiful day in Northport, fancy seeing you here as well Mr Guzman?' spoke Detective Malcolm Cassell in a voice that reminded me of Jason Troutman (if you do not know who he is, try looking him up, what a unique voice).

'Excuse me, Sir,' I said; 'We are not open yet.'

'Oh, that is OK, I saw Mr Guzman here, and we met already. I figured I could walk in and introduce myself to you. You go by Monk, right?' proclaimed Detective Cassell.

'Sorry. Do I know you?' I asked.

'No, you do not, Monk. My name is Detective Malcolm Cassell.'

In the most pleasant voice I could muster, I answered, 'I would prefer Mr Monk, but I do not think it would matter to you what I think, am I correct Detective Cassell? What can I do for you?'

Detective Cassell smiles with those reasonably good teeth showing and without looking at me he wanders around the store picking up books, pens, anything he fancied and placing them all in the wrong spot. He makes a statement in that horrid voice of his: 'You may or may not know that there have been a lot of burglaries in the metropolitan area. A few of the victims are customers of Mr Guzman, to whom I spoke with yesterday afternoon, and I thought I would follow up with him in the morning with a few other questions and fancy that, I see him in your store. So, I thought I'd introduce myself to you.'

Cassell continues: 'A little research by some of my fellow officers found that your luck seemed to have changed a little while back since you started associating with Mr Guzman here. I mean, you went from the lessor to owner in a manner of two years, modernised the store, upgraded it and all paid without bank financing. The retail business has proven very fruitful for you. Is that correct Monk?'

I did not like the tone of his voice or where the conversation was heading. Albert was standing there, cool as a cucumber, but I could see his lower lip twitch like it does when he has a little worrisome thing that he cannot seem to shake. For my part, I also was as refreshing as a watermelon, but I thought maybe there had been some minor mistake that I might have made during one of my excursions with Albert that stuck in Detective Cassell's research that might point the finger to me.

'Well, Detective Cassell, I am glad to know that you have noticed how well I manage my store and how I can sell my wares and how, after expenses, I manage to save money to expand my store. If you would like to check my cash register receipts, inventory orders, special orders, you will see that all I do is legitimate. If you need me to assist you with your financial matters, there is this book, *The Barefoot Retirement Plan* by Doyle Shuler that could help you reach those financial goals; it goes for $24.95.'

I give Cassell my biggest smile.

He too smiles back at me and continues pressing; 'No that will not be necessary. Those were the certain aspects of your recent 'growth' in your business that I found interesting. Just thought I would come in and speak with you to let you know how much you impressed me.'

With that, he nods to Albert and then me; goes to the door, notices that my sign is wrong and turns it over to the 'We Are Open' position and waves his hand as he walks out the door.

As Detective Cassell walks past my front window, he glances in and continues to smile, waves and moves out of our sight of vision. Albert starts to speak, but I stop him by placing my index finger in front of my mouth. I take out my RF signal detector from my top drawer and scan around all the areas that Cassell stood around in to ensure he did not leave any little bugging devices. I then nod to Albert to speak, and he blurts out: 'He knows Danny, he knows.' I took a moment to think and said to Albert; 'No, Albert he does not know. He suspects. Just that, suspects.'

'Oh, dear Danny, I never thought we would get caught at this. I mean, we both have taken as many precautions as possible, with resourcing information and then selecting the appropriate channels for distribution of our 'acquisitions,' all of which I can vouch for as not one of my resources wants to have the police get involved. I am worried, Danny. I just got wind of an opportunity for us too, what are we to do?'

'Tell me your impressions of Detective Cassell,' I asked Albert.

'What do you mean Danny, my impressions?'

'What you think of him, Albert?'

'I find him a total Neanderthal. Did you see how he dressed? I think he is merely a power-hungry man wanting to move up the political line and maybe become an inspector before he reaches retirement age, and he is married. Did you see that gaudy ring he wore? Why do you ask?' answered Albert.

'I get the impression that while he may suspect something, he is also fishing for something. NSW police officers have a dangerous job and while their pay is 100% above the average national pay in Australia, this salary is nothing compared to the risks associated with the job. In my opinion Albert, he wants something from us, but I do not know what, yet.'

'I do not know Danny dearest; it was quite a shock to me when he came into my salon yesterday late afternoon, asking me about the clients, victims as he called them, of the recent burglaries and hinting how I happen to know many of them. I assured him that during the time I have been in business, I have met many people in the type of business I am in. He did that smile he did for us this morning and walked off right before we closed the salon for the day. I just stood there thinking to myself what if he knew what we had done, I wanted to tell you what had happened, but you had closed for the day and I did not want to bother you in the evening. I thought it best to come in early this morning to speak with you and then he appears as if to spoil me by telling you about this new opportunity.'

'Albert, we continue doing what we do best and know that Detective Cassell may be watching us a little closer, that is all. Now tell me what this opportunity is?'

'OK sweetness, maybe this will keep my mind off the dreadful Detective Cassell,' whimpers Albert. 'Have you heard of the Apollo and Artemis earrings?'

'Other than the names being about the Greek gods, twins I believe and son and daughter of Zeus and Leto; nothing else comes to mind as far as earrings. Tell me more.'

'It turns out that Mr Bill Randolph owner of Pinnacle Minerals and a proud resident of Avalon Maison in Mosman he recently purchased said earrings for his missus, Mrs Philippa Randolph and they are worth a cool $78,000,000. One earring, the Apollo, is blue and pear-shaped while Artemis is pink and also pear-shaped. The Apollo Blue is said to be, and I quote (Albert makes those little quotation signs in the air with his hands), 'the largest flawless fancy vivid sapphire diamond ever to be offered at auction,' according to Sotheby's. The 14.54-carat gem earned a rare grading of 11b, which accounts for only 1 per cent of diamonds in the world. Meanwhile the 16-carat pink Artemis was classified as an 11a diamond, 'the most chemically pure' of its kind.' concluded Albert, proud of his knowledge of the gems.

'And' I said, prodding Albert to finish his dissertation.

'Darling, there is a wealthy married Chinese billionaire that would like very much to give these gems for his 'girlfriend,' said Albert, again making the quotation signs in the air. He is offering a nice $20,000,000 if anyone brings said gems to him, no questions asked. It is all posted on the 'dark web' said Albert finishing his spiel.

So that is how Albert finds his opportunities and buyers—on the dark web. Other than paying bills, an occasional email to my cousin, Gary, or Gaz like my mother used to call him, checking my bank account balance, and ordering books, stationery, cards, and other material for my store from my suppliers and using Australia

Post to ship my online sales - that is the extent of my computer skills - and of course, ringing sales up in the cash register. The dark web: how does anyone even get to the dark internet is far beyond my capabilities. I have learned how to pick locks, bypass alarm systems, utilise sensor reading instruments, and more. All this research was done the old fashion way, reading books. I know the police can track your past movements on the internet if you use your computer. I tried looking into the dark web using an internet café over in Parramatta but found the lingo; VPN, ISP, encryption, TOR, and such, confusing and then if you understand all that they expect you to pay with bitcoin. Bitcoin, what the hell is that, anyway? For one, I pay cash as I go. That is the type of guy I am. That is why Albert does his part so well, and I do my part just as well.

Perfect partnership.

Eventually, I would have learnt this black web or dark web or whatever colour it is, because everything in life is changing and I know I need to change since I do not want to wind up like Mr Hebert McCullum and have to quit this line of work since I did not keep up with the times.

'Albert, you think we should go after these earrings. Are you comfortable knowing Detective Cassell is looking into us as possible suspects in some of the past activities we have been involved in?' I query Albert.

'Yes, the prospect of increasing our 'shadow super' by our share of the spoils of this acquisition warrants the risks, don't you think Danny?' sheepishly asks Albert, leaving the last decision to me.

I seldom think of the risks associated with the 'acquisition' part of our partnership. There is a risk in everything in life and what is life without risk, boring, I say. The thought of Detective Cassell looking over our shoulders presented a new challenge, but as with risk, life is so full of them, so I gave Albert my answer.

'Albert, my friend, we may become one of the usual suspects in our next caper, but that is a chance I believe we are both willing to take, so yes, this 'acquisition' warrants its risks. Remember the quote by Jean-Paul Sartre, *'To know what life is worth you have to risk it once in a while.'*

The next step was to begin our planning so as not to become one of the usual suspects.

IN SPECIAL CIRCUMSTANCES

So far, we have been cautious and lucky, but a recent visit by Detective Malcolm Cassell has laid doubts as to our ventures being secret any longer. To quote my friend Albert; 'He knows.'

Well, I do not think Detective Cassell 'knows' but I feel fairly sure he 'suspects' and this brings additional concerns as we endeavour toward our new 'acquisition,' the Apollo and Artemis earrings belonging to Mr and Mrs Bill Randolph.

Through Albert's connections he had obtained information through the dark web that a Chinese billionaire will pay, no questions asked, $20,000,000 for those earrings, so he might splash them on his 'girlfriend.' Now I figure these earrings had to be fancy, and worth a lot more than the $20M offered, and Albert knew about gems for he gave me quite an excellent description of them. I remember Albert reciting these details from memory.

My thought is that these earrings would not be worn out in the world by said 'girlfriend' but that having these earrings was instead a statement by a man who has immense wealth, and it would not bother him to have his 'girlfriend' wear them around the house. What a shame, I thought to myself. Wonder what the wife thinks of that? Oh, well, that might be another story for another time.

Albert sources were able to provide us a detailed plan blueprint of Randolph's mansion, the gardens, a detailed schematic of the security system and a plan of the electrical systems protecting the grand expanse that is Avalon Maison. Albert could also find out that the in-house staff members occupy the same premises as the Randolphs, in this case, the head major-domo and the live-in house cleaner. The chef, gardener and both chauffeurs live in their own homes and depart each day unless needed for special occasions. Albert's proposed 'acquisition' would not be easy to get with a potential total of four individuals that could be in the home at any time.

As it so happens in life, a friend of a friend of a friend of Mrs Randolph was having her hair done by Miguel at *Cut Me Crazy* last week. After some serious sipping of numerous glasses of Château Mouton Rothschild Pauillac 2010 champagne she cheerfully told the entire hair salon that the Randolphs' will be on holiday in Aspen Colorado at their chateau for the next three weeks leaving that very Friday.

Our window of opportunity was short, but we were capable individuals, and we will make do, as I told Albert. Most times, Albert does not get involved in the physical aspects of our 'acquisitions' since he has a sensitive stomach for adventure, but I told him he had no choice this time. The landscape of the Avalon Maison was too vast for me to cover by myself and I needed an extra pair of eyes and ears, so Albert agreed to participate.

All my plans when making an 'acquisition' are simple. Avoid going into any home that is occupied and avoid complex integrated alarm systems at all costs. Those two caveats were not to be available to us this time. It could not be worse.

As mentioned, we would have both servants sleeping in the house and the alarm system used at Avalon Maison was not one but two systems in one. The first component was the Australian Vision System (AVS) with 28 cameras all recording 240 frames per second and including night vision and motion detectors. Now add to this equation the Burglar Immobiliser Territorial Entry System, which disperses a noxious gas 3000 metres square when triggered, most commonly known as the BITES system, and this presented quite a problem. I could feel the $20,000,000 just slipping away. I have to give this 'acquisition' a lot of thought.

A couple of weeks pass before I ask Albert to come over after closing time on Thursday night. We huddled in my unit upstairs to go over all the information we had. The reader may remember where my abode is since in all my previous stories, I have mentioned the fact that I am a person of privacy but alas I will share that with you again in case the readers have not grasped its location. Just above the *Village Books & Stuff* is my humble abode. An ample living area that comprises a lounge area, a dining kitchen combo, a small reading nook, a huge bedroom, big enough for a king-size bedroom set including a dual door walk-in closet and a bathroom that comprises a tub that would make Cleopatra jealous and a separate shower. Here is where I retire each evening after closing my store and prepare for the next working day. Now you know me a bit more, happy?

We had building layouts, the original home blueprints, landscapes around the house, the alarm system schematics, and the electrical blueprint. My experience with alarm systems has taught me one thing: not one system is impenetrable, and so was the case with the AVS system. The AVS system allows its owner to remotely view their premises with software enabling the homeowner to monitor all the cameras' views in real-time from a PC, laptop, or PDA anywhere in the world with an Internet connection.

So, the first thing is to know the routine at the house when the proprietors are not in and that was what Albert and I did over several days. When we finished monitoring the house, we would return to my place to go over the plans. Let me share we had many a late night doing this. We hoped that monitoring the servants when the owners were on holiday would give us a pattern and it did. Their routine told us that the house cleaner was an early riser when the Randolph's were out, but she went to bed around 9 PM and never left her bedroom, while the major-domo slept in the morning but stay up past midnight on most nights, going to the kitchen at about 1 AM for a snack or drink before retiring for the night. This information allowed us to find out that 3 AM was the best time to proceed with our 'acquisition.' The AVS and BITES systems were a concern to us still.

And yes, both Albert and I continue to work at our establishments every morning making us the envy of all small business owners around the world if they only knew.

Then one evening Albert and I are having a quick sandwich dinner on the kitchen bench and I walk over to the dining room table hoping for a revelation to reveal itself. I thought that it is just impossible for us to get into the house undetected, I took a deep look at Albert's outfit (today he was wearing a red tartan suit with a black shirt and a matching red tartan tie with black shoes and socks) and this outfit had to be the inspiration for my 'Eureka' moment.

'Albert, I think I found a solution to both our problems,' I said. 'Come here. Look at the blueprint, especially the side of Avalon Maison that is occupied by the servants. What do you see?'

Alberts gets off the stool and holding his Cuban sandwich (he makes one mean Cuban sandwich) he moves closer to the table making sure that his double-breasted jacket would not get damaged or get any stain on it. Munching away, Albert peers at the blueprint for a minute and looks up to me and says: 'I see nothing, Danny. What do you see I do not?'

Smiling at Albert, I say; 'My dear fellow, I for one sometimes in the middle of the night, get a craving for a drink or even a sandwich, so I get up and walk to my kitchen and satisfy that thirst or hunger. I bet you do the same sometimes?'

'Why yes, of course, I would imagine that just about everyone does that at one time in their life. So?' quizzes Albert taking his last bite of his sandwich.

'Well, Albert, if you look at the schematics of the AVS with its 28-camera consortium you will notice that they all point around key areas of Avalon Maison where the Randolph's live. Now look carefully, the servant's wing has one camera, and if you follow the blueprint that is the one camera that is not connected to the AVS system, it is a standalone system.'

'To make life even easier, look, there is a keypad in the servant's hallway's wing which connects to the BITES system. If either servant wants a drink or a snack, or leave their room for any reason, he or she must turn off the BITES system, he or she will go to the kitchen, satisfy their thirst, or hunger and return to the hallway, turns the BITES system back on before returning to their bedroom.'

Albert just stood there. We had been looking at these plans for a little over a week and had not noticed such a simple flaw in the system. Of course, the Randolph's felt secure. No one would burglarize them. The Randolph's, however, did not care if someone robbed their servants.

With less than four days before the Randolphs return from Aspen; Albert and I set our plan in action. Entry to the gardens of Avalon Maison from the servant's wing was simple, only a small wall from the road was the obstacle, be it a 1 ½ metre wall; small for me, but it felt like climbing Everest for Albert for it it took Albert a while to conquer. Having accomplished that feat, I used a Quantum RF Modifier to neutralise the single camera, giving us easy access to the servant's wing. The back French door proves to be an easy pick, and we were inside the house in less than one minute.

Here the reader might ask themselves; 'They got you now, Danny boy. Surely the alarm will blare out.' Well, not quite. Most rich folks believe that having the AVS system and the BITES system is enough to deter all burglars. The owner assumes, and you know what happens when you assume, most owners assume that having the AVS systems includes a door and window security combination - it does not. All I had to do was simply jimmy the French door lock, take out my OCD (Oscillating Camera

Disruptor) and aim it to the single indoor sensor, and we walked into the hallway and turned off the BITES using the keypad.

The reader again will think, 'But you and Albert do not know the security code? Got you!'

I will remind the reader that if they have a security system at home, as primitive as it can be, it will most likely have a keypad. The one thing all homeowners do when they clean their house, or in the case of the Randolph's have the house cleaner do it, is to dust, wipe and thoroughly clean every nook and cranny of their home — all their furniture, books, picture frames, etc. I could go on and on. But the one thing no one, and I am sure I include the reader here, that is not clean or even think of cleaning is the keypad to the alarm system.

The reader might be interested in knowing that the skin found on the fingers, palms, and soles of the feet of humans (and some primates) is known as friction skin. This skin is unique because it does not have hair follicles or oil glands, and because the skin is composed of ridges that are believed to be adapted for increased friction to help when handling various objects and walking. These so-called friction ridges are composed of rows of sweat pores or eccrine glands that constantly secrete perspiration. This perspiration—along with grease and oil transferred from other parts of the body—adheres to the friction skin and is transferred from the skin to other surfaces when contact is made with objects. The transferred outline of the friction ridges is a latent print.

So, I dusted the keypad and found the four digits for the code, punched them in, and the magical red light of the security system disappeared. The BITES system was now offline and said magical light was now green, ready to be armed once again. We listened through both servant's doors and could not hear a thing; They both seemed sound asleep, so we hurried to find the safe.

The blueprint shows that the Randolphs' safe was in the massive study, hiding behind a false bookcase, so we slowly proceed to the study, open the door, and turn on our penlight torches. We find the false bookcase wide open and Randolphs' safe even more fully open. We also see the body of a woman on the floor,

Albert almost faints on me. I grab him quickly before he falls onto the floor next to the body of the woman and steady him before I kneel to inspect the body. She had the back of her head cracked like a walnut, blood had dried up on the carpet and the white marble Napoleonic head laid close to her. She had been dead for a short while because when I felt her body; it was still warm, the warmth even penetrating the double gloves that I always wear.

A glance in the safe showed papers strewn all over the front of the safe, some files and no earrings. Someone had beaten us to the punch, and we had to get out of there quickly before the major-domo hears us or maybe hears Albert and his heavy breathing and wakes up to investigate.

We reversed our trail, rearmed the BITES system, reactivated the hallway sensor, locked the French door as we left, arrived at the same bushes we first hid in and activated the outside standalone camera and I heaved Albert over the wall and got ourselves back to my place as soon as possible.

Not since the Carmichael incident have, we encountered a dead body. We were fortunate that Carmichael died of natural causes but not the woman unless having your head cracked open like walnut is now classified by the NSW coroner as a natural cause.

The taking of a life is something that I have never done. I have never served in the armed forces. I do not own a gun and other than my steak knives and cutting kitchen knives at home that is the extent of my weaponry. Albert, well, he eats out most nights partying throughout the Northport nightspots and frequents the many exciting places in the Sydney Central Business District, so he is even less prone to violence than I.

'Danny dear, we will get the blame for this. I cannot go to prison. You see those people in horrible orange outfits all the time. That will not do, just will not do.'

I said, 'Albert, we are not going to prison. First, prisoners in NSW wear prison greens, not orange. You must be thinking of an American TV show you watched. Second, we will not come under investigation, and we are not even going to be suspects in anything. Third, we left no clues. I watched you every moment, and you did not fail me, you were incredibly careful. We both wore our hair nets and caps to not leave any hair follicles. You had your double gloves on, and your face powder-covered all perspiration so they would not find even a drop of DNA. I need you to do one thing for me though.'

'Yes darling, tell me anything. I will do it.'

'Go home. Try to get some sleep and before you get to work in the morning do your magic on the dark web and find the status of the Chinese billionaire's request for those earrings. See if he has withdrawn his offer on the net. Can you do that for me?'

'Of course, I can. I will do that tonight and get back to you early in the morning.'

'No, Albert, not early in the morning. All is cool. You open your store as normal, 8:30 AM. I open my store as usual at 10 AM and at about 11 AM you meander over here like you normally do on most days, and we chat.'

'I do not meander, Danny. I may amble, saunter or even stroll but I do not meander,' responded Albert, upset at my description of his walk.

'OK Albert, it has been a long night. I will see you in the morning.'

The next morning, I open my store at 10 AM sharp, unlock the door, turn my little sign to the 'We Are Open' position, and do the customary straightening of the books, the card section, etc. I take a glance at the stationary section, and before you can sip a Gloria Jean's coffee, it is 10:09 AM; time to toil and wait for that first customer of the day.

As a zephyr wind Albert rushes in, (so much for being cool and waiting until 11 AM Albert) and immediately starts: 'Oh Danny things are so bad, so bad. I checked my contacts online last night, and it turns out that there was a second bidder for the earrings. This time the offer was a cool $2,000,000 more than the Chinese billionaire's purchase order' said Albert, taking a deep breath. 'And the more I poked around the dark web; I found out that the earrings had already been 'acquired with hardship' by an 'independent acquisition team'. 'You do not think they mean us, Danny, do you?'

'We are not the acquisition team they speak of?' I said.

Before I could add to my answer to, I hear my little doorbell tingle and who do you think walks into my store, Detective Cassell 'Good morning, gentlemen. It seems I always find you both in deep conversation when I see you,' proclaims Cassell.

'Good morning, Detective, and why do we have the pleasure of your visit today?' I asked.

'I guess you have not read the morning papers this morning?' states Cassell. Albert and I shake our heads left to right, and Cassell continues; 'A burglary occurred last night in Mosman and some rare earrings departed the ownership of their rightful owners, but a forty-six-year-old maid was found on the study floor with an immense hole to the back of her head. You would not have any thoughts on what might have occurred?' asks Detective Cassell suspiciously.

Albert immediately takes his usual stance when he becomes nervous: he stares like a kangaroo in front of the headlights of a car, so I assume the lead in the conversation; 'I do not know Detective Cassell and I am concerned that you would think that Mr Guzman or I would have any idea as to the perpetrators of this horrible crime. What is your interest in us?' I charge the detective with my question.

'Easy, easy Monk, no need to get huffy here. It is just a question. The house where the dead woman was found is owned by the Randolph's and Mrs Randolph is a client of Mr Guzman. Yes, again another one of those coincidences that I look into, and this coincidence is not the first.' sternly answers Detective Cassell.

'Monk, I do not believe in coincidences, and my years in the NSW police force tells me you two are somehow involved in the burglaries, but my experience also tells me you both are not the violent type. So here is the deal, if you hear anything concerning this case, you get back to me and I am sure we can work around any difficulties,' said Cassell handing us each his business card and as quickly as he waltzed in, Detective Cassell smiles, turns, and walks out the front door, leaving behind my little doorbell tingling.

Albert, looking as if he was the aforementioned kangaroo, returns from his trance and says: 'Wow, he has come out and tells us we are suspects in all the burglaries Danny. What are we going to do?'

I thought, 'Well, I will be damned.'

'What Danny?'

'It only took two meetings with Cassell for me to surmise which side of the law the detective stands: the grey side.'

Albert does a Pauline Hanson on me; 'Please explain, Danny'.

'Yes, I will explain. Albert, Detective Cassell suspects us of the burglaries but not for the murder, and I am not worried at all.' I calmly told Albert. I continued expressing my thoughts to Albert; 'I believe Cassell has two sides to him. One side he presents to the public; the public servant, doing his job, day and night upholding the laws of the great state of New South Wales, but there is a second side to Cassell.' I stopped since Albert had that look of surprise which he seldom gets. 'Oh, you mean Danny…' I cut

Albert short. 'Yes, Albert, it seems to me from our last conversation that Cassell will overlook certain discrepancies on our part if we help him continue to maintain and elevate his public persona.'

'So, what are we going to do, Danny?' Albert asks.

'We will continue doing what we do and when possible or necessary help Detective Cassell in solving a crime.'

'Goodness, we are becoming private detectives now Danny?' blurts out Albert.

'Only Albert, my friend, only in special circumstances,'

AN EXCELLENT PROPOSITION

My store is on the vanguard in not using currency. Nowadays with all the devices able to either handle a transaction with a 'tap and go' or with a simple wave of your hand, placement of your wallet or tapping your watch or ring, you can purchase anything from a cup of coffee to a birthday card or book, as is the case in my store. I keep a miserly $100 in coins and small notes, everything else is processed electronically utilising the services of my local branch bank of the Northport Bank in Northport, and I get any additional small bills and coins from there also using, you guessed it, an automated teller machine. Long gone are the days when you walk into a bank branch, queue your way to a human teller, who smiles at you while they take your money from you. Yep, those days are long gone.

The bank is where I was headed this Friday at 9 AM before opening the store and changing my little sign on my front door from 'We Are Closed' to 'We Are Open'. Yesterday's receipts actually had more than the usual $100 I like to keep in my register. There is a small constituency of my regulars that continue to hold on to the past or are distrustful of all things electronic fearing someone would steal their fortunes. How suspicious we have now become. I can understand it, believe me, I can. There have been a few times in my second career that I happened upon cash and of course, I could not leave it behind. Serves them right for being so distrustful.

Walking into my local branch I see the row of automated machines to my left, a single podium where a branch person stands looking bored, but I am sure ready to assist if I wake her up. A little further to the back, again on the left side of the branch, you have three cubicles where the branch manager, personal loan consultant, mortgage loan consultant and investment banker (they share the same cubicle and alternate days of the week) to be at the branch, Friday is the mortgage banker and finally the assistant branch manager John.

John Barth is an interesting person. I struck a conversation with him once when he was substituting for the person at the front podium during a break, and the branch was empty of customers, and he hit me like a sharp, intelligent, and ambitious. Extremely ambitious young man. John is a well-dressed man; he certainly looked the part of a banker with his Brooks Brothers suit pin-striped grey with a button-down white shirt and a radiant blue tie. If I did not know better, I would swear that Albert outfitted him.

Starting a quick conversation with John and we come to address each other with our first names. John said he has been at the Northport branch for a little over three months and loves it here. The people of Northport are a bit more affluent than his customers from the Sydney branch where he previously was working for the last few years. More laid back, relaxed and trusting. A change of pace for him, he said.

I found John using an interesting choice of words during our conversation. We did not speak of the *Western Jaguars*; the weather did not come up but the words that stayed in my mind were the ones he spoke, and I quote him here: *'The people of Northport are a bit more affluent than his customers from the Sydney branch where… more laid back, relaxed and trusting.'*

As many of you know, the retail business is very demanding with long hours and many days are needed to appease the multitudes' desire for books, birthday cards, luxury pens and other paper necessities. So, I valued my evenings where I retreated to my humble abode for relaxation. However, Mr John Barth took my fancy. There was something about the young man that implies to me that there is a young man that would take chances, dangerous chances.

Banking is the profession that is at the centre of trust in a civilisation. Where the fortunes of many are in the care of one individual, in today's world, the branch banker or assistant branch manager, as in John's case. He has all the information he may need to see the entire fortune of a customer or a prospective customer sitting on his or rather the bank's computer. A couple of keystrokes on the keyboard and as if by magic, assets, numbers, figures, and allocation of all said assets appear to the viewer. If I had not entered into a lucrative partnership with my friend, Albert, owner of the premier hair salon in Northport, I would look at the potential of a second career with a bank. Something told me young Barth had also found his calling to this extracurricular activity while working for my local branch bank. I said this because a few weeks ago I noticed him driving off after work in a new Lexus LC 500.

So, I invited John to meet me for a few drinks at the local pub, *The White Sheep*, after work on Thursday night and here we are, John nursing a beer and me sipping an Evian.

'Banking must pay very well these days John. I mean a Brooks Brothers suit. Man, you always look so classy.' I said pushing the conversation in the direction I wanted.

John was taken aback but recovered and then said, 'Oh no Danny, these days Brooks Brothers are not as expensive as they were in the 'old days' (John was speaking of the 1950s, I am sure) and anyway, I need to look presentable. There is a lot of old and new money in Northport, and they love coming into the branch to talk about investments or get an additional mortgage to purchase another vacation home somewhere. Besides Danny, if you dress the part, you become the part.' explained John looking at me in my jeans purchased at Target and blue 'Bazinga' illustrated t-shirt from the show *The Big Bang Theory.'*

'You are right John, quite correct. If you dress the part, you become the part,' I said calmly sipping my Evian water, and then I drop my question; 'But a new Lexus LC 500 has to be beyond the $62,000 annual salary you make. So, tell me, just between us, do you do anything else at the bank besides attending to your wealthy customers?'

John looked at me with fire in his eyes. I had either struck a chord or insulted the young man insinuating he does something illicit at the bank. John takes a last gulp of his beer and gets up. I grab his arm, and he stops halfway and says, 'You can go to hell Danny saying things like that to me.'

The moment was there open to me. I saw a raw cut, and I was ready to pour salt into it. It will sting and make for awkward moments in the branch later on, but I needed to know something. 'John, are you embezzling funds from your customers? If you are, I am going to report you to Detective Malcolm Cassell; he and I go way back.' I showed him the Detective's business card.

OK, I lied about Cassell. We do not go back a way back. He rather suspects Albert and I of pulling several high-profile burglaries around the Sydney metropolitan area but cannot prove it. Just recently Albert and I encountered a poor dead woman at a Mosman mansion and because of this Detective Cassell thought we might have something to do with the recently deceased. We were glad when Detective Cassell said: *'Monk, I do not believe in coincidences, and my years in the NSW police force tells me you two are somehow involved in the burglaries, but my experience also tells me you both are not the violent type. So here is the deal, if you hear anything concerning this case, you get back to me and I am sure we can work around any difficulties,'* and he gave both Albert and me his business card. That was a direct quote of Detective Cassell, I did not make it up.

Having seen the business card John turns a little white, like the white sheep on the picture frame above the bar, and slumps into the chair.

'What do you want Danny?' glumly speaks young John. 'Why nothing, my friend! I want to point out to you that if I can spot certain particularities in you in a few weeks, imagine what the NSW police can do with all their resources.' 'John,' I firmly asked him, 'what have you been up to?'

Realising that the points I had made were valid and that at no time I honestly sounded like I was going to turn him into Detective Cassell, John goes into detail as to his recent adventures, post-work, mostly.

John explains that it all started in the second week of his arrival at the branch.

A customer approached him with a proposition, a small one he says, just a quick shoplifting job at *Missy's Book Shop*, just down the street from my store and from then on, he could not stop himself. This is a story for another day.

While shoplifting gave him a 'high,' John started looking into customers' accounts and he found plenty of customer dormant accounts with a few hundred dollars to several thousand and saw an opportunity. Just before the accounts were to be declared 'dormant' under NSW banking rules, he would place a small deposit, thus activating the account and subsequently creating several transactions in which the funds of the dormant account would be transferred offshore to his own Cayman Islands account.

John said he had been a prolific embezzler and that his overseas account now has over $136,342.56 in it. But John emphasises to me that is not everything he has done. Utilising the bank computers, he also knows all the assets of his customers, and other bank customers, the location, and the value of said assets.

John looks at me and grimly says, 'Danny, you heard what happened last week in Mosman where a woman was found dead, and some priceless earrings were stolen?' I nodded and asked him to continue; 'Well, I got into the mansion, please do not ask me how, (I did not) and when I entered the study to look for the safe, I find her, dead, blood all over the place. Man, the blood was still oozing from her cracked head.'

'What did you do next?' I asked him.

'I did what was sensible, I opened the safe, ransacked it as quickly as possible, took the earrings and fled, scared out of my wits.'

'So, the woman was dead when you walked into the study?' I stated.

'Yes,' answered John.

'You did not see anyone else in the house?' I asked.

'No,' answered John.

'Did you hear anything in any other room?' I asked.

'No,' said John.

'Where are the earrings now?' I asked.

'In a safe deposit box in the Northport branch where I work under the alias, Peter Smith.' How original I thought.

'The bank has a safe deposit box.'

'Yes. Many banks are now either refusing to take on new clients or offering to transfer their boxes to different, often inconvenient, locations. Some banks are doing the extreme by ceasing the service at local, regional, and national levels. But not Northport Bank. They feel that this is a very important core service that the affluent customers like and want and they have twelve branches scattered about the city in high money sensitive suburbs which offer this service. Northport is one of the lucky branches that has a large safe deposit base and only a few vacancies,' concluded John.

Several thoughts went through my head right then. Detective Cassell thinks Albert, and I lifted the earrings but did not kill the woman. I know John did not kill the woman but boosted the earrings. So, who killed the woman?

'So, John, what are you going to do with the earrings?'

'Dammit Danny, I do not know now. With a dead woman involved in the mix of things, these things have become hot, way too hot for me. I am not equipped to handle something like this. Maybe I could send them to the police anonymously, and they forget about it.' Sheepishly said, John.

'That will not happen. I can guarantee that to you. The police will continue to look for the person or persons responsible for the theft and the murder, but they have yet surmised that there is more than one person involved. John, if you just stole the earrings, someone else killed the poor woman.'

'I swear on my mother's grave that I just stole the damn things, I did not kill the woman, I swear it, Danny,' implored John.

'I believe you, John, I do. I also have a recommendation for you.'

'Go ahead Danny, right now I am open to anything to get these damn things off my hands and go back to my day-to-day routine at the bank.' Sighs John.

'John, I need you to follow my instructions to the letter and not deviate. First, I will give you $500,000 for the earrings. Second, you are to return the money you siphoned from the bank. Third, you resign your position, and once it is accepted, you take the money I have given you for the earrings and leave the country. Will you do this?' I asked John.

'But Danny if I do this what do you get out of this?' questions John.

'I will find a way to dispose of the earrings properly, ensure they are not traceable to you or me, and I will also help the police find the murderer. That is what I will get out of this.' Firmly spoken I thought.

John thought about this solution to his current dilemma and decided to order another beer. I waited for him to slowly enjoy his beer until he was ready to let me know what his decision would be. Finally, after taking the last bit of beer, he agrees with the solution I proposed.

'How long will it take you, John, to get the earrings from the safe deposit box, return the money you embezzled raising no suspicions and leave the country?' I put the question to John.

'I am pretty fast; so, it should take me only one week to put the funds back. I can ask for an immediate resignation which will take about two weeks to follow through and one week to get the earrings out of the safe deposit box without the bank knowing what has happened. So, for about one month. When can I have my money?' John said now with a bit of oomph and cockiness in him.

'You do all that, and when you are ready to turn over the earrings, we will meet at a neutral location, and I will transfer the $500,000 to any account you want me to. It will be immediate, and you can then go your merry way and so can I,' said I.

'That sounds okay by me,' as John got up and said he would get in touch once he had everything in place.

As John walked out of the *White Sheep* pub, I thought to myself and sounded a lot like Albert: 'Well Danny, darling, how are you going to pull this off?'

Suddenly, my eyes open wide. As John walks out, Alessia walks in with another woman who is laughing. Alessia sees me and comes toward me.

'Hi, Danny. What a delightful surprise to see you here tonight.'

'Well hello Alessia, so nice to see you again. You come here often because I have not seen you here before?'

'No, I do not. I wanted to, oh silly me, let me introduce you to Pat Owens, a co-worker at the library who is celebrating her fourth anniversary at the library today.'

I stood up and said, 'Hi Ms Owens. Congratulations on your anniversary. Please let me buy you and Alessia a celebratory drink.'

'No Danny thank you,' answered Alessia. 'Pat and I are having a girl's night out and no men are allowed,' as she winks at me and leans and gives a kiss on the cheek. Then they both wave to me as they move into a booth at the farthest part of the pub.

I grinned to myself, and I motioned to the server to get me another bottle of Evian but with a shot of 25-year-old Mortlach single malt (you do not want to know how much that set me back). Seeing Alessia really made my night and to get a peck on the cheek in front of her friend has to show that she likes me more than I thought. A good sign I thought, an excellent sign.

So, getting back to my thoughts concerning my conversation with John if Albert can sell the earrings for the original $20,000,000 promised by the Chinese billionaire, minus the $500,000 we will give John and solve the murder maybe, just maybe, we can make this an excellent proposition.

A SIMPLE CASE OF LOVE

My bookstore is seldom extremely busy. You can come in early in the morning just after opening hours and there may be one to three waiting to go in. Some days, not a soul is waiting. Take a gander at midday, and you might see three or more individuals, maybe browsing and maybe buying and at times in what appears as a 'rush'; there may be six to eight individuals, browsing around the store. Mid-afternoon to closing time you will get four to ten more, and that is a busy day I just described for you.

Today, at precisely at 10:01 AM, my front door tingles with its little bell and my friend Albert rushes in all excited.

Albert is wearing what I can only describe as a subtle outfit this morning.

A dark pin-striped suit with a bright pink shirt and a purple tie that does not go with the outfit, but I am not brave or fashion-conscious enough to tell Albert.

'Danny, darling I am here as per your voicemail. Have you decided what we are to do about Detective Cassell increasing curiosity into our private matters? I know you have a plan. I could tell by the sound of your voice when I got your message.'

'Albert, we need to come up with $500,000 by tonight to buy Randolph's earrings from the person who took them from their home last week.'

Albert became white as a sheet. 'Are you telling me darling that you know who killed the cleaner and took the earrings? I am happy for you, I am, but no way I am giving my hard-earned money to a murderer.' Emphatically stated Albert holding his arms with an embrace in front of him.

'That is not the case Albert,' I said. 'I know who took the earrings, but he did not murder the cleaner. I aim to find out who the murderer is with the help of Detective Cassell.' I responded.

'What? We are getting involve with that dreadful man. You are kidding me, right?'

'Well, I invited Detective Cassell to the store at noon so if you can join us, you will see how I get Detective Cassell to help us find out who the murderer is.' I smiled at Albert feeling that my plan was already developing slowly in my mind.

'You do ask a lot from me cariño but I trust you emphatically. OK, count me in. I will see you both at noon.' Said Albert as he left my store, again tingling my doorbell, but this time, gently.

A few minutes after noon my little doorbell sounds (you know I have not had one customer today so far) and in walks Detective Malcolm Cassell dishevelled as always wearing what has to be one of his trademark suit; charcoal with a white shirt and a paper-thin dark tie. The door has not closed and in walks Albert looking even more radiant than this morning (I guess he went home to change) because he is now wearing a bright yellow suit with a wildly looking blue tie that mixes into his dark blue shirt. Albert moves behind me as if afraid that Detective Cassell will jump him. 'Hi Detective Cassell, prompt as always,' I say. Detective Cassell looks at me.

'OK, you asked me here. Tell me what you have on your mind. You said little in your message to me last night.'

'Detective Cassell, I have had the pleasure of knowing you for a while now. May I call you Malcolm?'

'Whatever you want to call me is fine by me when we are in an informal conversation like now, but otherwise, Detective Cassell will be used. Understood?'

'OK by me,' I responded. 'Let me tell you why I asked you here today. I think we can help you solve the murder of Randolph's cleaner.'

I could feel Detective Cassell's eyes just boring through me and passing through Albert as well. 'What do you have in mind?' he says.

'First Malcolm, Albert and I need to accompany you to the Randolph estate to see the scene where the earrings were taken.' I wait for a reaction from the detective and seeing none I continue. 'OK, once we get there, we want to walk around the home to see if we can establish how the murderer got in and how he made off with the earrings. Will this be possible?' I enquire.

'Since when did I become your personal tour guide to a murder scene? What do you expect to see that my junior detectives have not already found? Or do you know something I do not know?' Sarcastically mutters Detective Cassell.

'Malcolm, do you want our help or not? I am sure that your superiors would be pleased if you were to solve a murder that has made the front pages of most newspapers in Australia. As far as Albert and I know something you do not know I can tell you we do not know who did this ghastly murder that you described. However, we are both very observant individuals and sometimes the untrained eye might see something you and your troops might have missed. If you do not want our help, that is OK, no worries. Today we call it a miss and leave it at that.' I explained to Detective Cassell.

Detective Cassell wanders around the empty store all devoid of any clients now for a good five or six hours (how can anyone make a profit in retail is beyond me). Cassell stops in front of the bestsellers bookcase section and runs his index finger through the books as if looking for a title. He picks up *Books, Pens and Larceny* by J. F. Nodar and opens a chapter and reads for a minute or two. He mutters a bit every so often but we cannot hear a word he says. Placing the book back on the bestseller bookcase, in the wrong spot I might add, he moves towards us and says: 'OK, we have a deal. You can come with me to the Randolph estate, and I will let you do your perusal, but I will be with you at all times. We all stick together and you will not wander off around the Randolph compound by yourselves. Is that understood?'

'Yes,' said Albert nervously, while I nodded. Detective Cassell continues: 'All information that you get is part of MY investigation. If asked, you are 'consultants' that I have asked to come in to look around. You do not speak to any of the other officers when I am around you. Again, understood?'

Albert and I nod in the affirmative.

'OK, let's meet at Randolph's place at 7 PM tomorrow.' Detective Cassell dictates.

'No-can-do, Malcolm. Both Albert and I run a business. I for one cannot close shop at that time - it is just not conducive for business and it is Thursday and I have late-night trading. So, I propose we meet there at 7:30 PM tonight after we both close our stores, miss the rush hour traffic somewhat and in the light of dusk we might see something your folks missed.'

By observing Detective Cassell's face, I could see that I was messing him up, but to my surprise, he said, 'You know. You are right. OK, let's meet at 7:30 PM as you suggested.' Suddenly he turns and goes through my front door leaving my little bell tingling for a while.

I walk over to the spot where Cassell placed the bestseller in the wrong spot and put it back in its number one position. This book seems to be a good seller I think to myself, I should order a dozen or so more from *Northport Booksellers* in case there is a good demand for it in the next week or so.

Returning to the front counter Albert looks at me and says: 'Sweetness, I hope you know what you are doing. I am going back to my shop for a fine drink of a Chivas Regal Royal Salute 21-year-old scotch I have been saving for such occasions.' Albert does a 'Malcolm,' and also departs leaving my little bell tingling for a while.

At 5:12 PM, just before closing an elderly man walks in, browses around the shop, and buys the last volume of *Antiquities of Central and South-Eastern Missouri Smithsonian Institution Bureau of American Ethnology Bulletin 37* by Gerard Fowke (the first edition from 1910) good for $234.99 which made my day and I close the shop promptly at 6 PM.

Albert decided he would drive us to the Randolph mansion, so we set off a few minutes after closing shop and arrived just shy of 7:30 PM to find Detective Cassell waiting for us on the large driveway.

As we exit the car, Detective Cassell comments: 'Well that is certainly an expensive car you drive Guzman. Cutting hair has to be a profitable method of making a living?' sarcastically he asks.

OK, I did not think this through letting Albert drive. He owns a Bentley Mulsanne 1998 which he inherited and has upgraded with some extra accessories with some of the money we earned from the other activities we have engaged in. If this does not confirm Detective Cassell's suspicions of our extracurricular activities, nothing will. 'He inherited that from his parents,' I said. 'Let us get started. Is everyone home?' I ask.

'Yeah, I asked the major-domo, what a silly name for a butler, to meet us here since he said he slept through the entire night of the murder. Both Mr and Mrs Randolph are not here. They are at the Sydney Opera House for an event. They were out the night of the murder and have solid alibis, so I do not think you need to speak with them,' answered Detective Cassell.

'Good, let's get started. Show us to the room where the cleaner was found,' I said.

'What? You do not know where that is?' asks Detective Cassell angling for a response that would incriminate us. 'No, I said I do not know where the room is. Neither Albert nor I have ever seen the front of this house, so how about showing us the way to where the body was found.'

We walk into Randolph's mansion through the front door, a pleasant experience by the way, and we find Gerard Fountaine, the major-domo, waiting for us. 'I asked the butler to wait for us here.' quips Detective Cassell. 'This is Gerard Fountaine, the butler.'

To which Gerard responds, 'I am a major-domo, not a butler Sir.'

'What is the difference?' asks Detective Cassell.

'The pay,' Gerard responds quickly and abruptly.

'OK, this is Mr Monk and Mr Guzman. They are my 'consultants' that I told you I was bringing tonight to review the room.'

'Nice to meet you,' said Albert as I nod towards Gerard, who looks uncomfortable. I say to the major-domo, 'Gerard, would you lead us to the room where the body was found?'

'This way gentlemen,' and we follow him into the study.

'Let us get started. Albert, you take the left side of the room, and I will take the right, and we meet back in the middle. Detective Cassell and Mr Fountaine, please sit in the divan and watch us making sure we touch nothing. OK?' I stated.

'Whatever,' said Detective Cassell while Gerard nodded solemnly.

We took a little under an hour to inspect every inch of the massive study. Albert did an excellent job of examining every nook and cranny making funny faces and the occasional 'Oh' and a few 'Ah' for more dramatic effect, just like I had coached him during our trip over.

While this was going on, I also looked around, but in reality, I was monitoring Gerard. He looked nervous about being in the room in the presence of two strange 'consultants' and Detective Cassell which surprised me since he was the one that 'discovered' the murdered cleaner at 7 AM and called the police and reported the burglary as well.

Gerard was in his late fifties about 175 cm tall, maybe 110 kilos with a round face, a crop of white hair and a white beard. He wore a distinctive black suit and tie that you would say was way out of Detective Cassell's league and budget. A Rolex, a pinkie right finger ring and Alessandro Demesure leather oxford shoes that would make Albert proud to own. As I approached the middle of the room, I thought it was time to prompt the question: 'Gerard, why did you murder the maid?'

Gerard stood up quickly, did not move and just stood there, flabbergasted, unable to answer, at least, not right away.

You should have seen Cassell face!

'I did not kill Michelle. I loved Michelle,' shakily answers Gerard.

'Of course, you loved her but you killed her,' I retorted to Gerard. 'But what happened that night? Did she say to you she did not have the same feelings towards you? Did it anger you? How did you handle this rejection?'

I pushed Gerard to get him to answer.

'Was she out of your league? I mean, she was younger than you. Did she imply you were just too old for her? Come, Gerard, I know you did it. Admit it, and I am sure Detective Cassell will put in a friendly word for you in the Office of the Director of Public Prosecutions to go easier on you.'

Gerard just sank into the divan. He seemed devoid of any colour in his face as if he knew that if he let it all out, it would be easier for everyone involved in this situation.

'Yes. We argue. I offered Michelle my hand in marriage, and she just laughed in my face. She turns around to leave the study. I do not know why, I mean I was angry, but a rage came over me, and I struck her in the back of the head with a bronze statue of Mozart that sits on the master's desk but now is at the bottom of the pond out the back. Realising what I had done, I took another similar bust from another room and placed it close to her and dabbed a bit of her blood on it so when the police arrive, they would find it but with no fingerprints on it since I wore my major-domo gloves when I placed it on the carpet next to Michelle.' slowly and sadly Gerard spoke.

'And then you took the earrings to let us presume a burglar broke in and was interrupted by the maid, and he murders her,' stated Detective Cassell.

'Oh no, I would not steal from the Master. He has been exceedingly kind to me over the years,' Gerard responded quickly.

'Okay, we will talk about this back at the station. Come on Gerard, off we go,' said Detective Cassell as he placed the handcuffs on Gerard's manicured hands.

Outside Detective Cassell tucks Gerard into the back of his car, closes the door and moves closer to Albert's car where we are waiting for him.

'How in the hell did you know he did it?' Cassell asked.

I answered, 'I did not know but suspected. Murder happens for one of the four Ls, loot, loathing, lust, or love. The local society papers went into a lot of detail as to how the house is organised, how the study is maintained. How long the servants had worked at the Randolph's and of course the newspaper had a photo of both Michelle and Gerard standing close to the Randolphs while they were serving them during one function at their home. You could see the way Gerard looked at Michelle. There was something there, so I thought it had to be a simple case of love scorn and I took a gamble and it paid off.'

'Well Danny boy, you and Albert did a decent job for me here, and I appreciate it, but I still think you had something to do with the stolen earrings. Why don't you both come clean now and let's make this a trifecta of honesty, how about it?' Bemuses Detective Cassell.

'Malcolm, I think you can read a person well in your many years of experience as a Detective. Look at me as I say to you: We did not take the earrings.'

Detective Cassell takes a few moments looking at me, collects his thoughts and then says, 'Well, you might be right for once. You guys did not take the earrings, but I am sure you know what happened here. Just beware that because you help me out here, it does not mean I will not be looking at both of you closely over the coming months. Understood?'

Gosh, he sure loves to say 'Understood'. I thought to myself.

Detective Cassell turns and heads back to his car and speeds off down the driveway and leaves Albert and me in a light dusty film.

'Danny, you were just divine in there, simply divine. What is our next move?' Albert asks me.

'My friend, I now meet with the individual that has the earrings and I will transfer $500,000 from our 'investment accounts,' to the Cayman Islands account he specified and once it is received in his account, he will hand me the earrings. While this is happening, you find our billionaire Chinese friend and tell him we have his Apollo and Artemis earrings, and we are ready to do business.'

With that, we get into Albert's car and gently drive out of the driveway not even raising a bit of dust.

THAT LITTLE BIT OF MONEY

O wning a small business can be a pleasant experience I know because I am a small business owner. My small commercial enterprise started with an idea, courage and doing things differently. The *Village Books & Stuff* is today one hundred per cent debt-free - all mine. The building, the stock inside of it, everything and it is all owned by yours truly, Daniel Monk, Danny to my friends, and speaking of friends, I can count them on one hand.

First, my next-door neighbour, Albert Matthew Guzman, the flamboyant owner of the most excellent hair salon in all of Sydney, *Cut Me Crazy* and second, Alessia Vassallo, who I would say is 'my steady,' in the American vernacular. Then there is Detective Malcolm Cassell, of the local police. The first two are staunch friends, while the last is yet to be determined in what category he is in.

My warm and honest friendship with Albert goes back a few years when we engaged in some extracurricular activities. I found these activities quite enjoyable and fruitful, while Detective Cassell, well he just wants to make sure he progresses up the seniority ranks of the Australian Federal Police force and does not mind if he gets there by hook or by crook. All he needs to do is nab us for our past 'acquisitions,' as Albert loves calling them, and we would both be residents in one of the fine correctional facilities in New South Wales.

As I mentioned my list of friends is not a large one and the main reason is that while running a small commercial business can be exciting and it is also demanding. These demands are of your time and they will reduce your social hours since you might be way too tired to party, which I never do much of. Now, do not get me wrong. I open my store at a reasonable time (10:00 AM) and close it at an even more reasonable time (6:00 PM) except on Thursday night which is deemed to be 'late trading hours' in New South Wales, and I go just a little later—730 PM. However, during off hours I also have to tend to a lot of things that require attention. Stocking, inventorying, cleaning, and going to the post office when I need to ship out any online orders. But I do have time to go out and socialise at the local drinking establishment in Northport—The *White Sheep* and that is where I met her.

Now you are going to think I am old fashioned, but the only way I could describe her when I entered the pub was; there is a young Sophia Loren. As tall as I am with beautiful long wavy auburn hair and hazel eyes which I could see because they were like beacons to every man and his dog in the pub. As I walked past her to my favourite booth, I sensed an aroma permeating from her, lavender, and it enveloped me as I sat where I continued to watch her as she sipped a cocktail.

The server came over and asked if I wanted my 'usual,' but tonight I thought I would spread my wings a bit in honour of 'Sophia' and asked for a 'breakfast margarita' which comprises of tequila, Cointreau, dry orange marmalade, fresh lime juice and Agave syrup. The server smiled, knowing that tonight was going to be a good tip night from me and went to get my order. I continued to glance at 'Sophia' and saw that frequently, men would sit next to her, start a conversation, and be entirely disregarded by 'Sophia.' That gave me some relief in thinking that maybe I had a chance to meet her or perhaps I would wind up like one of those guys: shot down.

My breakfast margarita arrived, and the bartender, Angus, did a great job of it, even having the right margarita glass and a slice of orange as garnish poured into a glass with fresh ice. One sip and I remember the reason I always come here, the food and the drinks, but particularly the drinks, or is it the food? OK, it is both. As I continue to look around the pub, my eyes lock on 'Sophia' and hers on me. We both smile and I nod to her, which gets a similar response from her.

'Sophia' is wearing a flattering fit-and-flare dress in draped linen-blend fabric. Featuring a tie-front neckline, adjustable shoulder straps and a smocked back panel that stretches to fit her shape just perfectly and blends beautifully with her tan skin and auburn hair. She stands, grabs her drinks and glides toward my booth, smiles and says: 'Hi. Mind if I join you?'

Super cool me responds, 'I will leave soon but sure.'

God, what an idiotic thing to say, I thought to myself. But my response does not affect 'Sophia' because she continues that infectious smile and slides into the booth across from me.

'You work at the bookstore, do you not?' she asks.

'Yes, I do. I own the *Village Books & Stuff*. My name is Danny. How do you know?'

'Oh, I just know. My name is Jezebel. Jezebel Ranford, I am the curator of the *Michael Rockford Gallery* in Northport. I go by JR. It is nice to meet you.'

'Likewise,' I say and stare at this beautiful woman sitting across from me. Then I ask: 'How long have you been at the gallery? I have not seen you there, but then again, I do not frequent art galleries much.'

'I just received my appointment last month, and I have been so busy in the back rooms cataloguing and researching the art artefacts the gallery has that I have not been on the gallery floor much. I walk by your store almost every day and always see you through the front window.'

'Well, I am easily noticeable since my store is not a hive of activity on some days. Do not get me wrong the store has its frequent customers buying the general office supplies, the occasional rare book but for the most, it entails the general store browser that just enjoys the smell of paper and ink and spending time in a small shop versus weathering the cold of winter or the heat of summer outside.'

Jezebel takes a sip of her drink, and her face turns serious on me.

'Danny, I have a slight problem, and I do not know who to confide in, and I was wondering if I could share something with you, get your opinion as a small business owner and maybe you might shed an alternative that I have not come up with for my situation.'

Intrigued at this spontaneous request for help, I gladly accept; 'But of course. How may I be of help, JR?'

'During my research in the gallery's backroom, I found what seems to be Arthur Conan Doyle's autographed manuscript of *The Adventure of the Dancing Men.*' A quick search of the records showed this article was donated in 1912 to the gallery's first curator and catalogue with a value of £2. It is worth at least $425,000 at today's prices and I know no one knows it is just hiding in the desk drawer in the gallery's backroom.'

'So, what is the problem, JR?' I asked.

'The gallery is running out of funds, and the last benefactors' funds are running out as well. Today's benefactors are only looking at a tax deduction, so the donations are quite low compared to the past contributions. So, I thought you might be of help to the gallery.' Jezebel smiled as she took the last sip of her drink.

'I am a small business owner, and I would love to provide you with a contribution if that is what you are asking for, but it will not be substantial.'

'No, Danny. That is not what I need your help with.'

'Then, how can I help you, JR?'

'I need you to steal the manuscript, sell it in the black market and give me the funds acquired, minus a small 'acquisition fee' of course.' Concluded Jezebel now sucking on the remaining small piece of ice on her highball glass.

My first thought is here is Detective Cassell setting me up with a beautiful woman as bait. I will not fall for it.

'Wait a minute, JR. Who do you think you are speaking to? I am a small business owner and would not know the first thing about stealing and even less on disposing of such an article,' I said.

Jezebel looks at me for a minute or two, smiles and responds with: 'Danny, I did not ask you to 'dispose' of the manuscript but to steal it. I know you have other resources at your disposal for these types of 'acquisitions.' I know you are an 'acquisition' expert and your other sources help you dispose of said 'acquisitions'. Am I right?' concludes Jezebel as she finishes the last of the ice in her highball glass.

Again, fearing a trap constructed by Detective Cassell or someone else I get up and say 'How dare you to make such a request. I have a good mind to report you to the authorities or at least to the board of directors of the gallery.' Jezebel smiles and softly says: 'Danny, I am Albert's cousin, so I know about your activities with him. Please sit.'

I could have passed out. Albert never mentioned a cousin to me in all the years we knew each other, so this had to be a trap for sure.

'Here,' said JR taking her mobile out of her purse, doing a quick speed dial, speaks, 'Primo, habla con Danny' and hands me the phone. A male voice answers with a high-pitched voice: 'Sweetheart darling, how are you tonight?'

I recognise the voice immediately; it is Albert's, so I answer back.

'Albert, it is me, Danny. How come you never said you had a cousin?'

'Crikey, Danny, darling. I never mentioned JR. So sorry, I do have a large family and I do not spend a lot of time speaking about them. What a pleasant surprise. Why did she hand the phone to you? Is she all right? Has something happened? Oh, dear, my sweet JR. What has happened?'

'Calm down, Albert. She is fine. I am fine. We are down at the *White Sheep*, and we just met. She has a proposition, and I thought it might have been our friend Detective Cassell setting us up, but it seems I was wrong. How about you coming to the pub and hearing for yourself the proposition your cousin made me?'

'I will be there in thirty minutes.' And he hangs up.

I hand Jezebel the phone and look at her. Here is a beautiful woman. Young, intelligent with an angelic face and she comes up to me with a proposition that speaks of pure larceny. I am falling in love, I think.

'So, JR, you go by Jezebel Ranford. Is that your Christian name if I may ask?'

'No, it is Josefina Ramirez, but I thought in the line of work I am in and not working in my native country, I better use a more Anglo name to fit in better. You do not like it?'

'I do JR, especially the Jezebel first name. This first name is not used that often these days, I think.'

Before the conversation got deeper and in less than the prescribed thirty minutes in walks Albert.

You cannot miss him.

Tonight, he is wearing a striking suit with neon and animal print. The long-sleeved fully lined jacket has functional buttons on the front, built in shoulder pads and fake buttons on the sleeve cuffs. The trousers have button and zipper fastening plus a concealed hook closure. The waist has belt loops plus hidden wide elastic on the sides of the waist for added comfort. The trousers have two functional side pockets and a fake back pocket. Completing the look of this suit is a matching tie which Albert is wearing with a button-down black shirt. It is truly Albert.

Albert sees us, and with his high-pitched voice, we hear: 'Hi you, beautiful people.' Albert then goes to the end of the bar and speaks with the bartender and walks to our booth and shortly afterward, the server comes with three drinks, which are the second round of my breakfast margarita, Jezebel's tonic water and Alberts's first Brandy Alexander and a glass of ginger ale on the side.

As Albert takes a sip of his ginger ale, he smiles at Jezebel and nods to me. He pronounces: 'Now JR, sweetheart, tell me this proposition Danny darling told me about over the phone.'

In the next twenty minutes JR describes the same conversation to Albert that she shared with me prior. This time Jezebel goes into the disposition of the funds with a little more clarity.

'Well, I thought after Danny gets the manuscript, you dear cousin Alberto, might find us a buyer for say, $400,000 and once payment is received, we could equitably divide the funds. Say $100,000 split between both of you, $200,000 for me and the rest goes to the gallery as an 'anonymous donation.. What do you think?' Jezebel proclaims before calmly sipping her tonic water.

As I look into those hazel eyes, I see not only a beautiful woman (gosh, I keep saying that to myself a lot) but also as I mentioned, one that has a purely larcenous heart.

'Wait a minute,' I interrupted. 'You ask me to steal the manuscript. Use our 'sources' which is your cousin to dispose of the manuscript and you get the an equal share of the loot. That is not an equal proposition, JR. Not at all. What do you think, Albert?'

'I agree with Danny. Not a fair distribution of the acquired funds at all.'

'But boys think of it this way. You did not know the manuscript existed nor its value. I can ensure you get your hands on it easily without fear of any compromise and you are $50,000 richer each. That makes for a genuinely delightful holiday in the south of France, don't you think? Besides, you now know how to get it and you need to have an accurate valuation of the manuscript as to its authenticity, and that is where my value comes into play. It is going to be my name on the appraisal valuation. So, we all take risks, boys, all of us.'

I have to admit that she made her position efficiently and to the point.

Jezebel went to say that the manuscript is on an old desk in the gallery's backroom. No one knows it is there and she can then say that the document was lost during some past period or misplaced during a move and it is never to be found, and the gallery can file an insurance claim and recoup the current value—$425,000—and no one gets hurt. Jezebel was emphatic that the paltry sum was nothing to a large insurance company these days.

After JR shared her proposition, she gave Albert a quick peek on the cheek and left us to discuss her idea.

'First, why did JR call you 'Alberto'? Did you change your name when you came to Australia?' I asked.

'Yes, I did. My name was a dead giveaway I was not from here so I just kept saying Albert instead of Alberto and over time that was it. I have never given it much thought so now I go with Albert all the time. Maybe I should legally change it but why bother.'

'You need to discuss that with an attorney Albert. It might get you in trouble one day.'

'Darling. Que sera, sera, as Doris sang. Now what are we going to do with Jezebel's proposition?'

A couple of more drinks and we decide that after hearing a very persuasive Jezebel that I would get the manuscript from the back room of the gallery and Albert would find us a buyer who would not be too fussy how the manuscript was acquired. There are many of those collectors of Arthur Conan Doyle that would bite at the chance to own such a piece of history.

My intention here is not to bore the reader with the fine details of our 'acquisition.' Let us say that as promised specific detailed plans of the building were presented by Jezebel and the schematics of the alarm system and the hours in which a security guard was roaming the inside of the gallery. Given the fact that we (actually it is I) because Albert seldom goes on an 'acquisition' with me since he finds them rather 'strenuous' or so he says.

Since we only had to get into the building and the back-catalogue room, the exercise was as easy as pie, as the Americans say. Given that I knew precisely which desk, which drawer the manuscript was in, it took me less than twenty minutes to navigate through the gallery, make the 'acquisition' and ensure that my exit was as clean as possible leaving no one the wiser of my participation.

While I did all the 'heavy lifting' Albert was busy reaching out to his various contacts, and it took him less than two days to find several bidders. We hoped that the fact there were several bidders for the manuscript would fetch us more than the $425,000 but alas these collectors are intelligent and worldly individuals, and they know the going rate for just about everything, so the bid was accepted at $375,000 a little less than what Jezebel had hoped for.

The local police released a press notice that a break-in had occurred in the *Michael Rockford Gallery* reported by the curator Miss Jezebel Ranford. She shared as much details as she could confirming the police report to the local paper, *Northport Advertiser*, the Sydney paper and all the national papers. The break-in was described as 'perfect', which flattered me a bit, and the police are at a loss as to the location of the missing manuscript.

A few months after the 'acquisition' the *Northport Advertiser* notes the departure of Miss Jezebel Ranford from the *Michael Rockford Gallery*. The reporter authoring the article stated that Ms Ranford 'was heartbroken over the loss of the Arthur Conan Doyle's autographed manuscript of *The Adventure of the Dancing Men*' and that she would go on a sabbatical to the south of France to *review her future in the art world*' or so said the reporter.

For our part, Albert and I received $45,000 each (yes had to take a cut), and we both know you really cannot go to the south of France with that little of money.

GOING TO RIGHT A WRONG

August is the windiest month of the Australian winter, at least it feels that way, in Northport. The way they build the main street of the village, it seems like you are in a wind tunnel and the wind chill makes a stroll a challenge. Not that I have to do any of that for I live upstairs right on top of my place of business, The *Village Books & Stuff.*

At precisely 9:45 AM, I walked down the back stairs to my store, turned on the light, turn off the alarm system and promptly turned on the air conditioner to make sure the store would be warm the moment I opened its door for business at 10 AM.

The routine is straightforward each day. Once the air conditioner is on, I do a quick review of the store to make sure everything is in the right place. My cash register is always ready to perform a transaction, even at 10 AM because I leave just $100 in small notes and coins overnight since everyone is now going the plastic payment method with either a PIN or a 'pay and wave' transaction. Cash, it seems, is losing its lustre which is something I do not mind because it saves me the constant daily travel to the bank to make deposits whereas now, only one trip is required, and I do that on Fridays.

Overall, I consider myself an honest small business owner even in these tough financial times and with increased transactions being electronically executed as I mentioned previously. If you do not know what that means by 'in the old days' I mean that I saw Mr

McCullum a few times do a transaction with the cash register open and not record the sale thus avoiding any GST and pocketing the entire proceeds of the 'sale'. You cannot do that with every electronic transaction.

When I bought the business, it was hard to make the mortgage payments, as well as the rest: utilities, insurance, buy stock and pay myself super and have spending money. Since partnering with Albert I have not had to worry about losing the business, just making sure the Australian Tax Office is happy. Of course, my challenge is now also making sure Detective Malcolm Cassell is off our backs.

This August Monday morning should have been a routine day but promptly at 10:10 AM my little doorbell jingles and in walks Detective Cassell (thinking of the devil) looking as dishevelled as he always looks with the blandest suit on needing a pressing.

'Good morning, Monk. How was your weekend? Profitable, I presume?' states Detective Cassell.

'Well, if it isn't Detective Cassell, the weekend is always okay with more people walking around the centre of Northport but nothing that I would claim to be a productive day. Just average. Why do you ask?' I query the detective.

'Oh, Monk, I am not speaking about this business. I am speaking of the 'business' which you run after-hours.'

'Detective Cassell, I am totally at a loss as to your insinuation. What are you saying?' I softly spoke since the little doorbell of my front door jingle for the second time, and I had a customer come in, and I wanted to make sure they did not overhear this conversation.

'Well, I am the one surprised this morning,' said Cassell. I guess you have not heard that the mansion of Immanuel and Adina Standerton was broken into on Saturday night. One of two known examples of a prototype design for the first shekel struck by the Jews in the Jewish War of 66 AD to 70 AD: the AR shekel, measuring 24mm and weighing 13.34 grams seemed to have vanished from their safe,' states Cassell. 'I just assumed you had something to do with the disappearance and I came in to speak to you about it since I could not find Mr Guzman in his store this morning,' finishing with a big smile.

Honestly, I knew nothing about this disappearance since on Sundays I do not read a newspaper. I turn on either the turntable with some smooth jazz vinyl records as background noise or the radio to listen to Oldies FM 108.7, which only has music and no news and spend the day cataloguing my personal rare book collection, which I hope never to sell. So, this bit of news was a surprise.

Glancing, I saw my customer was browsing the Australian history section, in particular, the NSW history section. He was holding in his hand one of the two volumes entitled *'Two Years in New South Wales; a series of letters, comprising sketches of the actual state of society in that colony; of its peculiar advantages to emigrants; of its topography and natural history'* by Peter Cunningham. The book set is quite valuable. I priced it at $225.

'Detective, I am not sure what you think my involvement was in the break-in, but I can tell you I had nothing to do with it. I do not know what a shekel is worth, anyway,' I finished with almost a grumpy face, something I am sure I picked up from Albert.

Detective Cassell says, 'Well these are worth $2,200,000,' and pivots, and I see him going out the door sensing that I probably was telling him the truth and he did not want to spend any more time with me. The man holding the two-set volume walks up to me, smiles, and presents his VISA card to make the purchase.

As my customer departs and makes my doorbell jingle, Albert rushes in.

'Danny darling, what did that dreadful man have to say to you this beautiful morning? I saw him walk past my store, look through the window, and I thought he was coming in, and he waves at me and keeps going. What is it with him today, sweetheart?' Albert queries.

'You saw Cassell go by but he did not go in to speak with you?

No. He did not. Why?

I repeated Cassell's story back to Albert, who stood in front of my register all astonished but looking marvellous. Albert started this Monday with a rainbow suit which incorporated everyone's favourite colour. The suit had bands of red, orange, yellow, blue, green, and violet all vibrant and he had a white button-down shirt with a suit colour matching tie. Add to this ensemble, a men's runners with LED lights that lit up every time Albert took a step, he looked like a Christmas tree. He looked 'royal' as if Elton John had crowned him; 'King of Northport.'

'Really,' said Albert when I finished relegating my version of events. 'That is his version of the story about not seeing me.

Wonder why he said that? Now you are saying these shekels are worth $2.200,000 and I knew nothing about them.'

My little doorbell rings once more and this time walks in Fredrick Holloway, proprietor of the *White Sheep*. He smiles at me, he waves and heads off to the office supply table, obviously looking for something for the business.

Albert turns to me and says, 'Danny, do you want me to find out what I can about the stolen shekels?'

Again, I had not thought about it. The article disappeared on Saturday night, and if it was a job done by a professional, the item would be in a buyer's hand already and maybe even out of the country, but it would not hurt to find out as much as one can about such a valuable piece. 'Sure, Albert, see what you can find out and get back to me,' I said to him as Fredrick came up to the register with several reams of paper.

'Hello Mr Monk, my office supply order from *Office Supplies Works* is running late, and I need to make some changes to the menu because the van with the fresh prawns is also running late. As always, your store is a lifesaver,' said Fredrick as he produces a $50 note to pay for the three reams of paper. 'That will be eighteen dollars, Mr Holloway,' I said, taking the fifty-dollar bill and handing him thirty-two dollars in change. I closed the register.

'Thanks, Mr Monk, see you on Thursday night.' He opened my front door and made my little bell tingle.

And he would see me on Thursday night since that was 'late trading night' in NSW and after a long day, I would go to the *White Sheep* for a drink and a meal.

Until Thursday arrived, the rest of the week was uneventful with some reasonable sales of office supplies, cards and my stock of rare and collectable books doing also well. As it nears closing time on Thursday night, the phone rings and I answer it to hear Albert's voice: 'Darling, I have news. Will you be heading to the pub tonight? If so, I can meet you there around 8 PM. I have someone I need to introduce you to.'

'Of course,' I said. 'I will meet you there.'

After closing the store on Thursday night, I walk up Main Street until I reach the *White Sheep* and see that, as usual, Thursday night is hopping with excitement. I walk to the back of the pub and find my usual booth as I notice Maire behind the bar nod to me and gesture with her hand as if pouring a drink. I nod back and settle in.

A few minutes later, Maire shows up with my 'usual'—El Presidente—a classic rum drink comprising 1½ oz, Havana Club white rum, 1½ oz. Dolin Vermouth Blanc, 1 bar spoon of Grand Marnier, ½ bar spoon of real grenadine. As Maire delivers my Presidente, she exclaims that these beautiful ingredients are stirred over cracked ice and strained into a chilled glass and garnished with a single cherry by Angus the bartender, who has to be the best bartender, nay, the best artist, in all of the Northport's pubs. I knew all that because Maire has told me this same spiel each time, I have my usual but she is wonderful and I always hate to interrupt her. Besides this drink has to be the perfect way to end a day; smooth and full of flavour and with Maire delivering it to my table with a beaming smile is an added bonus.

As I slowly sip my drink, I see the crowd of early diners is leaving, and the 'usual' bunch of late-night owls are coming in and then I see Albert walk in with a tall man whose face I cannot recollect ever seeing.

Albert sees me and unashamedly waves to me. Before coming to the table Albert speaks with the tall man and then Albert motions to Maire giving her a nod for his usual and indicating two, with his index and middle fingers. Then both he and the stranger sit at my table and Albert start his introductions: 'Danny, this is Marcelo Gutierrez, he works at *Ophelia's Pink Petals Flower Shop*, in the corner of Main Street and Hill Street. You know it, don't you, Danny?'

'Of course, I do. It is a pleasure to meet you, Mr Gutierrez, please sit down and join us,' I say.

'Please call me, Marcelo. Mr Gutierrez was my father back in Chile. I was born in Esperance Western Australia, where my father emigrated to start a fishing venture with his brother years ago. I found out early on that fishing would not be a life for me, so I moved to Perth, found it so slow that I then moved to NSW, and I settled in Northport. I find Northport is like living in the city with a country feel,' explained Marcelo as he gave me his life story in less than a minute. I already liked him. He gets to the point quickly.

'Great, now that the introductions are over let me tell you what Marcelo shared with me,' said Albert, waving to Maire to hurry with the drinks. My, he is so impatient sometimes.

Maire brings the two Cosmopolitan and I continue to savour my drink and enjoying the slow sips while I listened to Albert explain why Marcelo was here tonight.

'You see Danny, Marcelo is very connected to the Standerton family since he is currently dating their daughter, Allison,' quips Albert. 'The situation is one of complete rapture for both Marcelo and Allison, but there is a hitch. Her parents do not approve because they feel Marcelo is not the quality material their daughter should attract. Allison's parents mention on several occasions the fishing background and now the florist undertaking which Marcelo is engaged in,' sadly Albert says as he drinks his Cosmopolitan.

'Well sorry to hear that, Marcelo. You seem like a straight shooter to me even though I just met you. What has caused this friction between you and her parents?' I ask.

'I am not sure, and neither does Allison, but it seems that their entire analysis of me is that I am not as rich as they are or would even reach a lowly status as a simple business owner,' remarks Marcelo.

Ouch, that hurts because I am a small business owner, I thought as I continued to listen savouring the last few sips of my El Presidente. I notice Albert gesturing to Maire doing the helicopter blade sign ordering another round of drinks.

'This is where we come in, Danny,' interjects Albert. 'Marcelo knows where the shekels are.'

Surprised, I said; 'You do Marcelo?'

'Yes, I do,' answered Marcelo.

'I read the newspaper on Sunday morning of the reported theft. On Saturday night, I was at the Standerton mansion visiting Allison to watch a movie, and when she went to the kitchen to make popcorn, I saw Mr Standerton walk by and into his study. He did not notice me or did not care if I saw him. As I mentioned, Mr Standerton goes into the study, leaves the door open, and I see him take the shekels out of his wall safe and place them in his pocket.'

'Tell him what he did next,' quips Albert.

Marcelo continues; 'Well as he leaves the study and walks by, he notices me and does a simple nod and walks out the front door.' 'I do not know why but I think something strange is going on and I decide to follow him and see him go into his detached four-car garage and go inside. As I get closer, I look through a window and see Mr Standerton get down on both knees and then he goes under his pristine BMW Series 7 and places something, I am assuming it is the shekels, under the rim of the right front fender wheel. I then retrace my steps back to the house just in time for Allison to return with the popcorn.' 'Later Mr Standerton returns, bids us goodnight and retires. Allison and I finish our movie and popcorn, and I go home. The next morning, I read that there has been a break-in and that the precious shekels had been stolen, and a Detective Cassell shows up at my apartment that afternoon asking me all kinds of questions.'

'Did you tell Detective Cassell what you saw Mr Standerton do on Saturday night?' I ask.

'No. I was not sure what it would mean for the Standerton family, especially Allison, so I said nothing of what I saw happen other than Allison, and I saw the movie, ate popcorn and then I returned home,' answered Marcelo.

'Why do you think Detective Cassell came to see you?' I ask Marcelo.

'Why else! Mr Standerton wants me to be arrested and take me out of Allison's life, and what better way than for me to be in jail and Detective Cassell seems determined to put me there,' answered Marcelo.

'All you have to do is tell Detective Cassell what you have seen, and you are off the hook. What stops you?' I push Marcelo for an answer.

'I do not know what would be worse for Allison. An accusation of her father by me or the scandal that would ensue if the truth came out,' Marcelo answers shyly.

'And what do you expect to come out of this conversation Marcelo?' I ask him.

'Well, Albert said that you are a good man that sometimes right wrongs, and if you cannot help me, you would at least listen to my story and offer advice,' Marcelo says, taking the last few drops of his Cosmopolitan.

There is a pause in the conversation which offers me a chance to think of an appropriate response to Marcelo's plight and the penny drops and I respond to Marcelo.

'Marcelo, what are your business aspirations and your intentions with Allison?' I ask him.

'I have been working at *Ophelia's Pink Petals Flower Shop* for over six years and know the business pretty well. Ophelia Calderon is thinking of retiring next year and asked me if I would be interested in purchasing the shop and building from her. I would love to, but I am not sure the bank would give me a $1,875,000 loan. I have only $189,000 saved, and with a mortgage on my unit, I do not think I could make payments on both the shop and the apartment since most likely I would not be drawing a salary for the first year. As far as Allison, I plan to ask her to marry me as soon as this awful situation with her father is over. Why do you ask Danny?' responds Marcelo.

Turning to Albert I ask: 'Just wanted to hear you explain your plans Marcelo that is all. Now Albert, how well do you know Marcelo?'

'Marcelo and my cousin Jezebel were a 'thing' a while ago. Do you remember Jezebel?' smirks Albert.

Of course, I remember Jezebel, a youthful version of Sophia Loren with a larcenous heart that is to love, and I know she is today on a 'sabbatical' in the south of France, but that is another story.

'That was a while ago Danny,' interjects Marcelo, 'I am now completely devoted to Allison, and it is all over with Jezebel, I promise,' a humble-sounding Marcelo responds.

'OK, I will see if I can help you with your Allison and with Detective Cassell,' I tell young Marcelo.

'Oh, thanks a lot, Danny. What do I need to do?' he queries.

'Nothing. Just go to work as you usually do. Continue your relationship with Allison as you normally do and let nature take its course. OK?' I said to Marcelo.

Marcelo stared at me for a moment, nodded, got up and shook Albert's hand and then mine and walked out of the pub as if he was in deep thought but relieved.

Albert waves to Angus and in three minutes Maire shows up with our fourth cosmopolitan and El Presidente with an ever-smiling Maire bringing them to us to enjoy.

'OK, Danny, I know you. You asked Marcelo some personal questions, so it means to me you are interested in the young man's saga and might even have a plan to help him. Am I right? What are you going to do?' grinned Albert gulping his Cosmopolitan.

'I am going to right a wrong!'

'Excellent Danny. You are a wonderful man. Cover this for me dear. I forgot my wallet,' says Albert as he gets up and walks out of the *White Sheep* leaving me to handle the bill.

He is a doll!

DAMN IT, HE DID IT AGAIN

It is clear to me that Mr Standerton is quite a bastard to go to the length of staging a break-in, reporting it to the local police and maybe even insinuating that Marcelo might have a hand at the theft of the shekels all of this because he disapproves of Marcelo's lack of social standings. To top it off, he will probably file an insurance claim which will be paid out, and he then not only has the shekels but the insurance policy funds as well. Yes, he is quite a bastard I thought.

I have a plan which I will put into action this very night, but first a nice relaxing dinner while I work out some of the mental details. I wave to Maire for the menu, select something light and by the time I pay the bill, including all of Albert's Cosmopolitans, which is typical of Albert, and I go home.

I ring Albert who picks up his phone sounding already asleep. Time 11 PM. I would have thought he be out gallivanting. Maybe he is getting old as he is always telling me.

'Hey, you awake enough to speak?'

'I am now Danny. What's up?'

'To answer your question before you left the *White Sheep*, yes, I have a plan. Are you able to get for us a buyer for the shekels in quick-smart time? If so, what do you think we could get for them?' I ask.

Perking up rapidly he answers, 'I am sure I know a few overseas individuals, especially in Israel, who would even pay full price; The entire $2,200,000 - no questions asked - but then again, this day's offers are less. I'll see what I can do on short notice and yes, I could have something set up by this weekend? What are you thinking, Danny? I just love the way your mind works!'

'Well, Albert, I am going to retrieve the shekels from Mr Standerton. You work on finding us a buyer for the shekels and get us the best price for them as you can. To complete this scenario, we are going to go into the florist business in a week.' I gladly respond to Albert.

'Well, it is 11 PM here, and it is 4 PM in Israel, let me get to work on my contacts, and I will let you know by Friday morning. Hey, wait a moment. What do you mean we are going to be in the florist business? What are you going to do Danny darling?' asks Albert.

'I am going to visit the garage of Mr Standerton right now, make sure the shekels are still there and if they are. I am going to bring them home. Just make sure you have a solid offer from your buyers and quick!' I told Albert.

'Okey dokey, Danny, bye for now. Speak to you soon,'

Changing into the more proper attire for the evening— black—I put my gloves on and I sit down at my small desk at home and pen a brief note with some specific instructions. Finishing the note, I place the gloves in my pocket. I drive towards the pricey side of Cobbitty where the Standerton mansion lies and park in a dark spot about ½ kilometre from the house. Houses in this part of

Cobbitty are on the larger size, and the Standerton mansion was no different: large and its nearest neighbour a good acre away.

As I approach the mansion, I see the separate four-car garage young Marcelo mentioned and go towards the door. Locked, of course, people normally locked the garage side door and leave the car itself unlock so I quickly pick the door and I enter.

Seeing the BMW parked there gave me a good feeling since I did not think Mr Standerton would move the car under the circumstances and I hope that Detective Cassell and the local constables did not think to search the vehicle since there would be no motive to do so. Turning on my penlight, I am also confident that the car has no alarm on and I gingerly walk toward the car, slip around the right side, and kneel at the right front fender wheel and run gently my hand under the rim. I sense a small case and extract it, open it and inside are the oldest coins I have ever seen in two separate plastic bags. I place the bags in my pocket and slip the note I wrote into the small case and replace it where I found it. Carefully, I left the garage, locked the door and walked back to my car with no one seeing what had happened; a pattern I always try to maintain.

Friday at 10:01 AM promptly Albert makes my little doorbell jingle and smiles as he announces: 'Darling, I hope you had a great night for I have found someone willing to pay us $1,800,000, no questions asked for the shekels and are ready to meet us as soon as possible. Tell me you also had a great evening gaining our little coins?'

I smiled back, saying I did and would be ready to do the transaction. 'Great,' answered Albert pointing toward my stairs, 'I will get it set up right away. Mind if I use your unit upstairs to make the call?' taking his mobile out of his pocket. 'By all means, take your time,' I replied.

While Albert is upstairs my little doorbell jingles and in walks Detective Cassell. Cassell smiling at me and says: 'Well I am not sure how you fix things around here, but Marcelo Gutierrez is off the suspect list, and you are as well.'

Looking as perplexed as I can look, worthy of an Oscar I stare at Cassell: What do you mean Detective Cassell by off the hook?

'Well, it seems that Mr Standerton 'found' his coins after all. He remembered that earlier in the week, he had taken the shekels out of his safe and took them to his bedroom for a quick review of his insurance valuation form and left them there. So, when he went Saturday to his safe in his study, he did not find them. Forgetting that he had taken them out, he panicked and called the police. He now says he has them back in his possession and they are secure in his safe. What do you think of that?' Cassell asks.

'All's well that ends well as Billy used to write,' I said.

'Who said that? Who is Billy?' asks Detective Cassell.

'William Shakespeare is the Billy, and *All's Well That Ends Well* is one of his plays,' I answer.

'Monk, you are always a smartass.' As he storms out.

Out of the corner of my eye, I see Albert had been standing at the landing of the stairs and had seen Detective Cassell leave but probably did not hear the conversation, so I detailed to him what had transpired.

'So, Danny, Detective Cassell thought we had been involved in the theft of the shekels from the get-go, and you did not tell me. Why?'

'Well, I did not want to worry you,' I answered.

'So, tell me if we have the shekels, how is it that Mr Standerton says to Detective Cassell that he misplaced them and now has them safe and sound. How is this possible? Albert questions.

'I left Mr Standerton a brief note when I took the shekels, and the note suggested that he call the police and let them know he has found the shekels and to drop the investigation on Marcelo. The note also said that I had proof he staged the entire incident and I could prove it and that he better not double-cross me or I would point out all these things to the police.'

'You did not mention my name, did you Danny?'

'Albert, I did not mention any name! Why would I even mention your name? I just said I know what he did, and that I was keeping the shekels as payment for my silence and that he can forget the entire incident. That should keep Mr Standerton in check for a long time.'

'Indeed, that should keep him in check,' says Albert.

'Correct Albert. Now when do we exchange our acquisition?'

'I received some pretty specific instructions from our buyer, very much cloak and dagger, I feel. Tonight, we are to buy an attaché case at the Sydney International Terminal before security at the Forever Travel store. He wants us to buy this specific attaché case; an Ettinger nut and blue heritage St. James attaché case. We are to place the shekels in the case and then met him at the entrance to the international departures at 10:30 PM. We will recognise him for he will have the same attaché case. We are then to proceed with him to the male toilets, each goes into an adjoining toilet and 'slide and exchange,' the attaché cases. We then take a moment to open the case; once we are satisfied, we flush the toilet to let the other person know we are okay with the contents of the case and then he leaves first followed by which ever one of us has gone into the toilet a few minutes later.' Albert said, stopping to catch his breath. 'I do not like it. It sounds dangerous. I will drive you but I will not go into the toilet alone. Danny, will you, do it?'

For all I know the buyer could be Israel's Mossad, and I, for one, will take these precautions seriously for I do not want to mess with these folks so I give my answer to Albert in one paragraph.

'Yes.'

At the appointed time, after purchasing the attaché case, which by the way, was close to $5,000 in price, we waited, and we were approached by a tall, slender individual wearing glasses, a thin moustache wearing an elegant business suit and carrying the identical case. He nodded to us, and he and I proceeded to the men's toilet where we each got into separate but adjoining toilets. We slid the attaché cases to each other, I opened mine and saw nothing but crisp $100 notes bearing one of my favourite Australian authors, Banjo Paterson. I did not count the money and flushed the toilet as instructed. A minute later I heard the other toilet flush, and I left the bathroom after he left as instructed. I looked for Albert and motioned to him to walk next to me as we ambled back to the parking deck to get into his car.

A few weeks have passed, and everything went back to its routine, and as the routine goes, I closed my store at 6 PM. I went upstairs, changed, and picked up a large envelope containing some contracts from the kitchen counter and walked to the *White Sheep* to meet up with Albert and Marcelo.

Arriving at 7 PM I see they are already there and by the multitude of empty glasses, have been there for a while: Albert, Marcelo and what I presume to be the daughter of Mr Standerton, Allison, waiting for me and I even had an El Presidente waiting on my side of the table that Albert had ordered and started a tab. I sit down and lay a large envelope on the table and take a small sip of El Presidente, delicious I think, and start the conversation.

'Hello, all you beautiful people. How is everyone this evening?' I ask.

'Darling, as always I am ecstatic to see you, Danny,' answered Albert.

'Danny, let me introduce you to Allison Standerton, my fiancé,' speaks young Marcelo.

'Hi' and a massive smile beam from the young Allison as if I was Father Christmas, which they did not know I was.

'I am so glad all of you could come here tonight to meet with me. I have a proposition for young Marcelo here, which I hope both Marcelo and Allison will find interesting.' I stated.

'First, my dear friend Albert vouches for Marcelo, and that is all I need to know. I met Marcelo almost a month ago and was impressed with his upbringing, his composure and his attitude towards life, business, and love. For that reason, Albert and I decided we would love to make this business proposal for you both. We want to become silent partners in the purchase of *Ophelia's Pink Petals Flower Shop* with the condition that you pay the loan back each month in the sum of $1,000 until the loan is paid. Any profits made we will divide each year with 10% going to Albert, 10% to myself and you and Allison will keep 80%. What do you think Marcelo, Allison, ready for new partners?' I sip my El Presidente.

Both Marcelo and Allison were gobsmacked.

'Here, sign the paperwork, take the cheque and buy the flower store, get married and be happy,' I proclaimed.

Allison leaned over and kissed Albert and me, Marcelo, got up, embraced Albert, and shook my hand. Without reading the documents, signs the contract, passes the contract to Allison to sign, who peruses it for a moment and then signs. They both look at the cheque for $1,875,000, grab each other's hand and run out of the pub.

I look at Albert sitting there sobbing like a baby. As always Albert cannot contain himself, so I go to say something to him, but he got up and also rushed out of the pub.

A few moments later, Maire comes by and lays the enormous bar bill on my table.

Damn it, Albert; he did it again.

OH YES BABY. GIVE IT TO ME!

It was a typical Sunday morning in Northport. The sun rose early this spring day, and the temperature was already nice at 16C under the average but great walking around weather as long as you have a jumper on, which I did. It was going to be a lovely day today I thought as I am walking down Main Street and my phone rings; it is her!

I took Mary McCarthy out on a quick dinner date last night; Albert had set up this blind date. He told me his logic was, and I quote; *Darling, you need to really find out your feelings for Alessia. So, I have set up this date for you with wonderful Mary. She is adorable and I am sure she is your kind of girl.*

So, I gave in to Albert's logic because I needed to find out my feelings for Alessia and what a better way than to go on a date with another woman. My mother would shake her head at my logic. It turned out that Mary is a nice enough person and after being on this date I felt she is just not my type for a romantic relationship and I made it clear to her or so I thought last night. So, I wonder why she was ringing me so early in the morning when I saw her name on my mobile phone.

'Hello, Mary. Top of the morning to you today.'

'Hi Danny, I just wanted to let you know I had a wonderful time last night, and if you want to do it again sometime soon, I would be more than happy to see you,' proclaims Mary.

Oh, oh, I thought, this sounds like trouble brewing, as I walk past Albert's favourite morning break store, the *Java Hutt*, and continue walking.

'I also had a fun time, Mary. The food was delicious, the restaurant was splendid, and you were great, but, as we discussed last night, I am not ready to pursue any type of relationship at the moment. My shop is keeping me terribly busy and I, to be honest, asked you out because our mutual friend, Albert, asked me. So, if it is okay with you, let us part as friends for now.'

Suddenly I hear; 'Oh yes baby, give it to me!' over the phone.

'Okay, Danny, I understand. I was just wondering if maybe I might have persuaded you to progress into this relationship a bit more. Take it to another level sort of,' Mary repeated meekly. Again, before I could speak, I heard: 'Oh yes baby, give it to me!'

I am not sure what I was hearing. Was Mary suffering from a dual personality and communicating her feelings to me with two different voices at the same time over the phone and she did not realise it? Was Mary just a phycological stalker? What did Albert get me into?

'Oh, Danny, I was so much hoping that you would reconsider what you said last night and maybe give it another go. I opened up to you last night, and I was hoping, no wishing, that you would see the possibilities of us having a deep, profound relationship. Do you not feel that connection between us?' prompted Mary.

Oh boy, another fine mess you got me into Albert, I thought to myself. What have I got myself into without even noticing anything strange in Mary last night? Before I can answer her, I hear again, 'Oh yes baby, give it to me!' Now I am really getting concerned that if I answer Mary in the wrong way, she might just lose it and next time I see her she has a kitchen knife in her hand. I took a novel approach.

'Mary, on second thought, it is only 8 AM and I do not need to open my store today. How about I get us each a coffee from the *Java Hut* and bring it to your place and we can chat a bit? What do you think?'

'Oh, Danny, how wonderful that would be! A nice cup of coffee perks me up in the morning and I am already dressed. So please rush over so we can take as much time as we need to talk,' answered Mary anxiously. Before I could ask Mary how she likes her coffee, I again hear, 'Oh yes baby, give it to me!'

Startled, I asked Mary, 'How do you want your coffee?'

'Oh, just a double strength cappuccino please with extra chocolate sprinkles. Thank you so much, Danny, and Danny, please hurry!'

I literally ran to the *Java Hutt*, got the two coffee orders (I just had a latte) and walked to the back of my store, got into my car, and drove to Mary's. Her house was near the old, abandoned Northport Home for the Feeble-Minded (by the name you can tell how old the place is). I parked the car in front of her house and quickly crossed her front yard and knocked on her front door.

It took Mary less than thirty seconds to come to the front door, open it and usher me in.

'Oh, Danny, it's so nice of you to have your morning coffee with me. You do not know what this means to me. I am really so happy you offered me this chance to speak with you in person again so soon after last night.'

'That is Okay, Mary. I also wanted to ask you a question in person and this coffee idea just popped into my head as we spoke on the phone.'

Mary was ushering me into her lounge area as we spoke, and I got to see a better look at her place in the daylight since last night I just knocked on her door and she came out when I picked her up for the dinner date and then I walked to her front door. Yes, I am a gentleman and do not rush things.

The outside of the house was well maintained, clean and organised. The inside was also clean, organised and exotic. Mary really went into the red. A large red, velvety lounge with big fluffy white cushions. A side chair that looks expensive, but you could tell it was used a lot. No TV in the room so I presume she must have a media room somewhere else in the house. I notice no photographs. There were a lot of pictures of mid-1800s nude women - the kind you see in museums. These also were well-framed, and I have an eye for art and for the life of me I believe the photographs were replicas of original oil paintings and expensive. So, Mary had money or had inherited money to own these replica original photograph masterpieces.

'Please sit, Danny and drink your coffee here, next to me,' sheepishly states Mary.

As I sank into the red lounge, I almost spilled my coffee but recovered. Mary laughed and then said, 'You make me laugh doing just the simple things, Danny. Have I told you how wonderful you were to me last night?'

'Yes, you have Mary. In fact, you stated that to me several times last night and I appreciate it, but I am always a gentleman when I take a lady out to dinner.'

Mary smiles: 'See what I mean. A lady. That is what you think of me. You are so nice and wonderful. That is all I want to say to you, all the time. You are nice and wonderful.'

OK, this was getting weird and weirder as time passed, so I jumped right into my questions; 'Mary, did you hear a second person speaking while we were on the phone this morning?'

'No, I did not hear a second person when we were on the phone speaking. Was it at your end because if it was, I did not hear it?' answered Mary, feeling surprised at the statement I just made.

OK, I am not an expert, but it is possible that a dual personality person does not know the other person is around, so I asked again but differently.

'The reason I am asking you Mary is that I distinctly heard a voice say something unusual while we were on the phone and I can tell you that person's voice sounded like they were standing next to you while you were on the phone. Is there another person in the house with you Mary?'

You can see Mary's face move a bit as she processes that question as if to find me the right answer. The answer will no doubt surprise me since I totally have just figured out that Mary has a dual personality disorder. That has to be the answer. Remind me to thank Albert again next time I walk into his hair salon or he visits my store.

Mary suddenly laughs; 'Oh Danny there is no other person in the house, but I know where the unusual statement might have come from. Here,' as she grabs my hand. 'I want to show you something.'

I did not like where this was going but I was bigger than Mary so if she tried something funny, I am sure I could take her, I think.

Mary leads me out of the lounge area and towards her bedroom where the décor matches much the same as the lounge area. Lots of red and this time original oil paintings of nudes. No replicas here but actual expensive, and I mean expensive, oils. Mary's bed is what I would call a super king side in red, of course, and plenty fluffy white pillows and lots of mirrors. Next to the bed is a tall bird cage and inside I see a large parrot.

Its body is entirely green, and it has distinct feathers in vivid lilac and a big yellow spot on its forehead. Its cage had to be worth over $2,000 since it is huge and has almost everything a parrot would want in a cage. I am not sure what a parrot would want in a cage but for sure if I were a parrot, I would like to have the gold-plated bath it currently has.

'Danny, meet Marisol. She is my Mealy Amazon parrot I received as a gift from a friend three years ago. Is she not beautiful?

She has been a lot of good company since she has taught herself to speak. She is wonderful, just like you Danny.' Says Mary.

Okay, I was not expecting this, but then again, I thought Mary was one kooky cookie anyway so why am I surprised?

Mary sat us both down on the bed and explained: 'Danny last night you said a lot about yourself. Your store, how much you love your work and when you asked me what I did for a living, I dodged the question.'

I said, 'Yes, Mary I noticed that, but I figured you did not want to speak about it just then and you would when the time was right. Is now the time?'

'It is Danny, my wonderful Danny. The words you heard came from Marisol and you probably heard her favourite sentence; Oh yes baby, give it to me! Am I correct?' asks Mary.

'Yes,' I answered.

'Danny I am a professional 'model' if you get my meaning. Will that make a difference to you if we are to continue with a relationship?' states Mary.

I needed to handle this carefully, I thought to myself.

'Mary, last night I was very clear of my intentions and I do not want to lead you on. While you are a great person, I am not interested in you other than as a friend. What you do in your life does not change that. Am I clear Mary?'

I can see Mary's eyes go sad on me and then she says, 'I understand Danny, really I do, I just hoped that it was because we were not a match and not because of my 'modelling,' you know?'

How could Albert have thought Mary, and I had anything in common unless the oil paintings are worth more than I imagine. I am going to have to ask him later.

Taking Mary's hand I lead her out of the bedroom, I hear Marisol speak; 'Oh yes baby, give it to me!' and I think to myself; boy what a pair of crackers!

I bid Mary adieu and being Sunday I had no intention of working at the store doing inventory or cleaning getting ready for Monday. So, I drove back to the store and parked my car at the car park, and I walked back to the *Java Hutt* to get myself another cuppa and a cake.

After sitting there waiting for my cake and coffee, Alessia walks in looking marvellous.

'Danny! What a surprise. I thought I would get myself a coffee and here I find you this beautiful Sunday afternoon. Mind if I join you?'

What a delight. Alessia. A woman I really like and want to get to know and I have yet to ask her out. Now is my chance.

'Of course, Alessia, please do,' as I motioned for the server to come and take her order.

'What are you having Danny?'

'Today I am treating myself to a simple afternoon treat. A flat white and a small lamington. I am hungry because I missed lunch since I was in a meeting with a friend clarifying some things.'

Smiling Alessia walks to the counter and tells the young lady behind the counter pointing to my table: 'I will have the same.'

The young lady nods and goes to place the order and Alessia walks back to the table. I just stare at Alessia. She looks just marvellous. With khaki shorts and a bright red t-shirt and a simple Maltese cross on her neck, she looks like the very example of what a spring day should look and feel like.

'While we wait for the coffee and sweets, tell me a bit more about you Alessia. So far I know a few things like your taste in books but not much.' Boy, was I brave, very brave indeed!

Alessia smiled and without hesitation, she started her life story. She relished on her parents, how influential they were in her education and how they put the love of books in her at an early age. How this attraction to books and learning, for she is an avid reader and a devourer of information, got her started in her collection of books which now totalled over three thousand. How she loved going to IKEA and buying their bookshelves, especially the 'Billy' which she found easy to put together herself and store her cherished book collection. She also said that she had many other passions, too many, it seemed some simple, some more complicated but all fun, she assured me, but detailed little. Oh, well, maybe another time, I thought. During the conversation we each questioned each other on our goals, values, etc. We spoke about everything and anything and it was just wonderful. I asked her how much she enjoys collecting books and Alessia said; 'With a passion I love it. It is an expensive proposition but I manage all right with all my investments.' And left it at that. I thought to myself, she reads, collects, and invests. Definitely a keeper!

Coffee and lamington cake came and Alessia kept speaking.

I loved the sound of her voice.

I adored how she used her hands to express herself and how her hair just moved from side to side as she spoke and laughed.

The server interrupted us placing the bill on the table next to me saying that they will close in thirty minutes and if we wanted to order anything else. I glanced at my watch. Goodness, we spent 3 ½ hours at the *Java Hutt* and it seemed like just fifteen minutes had passed. Picking up the bill I told Alessia to wait for me outside while I paid it. In my mind today has to be the time where I ask her out and decide I would just do that as I walk Alessia back to her car.

Well, I got the date but not the way I thought. As I walked out of *Java Hutt* Alessia said to me, 'Danny. I like you. I like you a lot. Let me walk you back to your place so we can continue our conversation. I could never speak so openly, so comfortably to anyone and I feel so good now.'

'Alessia, I was going to walk you back to your car but spending more time with you would be just the topping on the cake, pardon the food pun, but I cannot seem to get enough of you either.'

With that sentence, Alessia comes closer and we kiss.

A long, slow, passionate kiss.

A kiss that brings me almost to tears for I knew I had fallen in love with her but was not yet ready to tell her. Was she in love with me? I hoped so.

As I walked alongside Alessia to my place, I thought of my life and how complicated it had become with my store and of course my extracurricular activities with Albert. How and when to tell

Alessia is something I need to think about but now all my thoughts were on getting to know Alessia even more.

Arriving at my place, I open the door and let Alessia into my home.

'Well, Danny, this is like I envisioned your place. Uncomplicated and comfortable. I love it.' She sat in the lounge.

'Can I get you anything Alessia? Maybe another coffee?'

'No thank you, Danny. Please come sit next to me and let's continue talking.'

So, I amble over and sit next to her. As I sit and before I say anything Alessia speaks; 'Danny, you know you are one quite special man. I am so glad we are friends.'

Oh, oh. The word 'friend' has come up. What does she mean?

'But friends can evolve into something else, can they not?'

Like a dummy, I nod and Alessia continues. 'Danny, have you ever wondered if you love a person because you need them or you need them because you love them?'

Wow! That is one heavy statement, but I know how I feel and answer her, 'It is because you love them that you need them.'

Alessia smiles and just leans into me, kisses me, and whispers; 'Yes that is how I feel as well.' With Alessia next to me I think about Mary and her crazy Amazon parrot Marisol and how my day started with the darn parrot squawking over Mary's voice while on the phone; 'Oh yes baby, give it to me.'

A GOOD AND PROFITABLE
DAY AFTER ALL

S ometimes friendships can really be pushed, however, genuine friendships will always prevail and if you can mix a wonderful friendship and a good business relationship, which is difficult sometimes to do, why let something like a bad blind date ruin it for you.

Monday, I got out of bed a bit earlier since last week I had worked on my special occasions card display and I wanted to give the final touches to the display to prepare for any rush that might come in the months ahead for the cards.

The *Village Books & Stuff* carries all kinds of materials. From office supplies to antique and exotic books to your normal run-of-the-mill celebratory cards for all occasions so I wanted to have the display finished by the time I opened for business at 10 AM.

At 9:50 AM I looked at the card display and, if I do say so myself, it is the best darn display I ever made. So, I made sure things were ready around the front counter and a few minutes before 10 AM, I unlock the front door and turned the little sign over to the 'We Are Open' side.

Let the masses in, I thought. However, my thoughts turned to Alessia.

I spent an interesting Saturday night with a blind date, Mary, set up by Albert. I found Mary nice but not my cup of tea. To top it off, I discovered her parrot Marisol, and it made for a strange morning on Sunday, however, the afternoon and evening turned out simply perfect for I bumped into Alessia Vassallo at the *Java Hutt* and started a conversation that ended at my place.

Alessia spent most of the night with me leaving around midnight since we both had to work. I know I have fallen for her and I had an opportunity to tell her that last night, and I sort of did tell her how I feel but did not come out and the three words: 'I love you.' Doesn't every woman want to hear that?

Oh, I wish my mother were alive. She would guide me through these emotions and let me understand how a woman thinks because I just do not seem to get those three words out of my mouth.

So here I am on Monday morning ready to take on the business world when I hear my little bell tingle and my mind clears of Alessia's thoughts and I turn to see Albert waltzing in. Albert has on pink shorts and a pink jacket covered in palm trees with a white shirt and matching pink palm tree tie. He complements this with a pair of sandals and an awfully expensive New Wave SL sunglasses from Saint Laurent. This pair of sunglasses would set me back a month's rent if I were paying rent. Albert is holding his favourite mug of coffee and without a hello Albert jumps straight into the conversation of the moment:

'Danny darling tell me how it went with your date with Mary last Saturday night? Is she not just fabulous!'

'Good morning. By the way, does that outfit come with volume control? Only you can wear that and still look good,' avoiding his question.

'Come, come Danny boy, give me all the goss about marvellous Mary. She had to be a blast, right?'

'Albert, I appreciate your good intentions, but Mary and I are just going to be friends, just friends, you understand. There is no romantic potential here, OK?'

'Oh, dear I was hoping for so much. She is just a magnificent specimen of womanhood if you know what I mean?' said Albert.

'Well, she is a fine lady, and we will be friends,' I firmly stated.

'Well Danny sweetie, how about I skip this lack of a romantic interlude in your life and ask you this; How much do you know about stamps?'

Lack of a romantic interlude I think, if only you knew Albert. If only you knew.

'Other than you get them at Australia Post, you lick them and off they go, not much, I might even have a book about them in the drawer here, why?'

'Oh, dear boy, you have so much to learn. Come closer, grasshopper, and let me explain. Stamps are exactly what you mentioned and so much more. Stamp collectors are called philatelists and they are peculiar people and some are rich, very rich. They are always, and I mean always, trying to expand their collection by whatever means. Follow so far?'

I nodded. Of course, I knew about philatelists and the fact that some actual stamps can be awfully expensive to add to a collection, but I always enjoy rattling Albert a bit and getting him to share what he knows.

Albert continues; 'So I found that Arnie Kimbell at the *Northport Stamp and Coin Shop* on Elizabeth Street just sold a stamp worth $75,000 called the Hawaiian Missionaries stamp and a United Kingdom Edward III Florin 1343 or 1344 gold coin for $689,000 to one of my clients. Can you just imagine walking around with $764,000 in your trousers pockets.? What do you think of that?' said beaming Albert.

As I spoke, I hear my security alarm on my front tingle and Alessia walks in looking, well, as always, wonderful!

'Good morning, Danny.'

'Good morning Alessia. Please allow me to introduce you to my best friend, Albert Matthew Guzman, owner of the premier hair salon in all of Newport, *Cut Me Crazy.*'

Both Albert and Alessia shake hands and Albert immediately gives her an embrace and hogs the conversation; 'Tell me, Alessia: I have seen you here in the store a lot of times - are you one of those people that loves books or do you just love my Danny!'

Oh boy, do not go there, Albert, I think.

'Well, I am so glad you brought that up, Albert. Danny has spoken so much about you.'

'And he has spoken so much about you Alessia,' Albert states, winking at me knowing that I have not done so. I am a private man as the reader knows.

'Well since you and Danny are such good friends, I am wondering if I should share something that I did not mention to Danny last night.'

'Alessia, Albert and I go back years, so I am more than happy for him to hear whatever you need to say Alessia. Shoot!'

'In that case,' Alessia comes around the back of the counter, leans close, kisses me, and then states, 'Daniel Monk, I am in love with you!'

All I hear is Albert screaming like a girl, running around in a small circle, clapping his hand, and saying aloud; 'I knew it, I knew it, I knew it' repeatedly.

Looking at Alessia the words slowly and sweetly come out; 'I fell in love the moment you walked into the store and have loved you every moment ever since, and I too love you' and this time I kissed her until the doorbell tingle indicating a new male customer has entered and looked at us kissing and walked toward the rear of the store as if nothing were happening.

'I need to get back to the library. I will call you tonight sweetie,' and Alessia leaves, stops and gives Albert a quick peek on his cheek and Albert is smiling as Alessia goes out the door.

The man returns with a first edition hardback copy of *The Bible Code* by Michael Drosnin.

'How much?'

I type the information into my computer and without going into the fact that it is a first edition expensive but not an antiquarian book, not yet, since it was published in 1997, and there are a few still around and it is not even fifty-years old, still a baby, but still, I look inside the cover and see the little tag on it; '$99.'

The man hands me a $100 note and I ring up the book, give him his change and place it and the receipt in a bag. As he opens the door, he turns around and with a big smile says: 'congratulations.'

'Well, Danny. When were you going to tell me about what has been happening with Alessia, never?'

'No, I was going to tell you, but it just never came up and all of this has happened so fast. Anyway, why don't you finish your story?'

Before Albert can restart the conversation my little bell over my front door tingles for a fourth time and in walks Detective Malcolm Cassell, Northport's favourite dees.

'Good morning gentlemen. What mischief are you both up to?'

Albert slowly moves around the corner of my counter, shying away from Detective Cassell so that leaves me to respond to the greeting from across my counter: 'Just comparing business strategies for the long scorching summer we will be having. Albert is cutting more hair since his male clients want their hair short and I am selling more books since people are getting ready to go to the beach and reading more for a change. Is your summer planning as exciting as ours?' I asked sarcastically.

'Listen you smart-arse; I walk in here friendly like so do not go about getting my temper worked up or I will take you into the police station for questioning,' snapped Cassell.

'Oh yes, I am sure you have grounds for doing that. All I have to do is call my lawyer and I am out, and you will face some serious trouble from her,' I barked back.

Albert exclaims, 'Boys, boys, please calm down. It is quite early in the morning to get our blood pressure up. How about I go get us all some coffee from the *Java Hutt* and we sip it together calmly? What do you think?'

I guess I started rattling Cassell's cage, and he responded so I backed up a bit and so did he. Tempers seem to have cooled a bit.

'No, that will not be necessary. I just want to remind you both that over the past months there has been a lot of activity in the break and entry arena over at the north shore, and I have my eyes on you both. You understand. I know you both are always up to something, but I have not found anything to pin on you yet, but I will,' comments Detective Cassell.

'Cassell after all we did for you with the case of Randolphs cleaner's murder. I would have thought you would be nicer to us,' I say.

Detective Cassell turns around and heads toward the front door and simply turns and says, 'Just watch yourselves. I am,' and walks out.

Albert moves to the front of my counter and sighs; 'Danny, why did you push him. You know he is just itching to catch us and then what will happen to us. I cannot do imprisonment, I just cannot. Those prison greens are just horrible, just horrible! Besides we have not been over the north shore for any 'acquisitions' so I am not sure what he is spewing about. He is one nasty man.'

'Do now worry Albert. We are smarter than that flatfoot anytime. Let us get back to those coins and stamps. Who bought them?'

'A Mr A. G. Michael from Bondi. He has a penthouse right on the beach. Quite a spread I have heard, and he has plenty of money if he drops these kinds of bills on stamps and coins, don't you think darling?' responds Albert.

'You think that through your sources you could find us a buyer because things have been slow so far this spring even though I exaggerated to Detective Cassell a bit? Also, do you know his address? I am sure he will keep those two items at home because I am sure those are not the only items in his collection,'

'I will get on it darling and get back to you as soon as possible. Bye for now, ciao. And I am so happy for you,' and he also comes behind the counter and gives me a peck on the cheek and off Albert goes through the front door like a pink wind since he was moving so fast and almost knocks down my second customer of the day.

'Oh, my, who was that rude young man?' Asks the elegant mature lady that had the misfortune to be bumped by Albert.

'Oh him? He is with the fashion police. How may I assist you today?' I ask as I quickly usher the lady into the store.

'Yes, yes, of course. I just returned from a tour of Belgium and found a wonderful apple dessert - of which I forget the name - but

I remember they made it from the Amorosa apple. Do you have a cooking book that has Belgian recipes?' the lady asks me.

'Please look around the store while I check my computer's stock list to see what I have in the store.' I point the lady towards more exotic books in my establishment and I punch into the computer. I have a good idea that I have something on Belgian cuisine since I actually made myself Belgian waffles a few months ago and took the book upstairs and used the recipe. Where did I place the book that is the question? Did I place it back in the right area in the bookcase?

Checking the computer, I see the location and head straight to it, pick it up, look through the pages and there is an apple recipe using the Amorosa apple. I am in luck and as I bring it to the lady, I exclaim; 'Here is a wonderful book by the title *'My Belgian's Mother Recipe Book'* by Monique Mertens and it has a terrific recipe using the Amorosa apple just like you wanted. The price is only $22.'

'Oh, my, that is amazing, and I will also take this marvellous book I found.' The elegant lady states.

'Oh, I see you found *'Bad Company and Other Stories'* by Rolf Ledgewood. It is the first edition. You are aware of that, Madam,' I ask.

'Oh yes. What is the price?' she asks.

Since I do not mark my books with price stickers to preserve their authenticity I said, 'Let me check the price for you and I will let you know,' and a quick lookup tells me the price is $60 and I quote her that.

The lady responds, 'Oh wonderful. I will take them both. Do you take AMEX?' excitingly she says.

'Yes, I do,' as I take the recipe book and place it and the first edition in a shopping bag, ring up the sale, take the lady's platinum AMEX card, notice her name, and tap it. The credit card company approves it in less than two seconds, I smile, return the card to the lady, and give her the shopping bag.

'Thank you for your patronage, Ms Lemmens.'

'My, you know my name. You have been excellent. I will have to tell my friends about this quaint store. Does it have a name?'

'Yes, it does,' I say; 'It is *The Village Books & Stuff.*' I smile at her as I think to myself, what, can you not read it? It is on the front of the store below the display window.

'Goodness me, what a nice name! I did not even notice the name when I came in. How did you get the name for the store?' she asked.

I now give her a brief history of the store. How it used to be a printer's shop in the late 1880s all the way until the 1980s and was owned by the same family all that and how the family ran into financial difficulty and closed down. How Mr McCullum open the store as bookstore with a pot-pourri of office supplies and cards. How I bought the store and building, renamed it, and I that live upstairs in a very enjoyable remodelled three-bedroom, 3-bath unit. I did not share with the customer that all this was possible because of the extracurricular activities that Albert and I have undertaken to supplement our retail income for the last four years.

She smiled all along with my story and left with a small wave at the door. Well, a second small sale before lunch. The rest of the day went well as well. A few individuals came in, browsed around and a few actually bought something; I sold four Happy Birthday cards, two reams of printer paper and a first edition book of poems by J. Farrell 'How He Died and Other Poems' and promptly at 6 PM, I turned my little sign around showing the 'We Are Closed' turned on the alarm and walked upstairs for the evening. I thought of what Alessia said and I thought, yes, another good and profitable day after all.

A VENTI COFFEE CUP TO CLEAN

My only thoughts are about Saturday night. So as soon as I got into the unit, I sat down in the lounge and called Alessia.

'Hey,' she says.

'Hey is for horses. How are you? I think that Saturday night we should catch a quick dinner to speak about what we both said and then catch a movie. What do you think?'

'Oh Danny, I am so sorry I have a prior engagement I need to do. Will you take a rain check from me for dinner and a movie? We can talk on the phone now about what we both said today.'

Disappointed as I was, I understood. While we both seem crazy in love, we also have other commitments, me with Albert and our other extracurricular activities and Alessia with... Well, I actually did not know what other activities she was in other than collecting books and investments, but I do not care. She told me she loves me, and I reciprocated. We are good.

'Oh, what a shame. The new movie from the James Bond franchise is coming out on Thursday, so I thought we could catch it on Saturday. What are you up to?'

Did I sense a hesitation right before Alessia answered? 'Oh, I and a couple of girls are going into the city. You know. Girls' night out. Had it planned weeks ago. I guess I forgot to mention it to you.'

'Not to worry Alessia. Now about this morning...'

So, we spent over an hour going over what we said and why we said it and I felt wonderful afterwards and could tell Alessia felt the same way so I ended the conversation by saying: 'OK, well you have fun and I will catch up with you next weekend, how is that?'

'That would be lovely,' as Alessia blows me a kiss and hangs up.

So, I was spending Saturday night indoors, and that is okay because staying at home will ease me into Sunday and I like Sundays.

Sunday is the only day that I do not open the store, and I just take it easy. No inventory, well sometimes I do my personal books, no accounting, no cash counting although these days almost all sales are swiped cards and, sometimes, those pay as you go apps.

This Sunday I plan to get up and have breakfast, clean up, and settle into my large LAZ-Z-Boy rocker-recliner to read. I am currently reading Richard Price's 1787 first edition *'A Review of the Principal Questions in Morals. Particularly Those respecting the Origin of our ideas of Virtue its Nature Relation to the Deity Obligation Subject-Matter and Sanctions,'* which I bought from a collector friend and found the title interesting enough to read before putting it up for sale in my store, with a little mark-up, say $660. My friend told me contrary to widespread belief, gloves are not recommended for handling rare or valuable books. However, I feel it is wise to use gloves made of nitrile or vinyl and I recommended to my customers buying unique and rare antiquarian books if there is reason to suspect a health hazard on the item such as mould or arsenic. My friend did mention that clean gloves made of nitrile, vinyl, or lint-free cotton are highly recommended when handling photograph albums, photographs, or books with metal or ivory parts. When I bought the book, he told me to wash my hands with soap and thoroughly dry them which I do and then I still put on my gloves. I made an investment in this book, for example, and I need to preserve its excellent quality so I can sell it and make a profit. So, I am good to go. I cannot wait for Sunday morning!

My mobile phone rings, I pick it up and see the name 'Hair Man' so I answer it; 'Yes, Albert, how are you this morning.'

'Just great Danny darling. I was wondering if I could come up and discuss the information you asked me about? Is it OK?'

'Of course, Albert. Any time. I am not doing anything tonight.'

'Oh, Alessia is not there? Well, then I will be there in a jiffy!'

I put down the phone and before I can think of what information Albert might have found my front/back door rings.

I open the door and there stands Albert; 'How did you get here so fast?' I ask him.

'Oh, I was in the car park when I called. I just did not want to catch you in your sexy pyjamas or interrupt you and Alessia but by how fast you answered I could sense you were up, alone, and already to take on the world and I was right. Now let me in because I have lots of gossips to share.' He marched in, sat in my lounge, and reshuffled all of my cushions.

It is amazing where Albert finds his clothes. Here we are on a Saturday night and he is wearing an original suit designed just for Albert, it has to be just for him because I would not be seen in something like this. Albert is wearing a suit which includes the jacket, the pants, the tie with an ocean blue background and goldfish printed on them with a white shirt and black shoes with no socks. He always gets away with it.

'Danny my love please sit next to me so I can tell you all the dope I found out about Mr A. G. Michael from Bondi,' as he pats my lounge and like a puppy, I sit next to him.

'It seems he has oodles of money. Has properties all over the world but makes his principal residence in Bondi at the Majestic Towers in the penthouse. It is breathtaking in design, views, and location. It is said to have unforgettable and uninterrupted ocean views from its balcony and a striking open plan interior and four immense bedrooms Plus, all the dining and coastal activities you need to complete your dream getaway are at your doorstep. Add to the open plan living a dining room where there's seating for up to twenty-four guests,' stops Albert to catch his breath.

Albert continues, 'A. G. Michael is the principal in Burton & Michael Investments one of the largest privately owned and operated financial services companies, which is big but not too big. Very client-focused from what I hear and the right size to provide both that client-focused service and be stable and strong at the same time. The company has offices in Sydney, Melbourne, Brisbane, Perth and even in little adorable Hobart. He also has branches in London, Singapore, New York, Chicago, and San Francisco. Large enough to be stable and strong, like I said, but able to pamper their clients and best of all make money for them. With just under $12 billion in funds under management, the Australian Financial Review deemed it a premier company and voted the company the best investment company in Australia in 2015, 2018, and 2020.'

Based on Albert's description I am quite interested in Mr A. G. Michael from Bondi.

Albert continues, 'Danny the main bedroom, with a super king bed, enjoys gorgeous beach views and an outside spa on its own separate and private balcony. The master suite enjoys a luxurious ensuite with double shower, a bath and a triple, not a double, basin,' explains Albert.

'Really nice Albert, are you now also a real estate agent? Where does he keep his valuables?' I ask.

'Oh, dear, I failed to mention; he has a walk-in wardrobe the size of a double garage and after walking through it there stands a vault. Like a small bank vault size where his precious paintings and other collections are,' a smiling Albert declares.

The size of a small bank vault. Interesting place to have one. Must have cost heaps to install. So, Mr A. G. Michael from Bondi is indeed loaded.

'What do you know about the Majestic Towers Albert?' I ask.

'This is what I know,' reports Albert, 'Majestic Towers stands four stories tall with two bedroom/two bath units all with vast private balconies and overlooking Bondi Beach. This luxury building sits on the east end of Bondi providing peace of mind both in location and value. They locked the building down like Fort

Knox with security all around it, CCTV cameras abundant in the lobby and manned-security reception which requires visitors to sign in and card access entry for tenants. I also found out the building hires good-looking, young, and attractive men for their security reception area. I say that is a bonus for me! Sorry, I got side-tracked, the building has three lifts; two cover levels one and two and the third covers the penthouse where Mr A. G. Michael lives - is this how we are referring to him? Mr A. G. Michael from Bondi? The ground floor has the building's facilities; pools, indoor and outdoor, gym, meeting rooms for the residents and a three-star Michelin restaurant, *The Royal @ Bondi*. The restaurant has two entrances, one from inside the building where residents come in from and one outside for the general clientele. Underground parking is also available to the tenants only. All units are owned, and no rentals are allowed, no Airbnb, darling, as well. No public parking. Is this enough information darling?' an exhausted Albert states as he smiles so proud of himself.

I needed to ask Albert who is the source of this valuable information but then again, Albert has never failed when he gathers intel so I answered his question: 'First, we will call him just Michael and not refer to him as Mr A. G. Michael from Bondi, too much of a mouthful, OK?' Now came the next question: 'Albert how in the world were you able to get so much information so quickly?'

'Well, I can tell you the extended version or the condensed version. Which do you prefer?' said Albert.

'The condensed version,' I say, and I lean on one of my many cushions because I know that with Albert the 'condensed version' is just a little shy of the 'extended version.'

Without a moment to catch his breath, Albert starts: 'You know Miguel from my salon? Well, Miguel is friends with Marta who is married to the commis chef Timothée of The *Royal @ Bondi*. who is dying to open his own restaurant by the way, which is how I got all this information so quickly! See how nice it is to go out and meet people and not stay in your place all weekend long?'

'Yes, that was fast and valuable information, Albert. Let me think for a moment. Would you like a coffee?' I ask.

'Oh yes, darling. Could I have my favourite, a Venti? Do you know how to make one? A Venti is made with half-whole milk, one quarter 1%, one-quarter non-fat, extra hot, split quad shots (1 1/2 shots decaf, 2 1/2 shots regular), no foam latte, with whip cream, two packets of Splenda, one sugar in the raw, a touch of vanilla syrup and three short sprinkles of cinnamon,' Albert explains, smiling.

I point to the kitchen and explain to Albert; 'There is the kettle and some instant coffee. Make it yourself what you want. I need a moment.'

Albert's face showed disappointment, and he said, 'Darling if you need a moment take as many moments as you need because I am going to the *Java Hutt* to get me a Venti before they close. Do you want anything while I am there?'

'No,' I answered.

'Okey dokey, I will be back in ten minutes then. See you soon. Leave the door unlocked so I can come straight up. Ciao!' and off goes Albert to get himself his Venti.

In thirty minutes (see what I mean, nothing is ever short with Albert), he opens the door proclaiming his arrival; 'I am back darling. What you devised?'

One thing I have learned over the years of working with Albert is that if he presents all the information, he leaves the implementation to me and really, I do not mind. I always think he will one day will give me a challenge that all that is required is for me to pick one door, walk in, go to the bedroom and there laying as plain as bread is something so valuable that makes the Mona Lisa look cheap, but no, all of Albert's acquisitions have been difficult, albeit successful, but difficult.

'Yes, Albert, your short thirty-minute outing for a coffee has given me a thought. How well do you know Marta and her husband?' I ask.

'They have invited me to several parties, well actually Felicia brought me as her 'wingman,' to Marta's and Timothée place in Leichhardt for parties they host to develop an interest in a crowdfunding campaign for his restaurant idea, whatever crowdfunding is. Why do you ask?'

'Albert, would it be possible to approach Timothée yourself minus Felicia or his wife?' I asked.

'Of course. He and I have grown to know each other over these parties that start early and finish into the wee hours of the morning. What do you need me to do, sweetie?'

'I need for you to ask Timothée to host a special dinner party for three, himself and you and I. Tell him you found someone interested in meeting him and speaking with him about his culinary ideas and maybe an investment in his new restaurant. You can do this for me, right? Make sure it is us, just the three of us. Do not include the wife, okay?'

'Of course, Danny, I can do this. I will schedule this as soon as possible. Any night you want it done?' Albert asks.

'No, whatever is good for him. Just allow enough time for us both to close shop, you drive us into Leichhardt and plenty of time for us to speak with him, taste his culinary skills and size him up.'

'Size him up?' asked Albert.

'Yup.'

'Consider it done. Speak to you soon. Ciao darling.' And off he departs leaving me his Venti coffee cup to clean up.

THE GAME IS AFOOT!

The first Monday of the month started with a beautiful morning in Northport with the sun shining brightly and winds at 12km/h which made for a pleasant cool breeze coming in through my bedroom window. My morning routine was quick. Shave, shower and have a quick breakfast and downstairs I go to tidy up before opening my little shop at 10 AM sharp.

Mondays are usually busy. Many folks believe Monday as a good day to come into the centre of the village, have a quick breakfast, do some shopping, do lunch, continue shopping until the stores close for the day and the evening crowd will start coming into town around 8 PM. Most establishments are closed on Sunday so Mondays the buying bug happens in little villages like Northport. Today was no different. As I promptly opened my store and turned over my little door sign to 'We Are Open,' I headed to my favourite spot, the high stool behind my front counter where the cash register sat and where I could see everyone come into the store and have a great view of all angles of the shop through the CCTV cameras that I had installed. I have some precious first edition books valued in the thousands and you cannot be too careful these days since the world is full of individuals of dubious character.

Waiting for the first customer, I peruse the hardcover first edition of the *New Larousse Gastronomique 2009*, available to purchase for $85 in case the reader is interested. Tonight, I should dine on French cuisine since Albert set up our dinner meeting with Timothée.

Flipping through the pages my little doorbell sounds announcing the entrance of a young couple with two children, these I do not like since sometimes children are a nuisance and I do not carry any children books. What people see in the little rugrats surprises me.

'Good morning,' I said, smiling and holding my breath.

'Pauly, Mabel, you go over there and play with the books while you father and I speak with this man,' said the woman.

Play with the books. That is my inventory you are speaking about lady, watch your mouth. Should they not be in school? I think to myself while making a mental note to place a couple of signs around the store which state the usual statement you find in a fine China store — 'You Break It, You Pay for It' but then again can you break a book?

'How may I assist you this morning?' I say while one eye is looking at the brats and the other at the couple. Can I get crossed-eyed doing this I wonder?

'I hope you can,' speaks the man. 'We are looking for a book on cricket for my father-in-law. He is a fanatic of cricket, and his 80th birthday is coming up. Do you have anything to offer?'

Before I can answer, the woman interjects, 'By the way, Ms Lemmens says hello. She recommended we come to you since she was so happy with your service and all your unusual books.'

Ah, Ms Lemmens, of course, I remember her. She bought a Belgian cookbook and a book by Rolf Ledgewood. Gracious lady with a Platinum AMEX if I remember.

Yes, Ms Lemmens. A lovely lady. I thought to myself.

'Well, can you help or not?' the man said, interrupting my thoughts.

'Of course, sir. Let me bring you one which is special since David Hookes signed it,' I say with a smile.

'Who is David Hookes?' the woman says.

'David Hookes is a South Australian cricketer, broadcaster and coach of the Victorian cricket team. An aggressive left-handed batsman if I remember correctly. The book is the first edition as well. Quite exquisite with its own dust cover. Let me get it for you. Please wait.' I say as I go over to the first edition area while keeping a hawk-eye on the two monsters fiddling with some books.

Quickly I find the book and lay it on the counter for the couple to see.

'That's it?' enquiries the man.

'Yes, sir, a pristine first edition. Quite delicious for the avid cricket aficionado.'

Before the man opens his mouth, the woman slaps her AMEX card, another Platinum card I notice, on the table and says, 'We will take it!'

'Don't you want to know what it costs? says the man. There is not even a price tag on it.' Looking at me thinking to himself I would probably rip him off. I am, however, an honest retailer, and I look up the book and find that I priced reasonably the book at $30 and so proclaim to this fact which makes the man look at the woman and she just nods to me and says to her husband: 'See Ms Lemmens said he had reasonable prices in his store.'

Thank you Ms Lemmens I think as I ring the sale quickly because I notice the kids are now getting edgy a bit since they have been in the store, what ten minutes, and they are bored. I bag the book and return the card and smile; 'Thank you for your patronage today, Mr and Mrs Zackary. Please say hello to Ms Lemmens for me.' I come from behind the counter to usher them out the door.

'Have a lovely day, Mr and Mrs Zackary. Pauly and Mable,' I said, startling the woman.

'Pauly, Mabel, let's go,' said the woman. As I held the door open, I felt a strong wind outside, and I hoped it was not bringing rain because that always cuts down the number of customers.

Luckily, it would not be that kind of day. The rest of the morning went smoothly with more customers coming in. Some bought cards, a few bought some office supplies, some bought some current bestsellers and one even bought one of the few copies I have of the Northport Writers Group anthology *Writing Can Be Fun—2020*' which I have in my store on consignment. Overall, a nice profitable day. I love supporting indie authors, I hope the reader does as well.

Right before closing time, Albert walks in all dolled up. I know everyone has a favourite colour. Mine is blue for example. For others, it might be red, the colour of passion and liveliness. Some steer towards orange which is quite an attention-grabbing colour. Several may lean toward yellow which is said to be the colour of happiness. More might go for green which is said to represent loyalty and nature. Finally, violet, the colour of royalty. In Albert's case, he is wearing them all.

If a man's suit needed a brightness control switch this is the one. All colours were vibrant and bold in a horizontal pattern with each colour in a wide band. A matching tie on a white shirt with moccasins, and no socks, of course, and again Albert radiated in it.

'Danny darling, what a delightful afternoon, how has your day been? Mine has been divine! The shop has been nonstop since 8 AM and it is almost 6 PM, closing time, clapping his hands, and we must have done over sixty heads and my profit for the day will be over $6,000. I am quite pleased with myself. Tell me about all your day!'

Of course, I had to go through my retail day with Albert, so when I do a recap, it takes about two minutes but with Albert, it will extend to ten minutes because of his questions. He needs to know all the details. Who came in? Who bought what? How did they pay? Albert is always looking for an angle, I guess.

'Darling after such a boring day you must be exhausted. Let me tell you about the wonderful evening planned for us. I have set up, as you asked, the meeting with Timothée to discuss our potential 'investment' in his new restaurant,' smiling Albert states as he winks at me.

'I set our business dinner up for 7 PM so I will pick you up at 6:15 PM sharp no dilly dally now. We will meet him at his place in Leichhardt, minus Marta, just as you asked.'

'Thanks for setting this up, Albert. I think we have a chance for two things. First a French dinner and maybe an opportunity to make some extra money so yes, I will not dilly dally, and I will wait out the back of the car park for you at 6:15 PM sharp. OK? By the way, is that what you are wearing to meet Timothée?'

'Yes, it is. I look smashing, do I not? Now, sweetie. I will go home. So, Danny, do not take a nap, no time sweetie. See you later.' As he turns to head out the door, I call out to him.

'Albert, I am glad you are wearing that suit tonight. You look smoking in it!'

'Oh, you are a flirt, Danny. Quite a flirt. I will see you at 6:15 PM. Ta!'

I look at the wall clock above the door and see that it is 5:55 PM so I walk to the door, turn my little door sign to 'We Are Closed' and lock the front door. I wished Albert is on time for he promises one thing and delivers another. I do not want to be late.

Walking to the rear of the store, I made sure the front window display was lit for the evening I turned on the store alarm system and headed upstairs. I think I need to do an outfit change; gosh, I am turning into Albert. First, I check the TV to see what I might miss tonight and find that nothing will be missed and nothing is worth recording for later viewing so after wasting three minutes in this activity I head to the closet. The last business meeting I had was four years ago when I went to the bank to ask for the loan to buy the *Village Books & Stuff* and I needed to look 'business-like' and since that moment I had no reason to wear a suit, well that is not true if you count Hebert McCullum's funeral. It is definitely decision time on what to wear and I am running out of time. Luckily, men have it easier than women. We only need to own two suits: a business suit and a funeral and wedding suit. Add a dozen white shirts, some button-down, some not and maybe twenty odd ties and one pair of black shoes, and another one brown and we are complete. So, my decision tonight was which style of shirt to go with the business suit and which tie. The black shoes for sure. All of this took another six minutes, and with time to spare I am dressed and by the anointed time I was downstairs in my store's car park waiting for Albert. I looked at my watch and smiled; 6:11 PM.

At exactly 6:23 PM Albert drives up in his 1998 Bentley Mulsanne and we head out of town via the Hume Highway towards Leichhardt. I do not say a word to Albert on his tardiness for at exactly two minutes to 7 PM we knock on the home of Marta and Timothée.

As Holmes would say, the game is afoot!

RESTAURATEURS

Albert, my friend, it is so good to see you. You look brilliant! Please come in. Bring in your friend, Mr Monk, I presume,' said Timothée as he ushered us into his home.

'Thank you Timothée for the opportunity to speak to you about our potential interest in investing in a new project with you,' said Albert. 'And you correctly presumed, yes, this is my dearest of friends Mr Daniel Monk.'

I take Timothée's stretched hand and give it a firm shake and find his handshake quite strong as it should be for a chef wielding heavy objects about a kitchen. 'Please call me Danny, all my friends do, Mr Bené.'

'OK, Danny, please also call me Tim then. Timothée is so difficult to say for some English-speaking people. Let us go into the kitchen where we can have a glass of wine and talk a little before our meal,' as he leads us to the large kitchen behind the lounge area.

'Albert, please leave your bag there in the lounge. We will probably end our evening there and you can retrieve it on your way home,' Tim said as he pointed to his three-seater lounge.

Immediately the aroma hits us as we reach the kitchen and realise, we are in epicurean heaven. The smells of sauces, spices, onions, mushrooms, garlic fill the kitchen and prepare you for what is ahead.

'What may I get you to drink, Albert? And you, Danny? May I suggest a wine to complement our appetisers?' Albert beats me to the answer: 'Of course, Timothée. I mean, Tim, whatever you suggest.'

'Excellent I have a 2012 bottle of Giaconda Nebbiolo which will go well with our conversation and is an excellent wine to complement our mushroom risotto.' Says Tim as he reaches for the bottle, opens it, and pours us each our glass to savour. As Tim continues working his magic in the kitchen. I had to ask: 'Tim, what creation are you making for us tonight?'

'Well Danny, I must confess I am nervous because I want to be at my absolute best tonight so you can see the effort, the love, the passion I have for cooking and hope that I can influence you with the flavours I create. If the flavours do not entice you, I will then get you to drink enough to agree to finance my, rather, our new venture,' Tim says, laughing a bit.

'Tim, the aroma in the room is splendid. If the food tastes half as good as it smells, you might get your wish tonight,' I say with Albert, nodding.

'Well, I already mentioned the mushroom risotto. A cold-pressed tomato soup will follow this with Fromage blanc and profiteroles. Then we will try Petits Pois a la Francaise with sliced Norwegian salmon. Just when you think you are full; I will present to you poached snapper with smoked baby potatoes and caviar. A small desert of roasted apple ravioli with star anise and white pepper and to finish a goat's cheese wrapped in puff pastry. Of course, we will complement each dish with the wine and top it off with one of my favourites after-dinner drinks, a Spanish sherry with the so not Spanish name of Harvey Bristol Cream,' smiles Tim, seeing our faces in awe at the feast we are about to embark in.

We continue to watch Tim prepare our dinner, and some small chit-chat occurs while we pass the time. Plates move left and right; saucepans swirl again from right to left as if gliding in the air. Nothing is spilt, nothing seems out of place. All six burners are going, each with its own delicacies. Tim makes it look like a ballet in the kitchen, and the smell continues to entice Albert and me. The hunger pangs were getting stronger as each minute passed. Then Tim says, 'Come, let's sit and eat.'

Tim points to several plates and lets us know the order of the meal but he adds that he wants to be informal and if we wish to, we can grab whatever catches our eyes. We did not stray from the course. Tim was doing a great job of guiding us in our digestive adventure. We continue to follow Tim's lead as we ate the food ensuring the right order, it does not matter if one person is ahead of the other in the meal. We waited for Tim.

'OK, we are here to eat tonight.' Both Albert and I looked at each other and said: 'We agree.'

The meal was like a slow, delightful waltz. We passed serving dishes back and forth and the conversation went from the dish to the ambitions of Tim and his wife Marta. Why did they want to open a restaurant? What are their plans? How much money have they raised? Have they received any interest from any individual to invest? What will be their personal financial investment in the venture? Have they decided on a locale? What about a menu? Who will manage the establishment if both Tim and Marta are in the kitchen? What is Tim's and Marta's experience in the business?

The questions poured out of both Albert and me and Tim had answers, excellent answers for all the questions and he volunteered some interesting facts. Tim also had his own questions for us: 'Well, my friends, what do you like most tonight? Anything that you did not fancy? Please, let me know. Was the wine delectable to your taste and the food it complemented? Be honest - that is all I ask.' Tim continues serving us, explaining his dishes, and having fun with his food. Both Albert and I looked at each other several times in delight over the three-hour slow degustation.

The one most interesting fact was that while there have been plenty of get-togethers to explore the possibility of investors joining Tim and Marta, Albert mentioned to me that no one has actually offered a proposition. Tim and Marta had explained in their presentations to the potential investors that the restaurant would cost in the neighbourhood of $1.5M to $2,5M which they had saved $550,000 and were just looking for the additional balance to get started. This point made both Tim and Marta wonder if now was not the time to venture into a business scenario in the greater Sydney area.

As Tim continued his lamentations, I did not understand why the hesitation of any potential investor. Tim was a superb chef, and he said that his wife was even better than him and he would always ask the potential investors why they did not want to invest in a restaurant and he never got an honest or straight answer. He always received an excuse. 'Tim, this is such a risky business.' 'Marta, have you thought of what happens if you and Tim want to start a family? Who will run the business?' 'Why have you not gone to a bank for a loan?' 'You are way too young to start a business in such a risky arena.' These were some answers Tim said he received at the get-togethers.

When Tim mentioned these opinions, I gave a quick glance to Albert, and we knew we had an opportunity here for both of us and so I started our involvement. 'Tim, what would you do if both Albert and I invested in your venture? Would you be open to a partnership?'

Tim almost dropped the last plate containing the goat's cheese wrapped in puff pastry and was speechless.

'Oh Albert, Danny, did I hear you say you are actually interested in investing in our restaurant? I cannot believe my ears. Wait till Marta gets home.' Tim got up to get three sherry glasses to pour us the Harvey Bristol Cream, and he asked us to move to the lounge area so we could sit a bit more comfortably.

'I can almost 100% state that Marta will be on board with your proposition once you explain to me a bit more of how the partnership will work,' said a smiling Tim as we settled in the lounge seats.

On the way over I had gone over with Albert the approach we should take with Tim and Albert was on board all the way with my thought process and he let me do all the talking for both of us until it becomes his turn to take part. I said, 'Tim, both Albert and I are impressed. With your culinary abilities and if you tell us your wife, Marta, is an even better chef than you, we believe you. Now we would like to go over the proposition for our financial support if you will hear us out.'

'Of course, Danny, Albert, tell me what you have in mind, I am eager to listen to your proposition,' excitingly Tim responds.

Okay, the bait is on the hook, let's see if he bites. 'Tim, we would like for you to speak to your wife and convince her that for one week both Albert and I will work at *The Royal @ Bondi*. Albert will work directly with your wife as an assistant maître d and I will work in the kitchen as a humble kitchen porter.' I let this statement settle in the air and wait for Tim's response.

'My friends, I do not understand, what plausible reason do you want to do such a thing? What do you expect to do by working with us?' a confused Tim says, taking a small sip of his glass of sherry.

'We want to see both you and Marta at work. See how you handle the daily challenges. See how Marta handles the front of the house and how you would handle the entire back of the house if you were to have your own establishment. This one-week experience would be at no cost to you since we would not expect payment for our work but rather, we would like to know—in as much detail as possible - how you conduct yourself with your customers, both in the building for example and those visitors that book your tables.' I stop and also take a sip of the delicious sherry and give Albert a quick nod for Albert to take over.

'Tim, we loved; I mean really loved your food tonight. It was a pleasure not only to the eyes, but all our senses were exploding with delight. However, this meal presentation was for two potential investors, not a crowded restaurant.' Albert pauses and also takes the last sip of his sherry and points to Tim to pour him another one before continuing.

'Tim I was at many of your get-togethers where some potential investors backed off before even asking a question or after asking you and your lovely Marta a question. I found that vulgar.'

'So, Danny and I thought if we spent some time with you both, sort of 'junior shadows' we may see how well you handle the business for someone else and if we are happy with what we see, and we think we will be, nay, we know after experiencing your culinary delights that you will be successful. We then wish to propose to you a proposition to finance your venture—100% - with a second proviso for our investment, once we completed our one-week 'work-tour' of the *Royal @ Bondi*,' said Albert, completely gulping down his glass of sherry.

'What is the second proviso?' Asks a hesitant Tim, thinking that an impossible hurdle is going to be presented.

I smile knowing that Tim will not find this proviso difficult to entertain; 'That you open the new restaurant in Northport, not in Bondi nor Leichhardt.'

Tim sat silently swirling his last few sips of sherry in his glass, taking a sip, and continuing to swirl the remaining sherry until he took the last gulp, pours himself more sherry and said: 'OK, it seems like a reasonable proposal but how do I know you will come through your end of the deal after the one week of shadowing Marta and me? What do you offer as a guarantee? I cannot just speak with my wife and just say there have been conversations, promises, but nothing concrete and suddenly she has a shadow for a week and the distant hope of our dream restaurant.'

It was now Albert's turn to take the spotlight. 'Tim, sweetheart, do you think that I have been coming to these get-togethers and I have not taken notice of what you and Marta are capable of? Do you think that I, we, would approach you with this proposition and not do our homework? Here, let me show you,' as Albert reaches for his bag and takes out a document.

'Tim, this is a new banking account that Danny I opened last month. It is our financial vehicle to funnel funds into our new venture, yet to be named, of course. Please look at the bank balance,' as Albert shows Tim the bank statement, his eyes open wide, very wide.

'You will put up all that money in this venture? You said you would cover 100% so Marta and I would not have a financial burden? So, what is the catch, Albert? There is always a catch in business,' a distrusting Tim says as he wonders if he is being set up for a disaster.

Albert begins 'So glad you asked Tim, here is our proposed partnership agreement which details everything for you. We want you to read it, share it with Marta, and then make your decision. No pressure. You either agree and understand the agreement and the two provisos we verbally told you, which of course are in the partnership agreement and the third written proviso which we like for you to read now, or you do not. We have nothing to lose and you, my dearest Tim, have everything to gain.'

Tim was numb.

He kept flipping the paperwork in the agreement back and forth reading the same paragraphs, stopping to take a sip of the sherry, and repeating this action for what seemed like ages but in reality, it had been only four or five minutes. He stops and reads the third proviso, points to it and turns the paper towards me. I nod yes.

Tim lays the agreement down on the coffee table, finishes his second sherry, pours himself the third one and says: 'Albert, my dear friend and Danny my new friend, I think we may have a deal here. Let me discuss it with my wife and I will let you know, say in two days?' shyly Tim states.

'Great,' said Albert, 'Now be a dear and make us a strong coffee for the road. It has been a long evening and we have a pleasant ride back to Northport tonight.'

'Of course, Albert, of course,' said Tim, getting up to make the coffee. Albert and I look at each other and smile for the new restaurateurs will be arrived in Northport!

The game is indeed afoot!

I THINK I HAVE TWO DATES

A few days pass and Albert comes into my little shop all excited.

'Danny, sweetheart, I just received a phone call from Tim, and he said he and Marta have agreed to our proposition, has signed the partnership agreement and posted it to me and wants to know when we can start our 'work tour' of the *Royal @ Bondi*?'

It was 10:01 AM, I had barely turned over the 'We Are Open' sign in my front door and Albert was ready to take up the challenge of becoming an assistant maître d.' I had barely finished my morning coffee and or settled behind my counter.

'Albert, my friend, it is so good to see you. Please come in. You are quite chirpy this morning.' I simply said to him hoping he would calm down so we could discuss our strategy before a customer walked in.

'Oh, darling I am fine and yes, I am ready to blast off into this new adventure. Imagine me a maître d'!,' exclaims Albert.

'Albert, you do realise that this is just a way for us to get into the Majestic Towers and pay a visit to our target Michael and see if we can make our 'acquisition' as smoothly as possible? 'We have no intention of becoming restaurateurs, you know that, right?'

'Of course, I know that Danny, it is just so exciting to play a direct part in our little escapade. You are the one who usually takes all the chances while I just provide you with information, valuable information at that, but this time, sweetness, I am taking a part, an important part. I know I have gone with you sometimes but this time I feel I am in the thick of it. Right there in the action. I am in the action!'

Albert's smile just radiated as he made this comment. His smile also complemented the outfit he had worn this morning. An aquamarine suit with a bright yellow button-down shirt and a matching tie with his favourite shoes; an Alessandro patinated Venezia-leather oxford shoes. The man was always at his sharpness.

'So, Danny, what do you think made Tim and Marta agree to our partnership agreement?' Albert asks as he picks up a book and pretends to read it in case someone comes into the store.

I answered him, 'It was the third proviso Albert you know that. The promise that if after one week of our 'work tour' around both of them and observing how a restaurant functions under their leadership and we decide that the restaurant business is not for us, a lovely sum of $2,000,000 would be fronted to them at a zero-interest rate with a monthly payment of $11,000 made until the entire $2,000,000 is paid back. That they will not have to pay interest makes the proposition good for them and in 15 years, they are scot-free of the loan.'

'That was brilliant, Danny. Paying the investment back at that amount. As you just mentioned, it would take fifteen years so of course, they jumped at it, but my friend your stroke of genius was the added sentence to the third proviso; a lifetime all reservation guarantee for either of us at the new restaurant in Northport. Divine! Just simply divine!' said Albert.

I smiled because I know that dining out is one of Albert's favourite pastimes and I also enjoy a good meal every so often and I have to admit that Tim was a superb chef after our introduction to his cuisine and if, as he said, his wife is even better, wow, I do not think we will miss out on much of the $2,000,000 we are fronting considering the potential profit ahead for us.

'Albert, before anyone comes into the store, what are your plans tonight after late trading hours?'

'Nothing at the moment darling, what do you need me to do?' Albert smartly states. 'Actually, I need you to come over and we need to plan our approach to this new venture. Is this okay with you on such short notice?'

'Of course, sweetness. I am at your command. I will stop over at the *American Monkey Bar* and pick us some of their sumptuous cheeseburgers that you love so much.'

'I do not love their cheeseburgers, Albert, you do, but that is OK, bring them on and bring me a strawberry thick shake. That I do like.'

'Ciao, darling. See you tonight,' said Albert as he rushes out the front door.

The rest of Thursday morning went well.

A few fresh faces came, browsed, they purchased a book, a couple of cards, some office supplies.

A typical day at the *Village Books & Stuff*. That is until she walked in.

As the little bell on my door signals the entrance of a new customer I glance up and see the most striking, breathtaking woman I have seen in a long time, after Alessia I say to myself. While expressing our love to each other, she and I have not said to each other that we would be exclusive, at least I did not read that into the conversation, and Alessia has not mentioned a word of this. I assume that this might be the reason for some weekends, and some weeknights, she is 'out with the girls' as she says.

A woman can be beautiful in many ways. The way she walks, the way she smiles, is not necessarily sexually alluring but at the same time, she is sexually attractive. This spectacle of womanhood brings my heart pumping faster and I have no control and then she speaks; I just stare.

'Good morning. What a lovely shop you have. I am wondering if you carry a particular title, I am looking for as a gift.' She sings to me. Well, at least that is how her voice sounded to me.

'What is the title of the book you seek Miss?'

'Please call me Laura. All my friends do.'

Taking out a piece of paper from her purse she recites, 'The book has a long title.' Holding the paper Laura reads me the title: '*Purple and Blue. The History of the 2/10th Battalion, A.I.F. [The Adelaide Rifles] 1939-1945*' and a Lieutenant Colonel Frank Allchin wrote it. I wonder if you, have it? I am looking to purchase it and give it as a gift,' Laura says with a smile that would melt all of Antarctica.

Why am I sweating?

Am I afraid that if I do not have the book, she will simply turn around, leave and I will never again see her? I did not recall the name of the book but then I carry a little over 12,000 books and I only remember some of the really expensive ones but this one by Lt. Col. Allchin does not ring a bell.

'Laura, my name is Danny and I am the owner of the *Village Books & Stuff* and I would be more than happy to see if I carry that title for you. Let's see what I have in inventory,' I proclaim and bring up the *Shopkeep* software inventory tab of my register (why do they still call it a register when it is not really a cash register), oh well, I punch up the details Laura gave me and guess what. I do carry it and it is a 'steal' for $550.

'Well, Laura, the lucky person you are giving this book to, is going to be thrilled for I have it. May I get it for you so you can peruse it at your leisure here in the store?' I think I am babbling also as I say these words to Laura.

'Oh yes please if you would be so kind Danny. My dad would be so happy to receive it as a gift,' says Laura as I continue to be in a daze at the sound of her voice.

I quickly go and based on the software inventory location I find the book and rush; no, I think I ran back to Laura and placed the book in her lovely hand. I watched her beaming smile and face radiate as she began looking through the book.

Laura is about 170cm tall with a slender sixty-five kilos frame and cascading auburn hair that just covered parts of her face which had a medium skin tone typical of southern European ancestry. Her eyes were hazel, which is rare and most beautiful, to see and enjoy. Her complexion was perfectly couture and with a coral or peach colour lipstick that made her face just stand out but not too much. Enough to admire that is for sure.

Taking in Laura's beauty made me think about Alessia and me.

Laura may be a bit out of my league, but I learned one thing in high school a long time ago. When asking women out on a date you should always start with the good-looking ones first and if they say no to your date request, you just work down the line. If you start at the bottom of the heap (and I do not mean that in a sexist manner) and she says 'Yes,' well you are sort of stuck then. Both Alessia and Laura are definitely at the top of the heap.

My thoughts are interrupted; 'How much is the book?' asks Laura.

'$550. May I bag the book for you?' I smile like a dummy at Laura. What am I doing? I am now with Alessia, right?

'Yes, please. My dad will be delighted. He is such an aficionado of historical warfare. I believe he will enjoy it since he mentioned it once before, and I made sure he did not have it in his collection. Do you accept AMEX?' Laura asks.

I would have accepted mud from her as payment. 'Yes of course.' Accepting the card and processing it through my merchant credit card POS. The magic words appear; 'Approved.'

Handing the card back to Laura I proceed in placing the book in a bag for her and tried making the moment last as much as possible.

'Thank you, Danny, you have been most helpful. If you ever head into the city or Bondi, give me a tingle and maybe we could grab a quick drink, Fridays are always good for me,' she says as she reaches into her handbag and reaches into her purse and hands me a business card.

The distinctive card shows her full name as.

Laura M. Burton

Gansevoort Promotions

CEO—Managing Director

Sydney, Australia, 2000.

+610246597444

Intrigued, I ask: 'Laura, what is Gansevoort Promotions, if I may ask?'

'I own and manage a public relations company. While not the largest in Sydney certainly, I feel, the most prestigious one. I have over one hundred of the ASX 200 companies as clients.'

Impressive, I thought to myself. 'Well, Laura Friday sounds good to me. I normally work late on Thursdays, you know, late trading hours, so Friday night would be a great way to unwind from a long Thursday. You can tell me then more about yourself and your company since you know everything about my empire,' I say this as I spread my arms showing that everything around us in this domain is mine. 'Is that OK?' I smiled and crossed my fingers.

'Of course, Danny. I will wait for your call to confirm Friday.'

With that, she picks up the bag, turns, winks at me and leaves.

About an hour later my door tingles again hoping for a prospective new customer and I look to find Alessia closing the door behind her.

'Hi, handsome. How is your day going?'

Oh boy.

'Hi, Alessia. The day is going great. Even better now that I see you.' Why am I feeling lousy? Am I coming down with the flu? Am I sweating? I feel like I am sweating again.

'Our supply of photocopy paper has not arrived, and I used that excuse to say I would get a ream of paper to tidy us over until the delivery comes. I also wanted to see you, Danny.'

'And I always like to be seen, Alessia.' Oh boy, I am going from dumb to dumber.

Pointing toward the office supply section Alessia says: 'Let me get the ream of paper, pay and return to the library for I do not want to be gone long. Oh, before I forget I want to ask you; what are you doing this weekend?'

'Which evening?'

'I am thinking Friday night. Are you available, handsome?' as she picks up a ream of paper and walks back to the counter with a $20 note in her hand which I take and give her change to and place the ream of paper in a bag.

'Of course.'

'Great Danny. I will call you to set up a place. Speak with you soon,' and Alessia leaves the store. As door gently closes and my little bell tingles signalling Alessia departure, terror strikes me: I think I have two dates.

A BAD NIGHT TO BE THINKING AS A BURGLAR

At exactly 6:01 PM I turned the lock on my front door, turned the sign over to say, 'We Are Closed', walked to the rear of the store, turned off all the lights except the front window display and turned on the store's security system as I walk upstairs. I am done for the day.

What a day it was indeed.

Sales were actually good about 13% above a normal day and certainly at least 27% over the same day last year according to my statistics from the *Shopkeep* software.

The highlight was of course; Miss Laura M Burton. I sort of had already committed to seeing her when I realised, I had also organised later a date with Alessia on the same night. What was I turning into? I know I love Alessia but what is this additional attraction to Laura? I was muddling in my thoughts when I heard the doorbell to my unit ring indicating that Albert had arrived with dinner.

Opening the door, I found Albert Matthew Guzman beaming in excitement and carrying two large bags holding our dinner from the *American Monkey Bar*. Albert rushes in. 'Come on Danny, I am starving tonight, and we have so much to go over with our plan to acquire A. G. Michael's coin.'

Albert placed the dinner bags on the kitchen counter and made himself at home. He takes out utensils and plates (for a cheeseburger), a couple of Great Northern Super Crisp beers from the refrigerator, salt and pepper, ketchup (no tomato sauce on an American cheeseburger Albert always says) and gestures me to sit at my dinner table as he takes out the cheeseburgers, chips but no strawberry thick shake for me. My thoughts are on today's outfit that Albert is wearing as he munches on his cheeseburger. Tonight, he is wearing what I would describe as a super skinny crushed velvet suit jacket in red with a wide-open white shirt and shows off his hairless chest and classic black shoes with matching red socks.

'The server at the *American Monkey Bar* said they were out of strawberries to make your thick shake, so I settled, no I decided, that tonight we both go for one of your beers. I hope you approve and if you do not, well tough.' There was a tone in Albert's voice, which I found interesting.

'Albert, my friend, you sound tense. What is wrong?' I asked him.

'The number of people waiting to be served was huge. I had to stand there for at least nine minutes waiting for our cheeseburgers. It was totally crazy. So, under organised, discombobulated, I would describe it better, it lacked organisation. The people were shouting, asking for their food and drinks. It was awful. I do not know why people get into the food business at all, I just do not know. Maybe we are going into the restaurant business so I can avoid all this hustle,' Albert stops and takes a mouthful of his cheeseburger.

Great, I think. This is the assistant maître d' that will work with Marta for a week. This may well be the worst idea I have ever come up with, but I will not pursue it with him now. Maybe when he calms down later on in the week, I will approach him on the style he needs to provide while being a maître d' at the *Royal @ Bondi.*

'Albert, please enjoy your cheeseburger and my beer. We have a little planning to discuss and I need you to be alert for this and not be distracted with the *American Monkey Bar* incident at this moment.' I sternly announce but I say to myself, maybe Albert has a point about the restaurant business. I will circle back to that thought later, I say to myself.

'You are right darling, as always, you are right. Let us enjoy our meal and start our plan.' A much calmer Albert stated.

Between sips of beer and bites of the cheeseburgers, Albert and I discussed what each other's role will be during the week's sojourn at the *Royal @ Bondi* and how we will make sure that Marta and Tim do not get a whiff of what our true mission is. The evening progressed well into midnight and after many more beers, Albert was feeling the effect. So, he called for an Uber to take him home and left his Bentley Mulsanne 1998 in the car park behind my store and I made sure he got into the Uber since he was a little wobbly.

As I laid in bed thinking of Friday and what new sales might walk into the *Village Books & Stuff,* my mind wandered between three other distinctive distractions; A. G. Michael's coin, my meeting Laura M Burton and my commitment to a Friday night's date with Alessia and Laura. Before you knew it, the alcohol kicked in and I was no longer in this world as I drifted away in my bed.

Friday morning like a cyclone Albert comes into my little shop all excited.

'Danny darling, it is a go! We are to start in three weeks on Tuesday night at 7 PM, which is one the busiest they have according to Tim. It is in three weeks because he had to make sure he could come up with a plausible reason to give the current owners why he would need two additional staff for a week. He said he came up with something that satisfied the owners and we are good to go. This is most exciting!'

'Excellent news Albert. Just a normal day at work for us with just an earlier closing time which I can easily be explained with a sign. Excellent indeed. Now were you able to purchase the old car as I said we should?' I also felt a little excited and then I remembered I needed to call Alessia and cancel. I wonder how she will take it.

'Yes, I purchased an old Ford Festiva. It is an awful little car to drive. Straight shift, or is it stick shift, I do not remember. Thank goodness I learned as a teenager. Some things you never forget, right sweetness?' winking at me.

With that, Albert pirouettes and walks out of my store as if he were floating on air.

I look in the top drawer on my front counter and I freeze.

Next to Alessia's card, I find the other card. I shivered at the thought of seeing both women's cards laying side by side. I withdrew Laura's business card.

Laura M. Burton.

Gansevoort Promotions.

CEO—Managing Director.

Sydney, Australia, 2000.

+610246597444

Why am I making this call? What is wrong with me? Alessia is, well, perfect and yet I take out my mobile to call Laura now that the store is empty of customers.

Punching the numbers, I actually start sweating again. What is it with me and this woman I ask myself?

A male voice answers; 'Ms Burton's office. How may I help you?'

Taken aback, I introduce myself and ask for Laura.

'One moment please,' the male voice says.

'Danny, what a pleasure you called. I was not sure you were interested in catching up with me and having a drink. Thank you for your call.' I could sense a little excitement in her voice, so I plunged right in.

'Laura, I can make the Friday night drinks. I can come into the city and meet you where you will feel is best for you. You name the time and place and I will be there with bells on.' God, I sounded so corny!

'Excellent, Danny. How about 8 PM at the *Royal @ Bondi?* You know where that is? Hello, hello, Danny, are you there? Has the line dropped? Hello, Danny?'

For a moment, time stood still for me. Laura suggests the *Royal @ Bondi*. Why? Quick answer the woman before she hangs up. Think, man, think!

'Oh, hi there. Sorry, my mind wandered for a moment. Yes, I know the *Royal @ Bondi*. It is a lovely place I hear. Any reason you prefer this place rather than somewhere else in the city? I mean, I just want to make sure you are comfortable with our first meetup. That's all.'

'I love the place and besides, I live in the building, so it makes it extremely comfortable for me after work to have a drink there, but if it is an inconvenience, we could go somewhere else. What do you suggest?' Laura says with a sad tone to her voice.

Quickly I realise that if I change the location Laura might decide not to meet, so I agree to the location and the date is set.

After I hung up the phone, I pondered the situation. Laura lives in the building that brings me so many positive and negative points to consider. On the positive side, I get to see the restaurant earlier and the locale from a customer's point of view, and I will have quite a distracting date that most men, and some women, would see first before me and I would be almost invisible. On the con side, there is always someone like Mrs Mangel from the TV show *'Neighbours'* who is on the lookout and might recognise me later while working during Albert's and mine 'work tour.' My mind went in different directions all at once, thinking of different alternatives, scenarios and tossing them out as not good enough until my inner smile came up. There is always an answer to every opportunity.

With the phone still in my hand, I ring Alessia.

'Hi, Danny, what's up, sweetie?'

'Alessia, I am so sorry. Something has come up on Friday night and I cannot make it. could we do it at another time?' asking as sheepishly as possible.

'Oh, I am disappointed, but I can understand. Nothing serious?'

'No, I set up a business meeting and double-booked you. I promise to make it up, promise.'

'Don't worry, Danny. I am a big girl. I can wait. Maybe I can go out with the girls instead. I can always plan something kinda quickly so do not worry. Good luck with the business meeting. See you soon,' and blows me a kiss before hanging up.

Before you know I close the store, Uber it to Bondi and I walk into the *Royal @ Bondi* precisely at 7:50 PM to make sure I can see Laura when she walks in. The lady maître d,' who I presume to be Marta, whom I have not met before, points me to the bar and I sit and make myself comfortable ensuring I have a view of both entrances.

I felt anxious for reasons unknown to me. I have been out with attractive women before but this time it just felt different as if destiny had brought us together. I gesture to the bartender to bring me one of my many favourite alcoholic drinks, a Mojito, and after a few minutes the bartender, who introduces himself as Antoin, brings me what turns out to be one of the best Mojitos I have ever enjoyed. As I am savouring the Cuban drink, I see her walk in.

Laura looks smashing. She appears to be wearing an expensive pastel Veronica Beard Gamila mid-rise ankle pants with a companion Dickey jacket. Both the blazer and pants are composed of Italian stretch wool, giving Laura both style and panache. A silk camisole brings her to almost perfection. She has a matching pair of handmade Italian shoes that you could see a mile away that were made with care from fine leather and a sensual stiletto heel. Before the evening started, I was already defeated. I wave at her.

As Laura reaches me, she takes my hand and lands the sweetest kiss on my cheek and I feel my knees buckle a bit.

'Hi Danny, you found the place. So good to see you. What are you having? It looks delicious! I will have the same please.' She sat next to me. I motioned to Antoin to bring two more Mojitos, and he smiled.

Before you knew it, the drinks became a meal and then dessert arrived and a coffee and at 10:35 PM Laura said, 'Danny I would love to show you my father's book collection to see if you can suggest something else to purchase and add to the collection for his Christmas present. Would you mind?'

Normally, I would jump at the opportunity of visiting an attractive woman's apartment, but it was getting late, and I needed to open shop on Saturday and then prepare more the debut of our 'work tour' and as I was about to make up an excuse Laura interrupts my thoughts and continues her statement.

'Besides, I could show you the view of the moon over Bondi Beach. What do you say?'

What could I say? I nod to our server to bring our bill, which I immediately grab from Laura. 'Come on, Danny. We can go Dutch tonight,' she said, smiling.

Laura said, 'Well then since you decided to be a gentleman and pay the bill how about we finish the evening on the balcony of the penthouse and like I said, watch the moon shinning over Bondi Beach.'

Wait one minute!

There is only one penthouse at the Majestic Towers, and it belongs to A. G. Michael of Burton & Michael Investments. Oh, my goodness, Laura M Burton. How is Laura associated with A. G. Michael?

Providence, coincidence, destiny, call it what you want tonight I was going to visit the very place Albert, and I wanted to case for a week and see more in detail, although I must give Albert plenty of credit since his sources provided an excellent description of the place but there is nothing like seeing things for oneself.

After paying the bill, Laura locks her arm in mine for two reasons. First, to steady herself, there was plenty of drink tonight and second, I think she likes me. A lot. We passed the security reception where I made sure I was on Laura's left so the security guard and camera did not get a glance of my face too well.

Laura opens her handbag, takes her purse, and taps an FOB card on the third lift access card pad and I see the lift arrow point down from the third level and it arrives shortly to the ground floor. Taking the lift Laura fumbles with her purse placing the FOB card in the purse of her handbag and, just as Albert described. we quickly arrive at the penthouse. The lift door opens, and a magnificent layout is sprawled in front of me. A huge open plan and decorated with excellent taste. There is definitely a lot of money here.

'Wow. What a place you got here.' I exclaim to Laura as she lets go of my arm and throws her purse on the lounge.

'Dad loves to collect all kinds of fine art and collectables. He has them scattered all about the place. Please go to the balcony and start taking in the view. I am going inside to make myself comfortable. Would you like a nightcap?' Laura states.

'Yes, that will be great.' I walk slowly toward the balcony as Laura disappears into the bedroom, I hear water flowing so I am assuming Laura has decided on a quick shower, so I quickly turn and rummage her handbag and purse and extract the security FOB and I hastily return to the balcony and stare into the moonlit ocean. What a view I think to myself.

After several more minutes, Laura arrives barefooted with two glasses and she is wearing an evening gown of luxurious sheer silk tulle with panels of hand-cut lace and soft satin trims and a satin tie for around the waist. I had to make sure my eyes did not fall out.

'Danny, I hope you like apple brandy. I love Calvados after dinner. Straight out of the fridge and neat. I hope you like it,' Laura said sheepishly.

'I am sure I can get used to them very quickly,' as we toast and we both take a sip.

'It is a beautiful night and a fantastic view but please let me show you my father's book collection before the night slips by,' as she takes my hand and walks me into a supersize office where a massive collection of first editions is immaculately presented.

'Impressive,' I say, walking around the study as Laura takes a seat in one of the large chairs and watches me look around. After a few minutes, I say, 'Laura, I might have an idea or two for your father's Christmas gift and I will ring you with my suggestions in a couple of days. Is that, OK?'

Laura smiles, walks over to me, and lays a passionate kiss on my lips. I respond appropriately and again Laura takes my hand and leads me into the bedroom.

'Are we alone tonight, Laura?' I ask knowing that I have Alessia on my mind so no, there will be three of us.

'Yes, Danny. It is just us tonight and for the next two weeks. Daddy is away on business and I leave tomorrow on a business trip of my own for two weeks as well. I want tonight to be special! Don't you?'

It is going to be a bad night to be thinking like a burglar.

THE GAME IS ON!

At exactly 5:11 AM I quietly close the door to Laura's bedroom and take a quick peek inside the master bedroom knowing that her father was out of town. Just like Albert describe it there past the master bedroom is a walk-in wardrobe the size of a double garage and as I walk through it it reveals the Chubb Holsworthy vault. Quickly I snap several photos I and still wonder how in the world did they manage to bring a small bank vault into the building and what kind of goodies Laura's father keeps in it. Probably all his precious paintings and other collections and the target of my visit; the Hawaiian Missionaries stamp and the United Kingdom Edward III Florin 1343 or 1344 gold coin with a combined value of $764,000. Seeing how the entire penthouse is laid out made me feel a bit more comfortable. I gingerly leave down the lift and ensuring my head is covered as best as possible I walked out of the Majestic Towers and head back to Northport. I had work to do.

Arriving at my unit at 6:50 AM, I take out my RFID copier and scan the FOB key Laura used to get the lift going. The RFID copier goes and accepts the information on the FOB quickly. I then retrieve a second FOB and reverse the code back into the second FOB. The correct light comes up, and a short beep emits from the RFID copier showing a successful copy has been created. I now have access to the lift to go up since I notice it is not needed to go down the lift from the penthouse. Knowing that I will not have to hurry to return Laura's POB today, I place the original FOB in my pocket. I leave my 'new' FOB on the kitchen counter knowing that

I will use it tonight when Albert is on his 'work tour,' as I will also be on my 'work tour' and I walk downstairs to prepare to make an honest living at the *Village Books & Stuff.* I glance in the mirror, see myself and wonder what the day will bring.

As usual Saturday morning, I open the store and get the customary early traffic in. This traffic falls into two categories. The first are those individuals, both male and female, with no weekend plans and nothing new to read so they come and grab one of the recent bestsellers in paperback format and at the front door they leave. The second is the office and small business individuals who order their supply of paper, inkjet toner or staples from the local big box office supply and run out before the order comes in. Either way, they both represent some good sales every Saturday.

During all this I do some research on the Chubb Holsworthy vault. With over 12,000 books in my shop, I knew I had a reference book on safes. The *Sandford Book on Safes: The Mechanics of Engineering of a Safe* by Michael Jay Brown (second edition), a steal at $220 if the reader is interested. A couple of solid hours of reading and studying should be enough to handle this baby I believe. As I am finishing my research, the store phone rings and I answer it; Laura is on the other end.

'Danny, I am so sorry I just had too much to drink, and I could not see you out this morning. I am so sorry. What time did you leave?' Laura asks.

'About 5:15 AM or so, Laura. I did not want to disturb you, so I left early enough to have a leisurely drive back to my place and get ready to open my shop. I too am sorry I did not bid you adieu.'

'I understand Danny, you have a business to run. Did you enjoy our time together? I know I did.'

'Why do you ask that, Laura? The evening was fantastic. Everything. The location, the meal, the view on the balcony. Us. Everything.' I answered her honestly.

'I am glad because I would like to do it again when I return if that is okay with you Danny.'

'I already have pencilled you in.' I responded. 'By the way, Laura, as I left this morning, and the lift started going down I noticed you had dropped your FOB in the lift. Do you need it right away?' crossing my fingers.

'Really? I was tipsy last night, so it does not surprise me. Why did you not come back and return it to me? We could have had a quick coffee and whatever,' a slight chuckle came from her sweet voice.

'I almost did, but I saw how delightfully serene you looked under the covers as I left so that I could not bring myself to disturb you. Besides, as you mention, I have a business to run single-handed.' I too let a little chuckle come through.

'Oh, OK, then. Do not worry about the FOB. I will send a courier to pick it up today and return it to my office, so I have it before I leave later this afternoon for my two-week business trip. I am going to miss you so much, Danny from the *Village Books & Stuff*. Hey, I do not know your last name. What is it anyway?' Laura sounded surprised that during our extended conversation last night, the last name never came up. It did not come up because I did not volunteer it, but I saw no way to not respond. 'It is Monk. Daniel Monk. At your service, Ms Laura M Burton!'

A big laugh emitted from the phone.

'I will see you soon Danny Monk.'

'I will see you soon too, Laura M Burton,' and the phone went dead.

Danny, my boy, you are one lucky son of a gun I think to myself. Not only can I duplicate her FOB undetected, but I quickly give Laura a reason why she does not have the FOB in her purse this morning. To top that, Laura is sending a courier to pick it up. I might not have the luck of the Irish, but my Anglo-Scottish surname is not doing too badly in the luck department.

A courier walks in at exactly 12 PM.

'I am looking for a Mr Monk. I am supposed to pick up a package for Ms Burton.'

'I am Mr Monk. One moment please, I will get the package for you.' I gallop to the rear of the store and grab the smallest shipping box I have. Wrap the FOB in bubble wrap, tape the box and write Laura's name on the box. I return to the front and hand the courier the box. The courier completes a transit slip, gives me the pink copy, nods to me and walks out the door and almost knocks Albert down since he was strutting in like a peacock, at least in the colour department. Today Albert had decided that wearing a multi-colour running lengthwise rainbow suit with a matching green tie and a white shirt would be the ideal day.

Albert could have stopped traffic.

Before speaking Albert looks and gives the courier a quick glance in the backside department as the courier is exiting and then Albert looks around and sees that we are alone. 'Danny, how exciting. In a couple of hours, I will be an assistant maitre d. By the way, if you are working in the kitchen, what will be your title?'

'The title of the position is a kitchen porter,' I answered.

'OK, but what are you going to do in the kitchen then, what is a kitchen porter?'

'As you know Albert, Tim is a commis chef or a junior chef that means he works for the station chef or chef de partie. A kitchen porter's responsibility includes such delights as basic cleaning tasks as fast as possible, cleaning the crockery and cutlery, ensuring the food preparation sites are clean and ready and the most exciting tasks of all, collecting and washing up pots and pans. This brings us to a change in plans, my dear friend,' I soberly announce.

'What change of plans? Are we not going tonight to the *Royal @ Bondi?*' a slightly confused Albert inquires.

'Not only are we going to the *Royal @ Bondi* tonight but we are also going to get our two collectable articles and we will be done in one night. We will not need an entire week to do our acquisition.' I proudly announce to Albert who feels like he will miss out on his chance to be a maitre d.' Then I drop the change of plans on him.

'One more thing, Albert, I need to be the assistant maitre d' and I need you to be the kitchen porter.'

'Think you can handle that for one night?'

I could have sworn that Albert's rainbow suit had gone dim suddenly as soon as I finished the last sentence.

'Me, a kitchen porter. Look at these hands, Danny dearest, they are not meant for menial labour. No, no way. I will not do it. It is just not, well, me,' an insulted Albert declares.

'OK, then I leave it up to you to get into the penthouse. Think you can handle that instead?'

'Danny, my dearest. My inspiration in life. Why are you doing this to me? I am so hurt,' and I swear I saw a tear come out of his left eye.

I decide then to relate everything that had happened last night with Laura and how easy our venture will go with my proposed plans and how confident I am that one night is all we need in our 'work tour' at the *Royal @ Bondi*.

After listening to my logic, Albert nodded and said he thought the plans would work out better just like I suggested, and we agreed he would pick me up at 5:15 PM for our drive to Bondi and he quickly and sadly turned and left my shop.

Watching Albert go out the front door I really did not feel bad with the change in plans after all I knew Albert's level of criminality is limited to charging astronomical prices in his hair salon to his hoity-toity clients and taking risks such as being caught doing a burglary is something Albert is not into. He is a planner. He is an information man and now he is going to be a kitchen porter. So, as I glance at the store clock, I smile knowing that the game is on!

A TOAST TO A SUCCESSFUL NIGHT

As we walk into the *Royal @ Bondi*, an attractive woman greets us to whom Albert immediately extends his hand. 'Marta, my dear friend, so nice to see you again. It has been so long.'

'Albert, sweetheart, so good to see you again as well. You rather look different today. Not your usual self I think, but still carrying that beautifully designed satchel as you always do.'

Albert indeed was not himself. Having agreed to be the kitchen help for one night he walked into the restaurant looking, well, bland, for him. He actually wore Emporio Armani jeans with a short sleeve Dolce & Gabbana shirt and the Fendi messenger brown satchel that I am sure Albert must have paid over two thousand dollars for. I on the other hand looked smashingly dapper with my outfit comprising an Anthracite maitre d' jacket, with some slight modifications I paid the tailor to add and matching pants with a superbly crisp white shirt and brilliantly looking tie, Daniel Craig, eat your heart out!

'You must be Mr Monk. Tim has spoken so much about you. We are most thankful for this opportunity you both have presented to us and we will work alongside each of you this month to ensure you see the best of what Tim and I do. Shall we get started, for we are about to open the door to our clients,' Marta said.

'Please Marta, call me Danny. We will work together for a while so no need for formalities.'

'Thank you, Danny. You have a familiar face. Have we met before?'

'Oh, I just have that average looking face. I get that a lot.'

At that moment, Tim comes out of the kitchen and greets us as well.

'Albert, Danny. Great, you are both here. So, by the looks of things Albert, you will be with me tonight. I promise you will do just wonderfully working alongside me. I will make sure you see how hygienic and efficient we work. It will be a pleasure to spend the next six hours with you. Come on now, things to do in the kitchen. I need to introduce you to our executive chef, then our chef de cuisine and our sous chef and finally my boss the chef de partie and of course the rest of the kitchen crew,' and Tim grabs Albert, and I thought I saw another tear in Albert's eye as he disappeared through the doors into the kitchen.

'Well Marta, it is you and me. Teach me the business from your perspective,' I say as Marta smiles and starts detailing the process of opening the restaurant to the public sharply at 7 PM.

Before you know it was almost 10:30 PM, and the restaurant was still excitingly active with the patrons busy eating their meals and savouring their drinks. It was time to act and just as I am about to ask for a break, my mobile rings and I answer it.

'Danny, it's Laura. How are you darling?' asks Laura all chirpy.

'Oh hi, Laura. How did you get my number? I do not recall sharing it or maybe I did, I honestly do not remember,' a quizzical tone in my voice can be felt.

'You wrote it on the courier form, so I jotted it down and I am calling you from the plane. I am being naughty. I am in the toilet,' a giggling Laura says.

Putting my hand over the phone I said to Marta: 'Marta, is it okay if I take a thirty-minute break? I have an especially important call right at the moment,' I said, having another Oscar performance moment if I do say so myself.

Marta looks at her watch but I know the time; 10:40 PM since I had looked at the time on the phone.

'Of course, Danny, please go ahead. I realise you already worked all day at your own place of business so this must be a long day for you. Take more time if you need it. It is slowing down a bit and we will close the doors at 11:45 PM anyway to let our patrons finish their meals and after-dinner drinks by 1 AM. So go, go, take your time,' a very generous Marta said.

'Thank you, Marta, in that case, I might take forty-five if you do not mind,' I said as I went into the kitchen.

'Okay, Laura, talk to me. What in the world are you doing in the plane's toilet?' As Laura starts her recital as to why she is in the plane's toilet I enter the kitchen. The place was still in an organised turmoil with each individual at their station and all performing acts of magic. I saw Tim, and I smiled at him, and he nodded back. I did not see Albert, but I figure Tim would not have him too far away. I headed toward the kitchen exit door where I found Albert's satchel just where I hoped he would place it as we discussed. I quickly grabbed it and stepped outside and closed the door behind me.

Laura finishes the conversation with: 'Danny, what do you think I am doing right now?'

'Okay, Laura, listen I can only wonder what you are doing but I cannot carry this conversation right now with you.'

'Oh Danny, it is such a shame for you are missing out on a treat. Oh well, guess it will have to wait until I get back and when I do, I will not tell you what I was doing on the plane's toilet I will show you,' and she hangs up laughing.

With that scenario burned in my mind, I take things out of Albert's satchel. First, I reverse my jacket now a beautiful darker shade of grey and put it back on again. I lay the following articles on a couple of chairs outside which must be used by the kitchen crew for their breaks. Mirror, moustache, wig, glasses, comb, photograph, FOB, decoder, and a pipe. Using the mirror, I carefully arrange the wig into place making sure that the hairline tilts exactly right to match the photograph and then put on the moustache again ensuring that the photograph is represented in the reflection in the mirror. A quick touch-up with the comb and both the wig and moustache are ready. I look at myself in the mirror. Almost a spitting image, I would say. I now place the pipe in my mouth and look again in the mirror. Mr A. G, Michael has been out on the town, which is what I look like, pleased with myself. All that is left to do is to place the decoder and the FOB in my front pocket.

Placing the mirror back into Albert's satchel, I hide the satchel behind several discarded cartons. I take a deep breath, put the glasses on and begin walking toward Campbell Parade, Bondi's main drag. I take a quick right and in 478 steps I am entering the Majestic Towers and quickly go towards the third lift.

'Good evening, Mr Michael,' the security person at the reception desk says.

I grunt something unintelligible and nod to the security guard and take out the FOB and tap the lift reader to allow access to the penthouse. Since Laura had left for her business trip and her father also away on a business trip, I knew the lift doors would be on the ground floor adding valuable time to my schedule. The lift doors opened immediately and in less than twenty seconds I arrived at the penthouse and the doors opened again to that spectacular view.

Without hesitation, I started putting on my gloves and I walked to the master bedroom and immediately found the vault just sitting there as if beckoning me. Having researched the Chubb Holsworthy vault this morning when I returned from Laura's, I knew exactly what to do.

The time on the phone with Laura took five minutes, so I set my stopwatch on my watch. Forty minutes to do everything. I knew I had exactly twenty-two minutes to do what I needed to do inside Michael's penthouse since I had already taken four minutes to put on my disguise (taking it off would require much less time) and walk to the Majestic Towers took less than 2 minutes that left me plenty of time. Then I would need four minutes to go down the lift, go outside, retrace my steps, remove my disguise, and walked back into the *Royal @ Bondi* as if nothing had happened. So, to work I said to myself.

The challenge of a Chubb Holsworthy vault is that it has both a key entry and a digital entry to it. The lock I was able to unlock in an impressive time (eight minutes) since it took several turns to get into the KCL locks correctly. Now the digital proved to be a little simpler. Using the small and portable RKB 6700 digital decoder, I took less than five minutes to go through the thousands of combinations for the digital lock to open. I then simply turned the three-handle lock, and the door opened. A light automatically turned on and what I saw was indeed impressive.

Picture frames for what had to be original masterpieces hanging on the vault's wall. At the back of the vault stood a wall containing at least one hundred smaller drawers, and each drawer had a tag affixed on the front. In the centre of the room was a large table and two chairs for what I presume was Mr Michael's enjoyment of sitting in the vault and contemplating his possessions and/or taking a drawer out and scattering the contents on the table to examine.

My mental note told me what I need to grab; the Hawaiian Missionary stamps and the United Kingdom Edward III Florin gold coin. As quickly as possible but with a keen eye for the prize, I searched and my eye caught a tag on one drawer: 'Misc.' I opened the drawer, and not one silver dollar but two coins lay solitary in the drawer. One appears to be in mint condition and encased in a protective casing with a small label: 'uncirculated' while the second one is also encased with an even smaller label: 'Misc. Find$$$.' It did not take me a moment to pick them both up and place them in my pocket and continue looking for my prize. Time left: twelve minutes.

Scanning quickly, I see another drawer and I hit the jackpot: 'Missionary Stamps' details the tag on the outside of the drawer and just four drawers above. I felt like I had won Lotto; a drawer labelled '1870-S Seated Liberty Silver Dollar.'

Time left: eight minutes.

Ensuring all drawers are closed. I step out of the vault and the same automatic light turns off and I close the door, reset the vault, and hastily walk to the lift and go down the lift. I check the time; six minutes left, and I notice I have done all this effort while holding the pipe gently in my mouth. Maybe I should look at using one for real.

Arriving on the ground floor I again grunt something to a new security guard (shift change must have happened just like Albert had researched) and this time I did not even receive a 'Good evening, Mr Michael' from this new guy. It is difficult to get good customer service these days. Going out the front door I retraced my steps back to the rear of the *Royal @ Bondi* where I quickly place the wig, moustache, glasses, the pipe, FOB, and decoder back into Albert's satchel. Taking the comb out and the mirror I do a quick comb through so I straighten out my hair that was messed up a bit from the wig. I look in the mirror and all is good at this point so I return the comb and mirror to the satchel. Reversing the jacket, I look exactly as I arrived, an aspiring maitre d.' Composing myself, I glance at my watch; 11:21 PM. The entire operation took forty-one minutes and I will be back to my duties in no time.

As I enter the kitchen, I place Albert's satchel in the same location, and I start toward the dining area when I spot Albert. Poor Albert, he looked dishevelled, ruffled all over and totally exhausted working feverishly on some pots and pans. This time I do not see Tim and as I enter the dining area, I see him and Marta speaking with the last customer in the place, so I walk over to the table to join in.

'Oh hi, Danny. Let me introduce you to the Lord Mayor of Bondi, Mrs Sandra Bakersfield, a wonderful counsellor and a great patron of the restaurant,' said Marta.

'A pleasure, Madam Mayor.' I took her hand and smiled.

'My, he is a charmer just like you said, Marta. So, Tim, this is the individual who might just steal you away from the *Royal @ Bondi*?'

Well so much for secrecy I thought and before I could say anything Tim speaks; 'Sandra, please keep it down. No one is supposed to know. I appreciate the fact you thought of providing some seed money but decided against it, but Danny and his friend Albert are just seeing if they may want to invest in the restaurant. Besides, I do not want Mr Michael to know I might leave his establishment.'

'Mr Michael,' I say. 'Who is Mr Michael if I may ask?'

'Oh, that would Alphonse Michael, he owns 85% of the *Royal @ Bondi* while a small confederation of us owns the rest,' said the Lord Mayor of Bondi.

'Well, I am not aware of the gentleman. I do not want to start a bidding war for Tim and Marta, or yourself, Honourable Mayor,' I added quickly.

'Oh, my, he is quick on his feet, is he not Tim?' says the lord mayor. 'Do not worry, I have been trying to steal Tim and Marta for a few months on my own, but I have a liquidity issue at the moment and all my eggs are, well, somewhere else now, so you go for it Mr Monk,' stated the Lord Mayor as she sipped the last of her drink and got up to leave. 'Put the meal on my tab, please. Please, everyone, continue to enjoy yourselves of what is left of the evening. Good night!' and as a breeze out goes the Lord Mayor of Bondi.

'I will lock the front door. Be back in a moment,' said Marta as she follows the lord mayor to the front door and ushers her out.

'And I will finish in the kitchen so we all can go home early for once,' said Tim.

'Danny, ask Michelle to pour us a brandy. I will be there shortly. I just need to tally up the cash register and take care of the lord mayor's bill,' said Marta so I gingerly walk to the bar and ask Michelle to pour us two brandies — 'Two Bardinet XO's, please Michelle,' I say. 'Make that four,' I hear as Tim and Albert come out of the kitchen. 'Finish pouring the brandies Michelle and go home. It has been a good night.'

'Thanks, chef!' Michelle pours the last of the brandies and goes toward the kitchen.

Marta joins us and Tim shares that everyone has left and we are the last ones in the place so he calls out. 'A toast to a successful night' As we all toast and clink our glasses together I think to myself.

Yes, a toast to a successful night.

DANNY MONK IS READY FOR BUSINESS

Driving back to Northport, Albert asks; 'Well, how did it go? I saw you pick up the satchel and not come back for over 40 minutes.'

'Albert, you saw me exit through the rear kitchen door. Did anyone else see the same?'

'No. I was on the lookout to make sure, just as you had suggested in our plan,' as we hit the M5 toward Northport, said Albert.

'Good. To answer your question. It went exceptionally well. Well, enough that you are going to have to call Tim or Marta at home on tomorrow to tell them they impressed us and do not need to return to our 'work tour' since we are happy with what they do. And to answer the question with the answer you want to hear Albert, yes, it was indeed a remarkably successful night for I walked out with our two targets; the Missionary Stamps and the United Kingdom Edward III Florin gold coin and more!'

'More? What else did you grab?' asks Albert excitingly.

'Albert, I am not sure, but something labelled 'Misc.' and when I open the drawer my instinct knew that they were valuable but I have no idea how valuable, that my friend, is going to be your task over the next few days after you dispose of our two original targets. Now drive on so we can get some sleep.'

An hour later Albert stops the car in my car park at the rear of the store and I get out. I leave the four items I got from the vault on the front seat. 'Albert, you know what to do with the car in case someone notices it. Here are the stamps and the three coins. Go home, rest and do your contact work and try to get rid of the coins and stamps as soon as possible. I will speak with you later. Good night, Albert,'

'Good night, Danny. Speak with you soon,' as Albert gently pulls out of the car park, heading toward his home.

Opening the door to my unit above my shop, the *Village Books & Stuff,* I open the fridge and take out a nice cold Great Northern Super Crisp before going to bed. My mind is racing. I remember Albert said that the Missionary Stamps were worth $75,000 retail while the United Kingdom Edward III Florin 1343 or 1344 gold coin went for $689,000. In the fencing world, sometimes you luck out and find a buyer willing to pay the going retail rate. A buyer could say they will pay a reduced price since they know the items were acquired illegally and thus is of no 'show off value' and the item becomes more of a 'closet collection' knowing that they would be the only individual able to see the item obtained. So, in my mind, I knew we could fetch through Albert's connections anywhere between $382,000 to $764,000. It would be a matter of finding a buyer or buyers if one buyer was only interested in one item. Sometimes it takes time and Albert and I are patient, but occasionally we like to dispose of the items as fast as possible and get what we can. Beggars cannot be choosers as the old saying goes; however, my mind was circling around the two coins I snatched from the drawer labelled 1870-S Seated Liberty Silver Dollar and

Misc. and the other one with the strange label Misc. Find$$$. I would have to wait for Albert to do his magic.

The issue of Mr Michael will resolve itself, but I need to have a plan just in case. Drowning the last of the beer, I place the beer bottle on the kitchen counter and amble to the bedroom. So, I hope tomorrow will be just another ordinary day at work.

Morning arrives, and all is well in Northport. The sun is up, the sky is blue and not a cloud in the sky. It is going to be a momentous day; I can feel it. After a leisurely shower and then a shave, I make myself a quick breakfast of bagels and cream cheese and a cup of coffee and turn on the radio to listen to some jazz. My small Sangean radio on the kitchen bench smoothly flows out Stan Getz and Astrud Gilberto's, *The Girl from Ipanema.'* What a way to start the morning I think to myself.

Finishing the last bit of the coffee, I place all plates and cups in the dishwasher. I turn off the radio and I head downstairs to open the store and let both old and new clientele come unto the wonders of the *Village Books & Stuff*. Daniel Monk is at your service. Goodness, I am in a great mood this morning.

Unlocking the front door and turning over the 'We Are Open' sign, the day begins at 10:01 AM. Danny Monk is ready for business.

The first potential customer walks in at 10:34 AM (yes, I have been watching the wall clock) and it is an elderly gentleman who smiles at me and introduces himself.

'Good morning, my name is Ewan Carmichael, where do you have the Newport News, young man?'

I think to myself (am I the news agency of Northport?) but I also smile back at him and walk around the counter and usher him outside the front door and point to the news agency one block away south. 'Thank you, young man,' he said as he started walking towards the anointed spot I pointed to. I glance at my TAG Heuer watch, a gift to myself after a much successful acquisition, and see that a grand total of eight minutes has passed. This day I might have felt great, but at this point in time is sucking.

I puttered around the store a bit. Move a couple of office supplies around. Tidy up the card section and I hear the front doorbell tingle. I turn and see a young man in his 20s come in.

'Hi, are you the manager?'

'Yes, I am. Can I help you find anything,' I think hoping for that first sale of the day!

'Hello again, my name is Peter Bozeman and I work in the *Northport Sunrise Centre* on Smith Street,' he said, extending his hand.

'Yes, of course. I believe your organisation helps runaway children from troubled homes. Correct? By the way, my name is Danny, so please no need to call me sir.'

'Yes sir - I mean, Danny - that is the purpose of the organisation. It was started twelve years ago by my mother, Phyllis Bozeman when I was ten and over the years, I helped her build it and now I work for the organisation full time.'

'So, Peter, you came into my store for a reason today. How can I assist you?'

Showing me an A3 poster, Peter said, 'I was wondering Danny if I could place this poster on your window display. It is for a noble cause.' He handed me the A3 poster. I gave it a detailed review, raising a couple of questions.

'Peter, so this event you are proposing next month is to raise funds for the *Northport Sunrise Centre* to buy the building, land and expand on the land it sits on?' I asked.

'That is correct, Danny. The owner of the land and building is giving us the first option on a very reasonable basis. The price is $3 million and an additional $1 million will expand the centre in ways that could accommodate more runaways in an overnight facility. So far, the Northport Council has allocated $1,500,000 and the few donations we have already received brings the total funds raised to $2,752,345.65 as you can see from the poster. All the funds are already in our bank account at the Northport Bank. We are hoping this fundraiser at the centre can bring the rest because we have little time as it is.'

'So, you need an additional $1.250,000 million or so and you can purchase the building and land and expand. The idea of a silent auction is great also, which means individuals that could not make a large contribution, for example, a small business, could take part and get some prizes for their contribution. I think it is a great idea so yes, Peter, place the poster on the display window. More than happy to help. I see you are having a band and you are calling the event—the *Northport Sunrise Centre Ball*. Excellent,' I said.

'Great Danny. Do you think we might see you at the auction also? It would be just great to have as many business owners and managers as possible come thus making quite a successful local event.'

'Of course, Peter, count me in. I will be there representing the owner of the *Village Books & Stuff.*'

'Great Danny. I will let my mother know you will support us with your appearance and an auction item. Do you have any idea what item you will offer for the auction?'

Damn, the kid is quick. I had said I would attend, not that I would donate anything. But quickly I thought about getting a tax deduction, so I said, 'Yes. I have a collection that includes three signed and inscribed books, plus two inscribed photographs and an autograph note in English signed by Fidel Castro. I have the collection for sale for $24,000. Would that be something you would be interested in?'

'Oh, my goodness, yes, of course. My mother will love you for it. Thank you so much. Before I forget, is there a particular side of the window you want the poster to be displayed?'

'No, Peter, you pick the location you deem best. I am open to your creativity in window displays of posters.'

Peter goes and places the poster on the left side of the window which makes it a strategically placed poster since it forces individuals coming in to at least see the poster when they enter the store and can actually read it on their way out.

'Danny, do you mind if I place a stack of flyers on your counter for people to pick up as they make a purchase as well?'

'No, by all means. If you have a good stack, give them to me and I will place one flyer in each bag when a customer makes a purchase,' I add.

Grabbing a huge handful, Peter hands me most of the flyers and places a few others next to the cash register.

'Thanks, Danny, hope to see you in a couple of weeks.' Peter then marches off, closes the door and waves at me as he passes the front window. I can just see him approaching the rest of the business owners on the street and making the same spiel.

Good on you, Danny boy. No sale, but you might help these folks and you have to make a mental note to call your accountant and see if the item you just offer can be a tax deduction. If it can be, great and if not, well, it is for a noble cause.

Again, I glance at the wall clock; 11:54 AM, the morning has flown by and not one buying customer. I am sure someone will come in and bless me with a purchase. Someone always does. So, at 12 Noon, I turn the little sign back to 'We Are Closed' and turn the little clocks' hand to the 12:30 PM position, lock the door and head upstairs for a quick lunch. I seldom close the store for lunch but today I felt like it. The privilege of owning a store makes it easy to make these decisions.

At exactly 12:32 PM, I turn the lock of the front door, swing the door sign back to the 'We Are Open' and again settle into the stool behind the counter and wait for the first customer to enter.

My mind wonders about the information I garnished last night from the Lord Mayor of Bondi. Alphonse Michael owns 85% of the *Royal @ Bondi*, while others have the balance of the ownership. Albert and I are backing the opening of a new restaurant in Northport from two individuals that work at said restaurant.

I have never been one for coincidences. That Alphonse's surname is Michael is coincidence number one. I have met a lovely woman by the name of Laura M Burton - that is coincidence number two. Finally, the owner of the two target collectables Albert and I acquired on Saturday goes by the last name of Michael making it coincidence number three and it is just not ringing well with me.

Looking around the store I sigh knowing that today might not be a good sales day. So, I did a bit of information research while the place is empty. Looking through several volumes of *Who's Who in Australia* which was Fred Johns's brilliant idea back in 1906. He started compiling a volume of biographies of notable individuals in the country and as far as I know I have all the publications from 1906 to present time. The only other place you can find the same collection is in the National Library of Australia. I obtained my collection from several deceased estates and got a subscription to it from its current publisher to receive future updates. I figure that eventually I can unload this magnificent bit of Australia history for a kingly fee since you can only look at these volumes in the national library. So, a quick look through the volumes tells me what I knew at heart. There is no such thing as coincidences. It all fits in. What a mess are we into, Albert, I think to myself.

Everything is connected.

First, A. G. Michael is Alphonse Gansevoort Michael. Second, Laura M Burton of Gansevoort Promotions is Alphonse's daughter, for she kept her mother's family name for the business. Third, Alphonse owns the restaurant we are trying to steal the commis chef and open a new restaurant in Northport. Fourth,

Laura and I have been intimate, really intimate, and she likes me, and I sort of like her as well. Finally, Albert and I just connected all this by acquiring some unbelievably valuable collectables from Mr Michael.

Albert, what a mess we are in, I said to myself a second time.

I glance at the wall clock; 3:45 PM and still no customers have made an appearance.

Needing to process all this information, I again meander around the store. This time I am doing a bit of straightening things out. I do a little dusting around the bookcases, occasionally taking out a book and dusting its dust cover and spine and top of the pages.

Adjusting the chairs, lounges and loose cushions also takes some available time. A quick sweeping of the carpet floor using my trusted Vileda broom carpet sweeper and as I am finished, I hear my little doorbell telling me someone is coming in. I look and see the same gentleman for this early morning come in towards me.

'Good afternoon, young man. I have a question for you.'

'Yes Mr Carmichael, how may I be of help?' expecting a sale.

'Why do you not sell the *Northport News*? I really had to walk a long way for the paper today. Would it be more convenient if you sold the paper in this establishment?'

As I again usher Mr Carmichael out the front door explaining why I do not carry newspapers, and I think to myself again: Danny Monk might be ready for business, but business did not walk in the door today!

WHAT COULD GO WRONG?

After a disastrous sale day yesterday, I hope today is going to be better. I open the door for business and go to my counter and wait. I have not even sat down when my little doorbell tingles, indicating a customer. I look and yes, there is a customer.

A distinguished-looking lady walks up to me and says: 'Are you Daniel?'

'Yes, I am. How may I help Miss…?'

'Mrs Addington. Yesterday I visited Miguel over at the hair salon and I commented that I had nothing new to read and the owner suggested I visit your little store.'

My mind tingled at the sound of her last name. Could she be the same Addington Albert and I 'acquired' the baseball collection from? Is this a setup by Detective Cassell? Be cool Danny boy, stay as cool as an esky!

'Well, welcome Mrs Addington. Is there a particular genre you like to read, or would you like to browse the store and see what catches your eye?'

'I am not much of a browser. I am a fan of British royalty. Anything to do with Queen Victoria and later is my fancy. Do you have anything that might pique my interest?'

'Please, one moment as I look into my inventory,' I said. Quickly I type into my inventory system *Shopkeep* and my results quickly pop up providing me with an answer: *'Princess Alice, Queen Victoria's Forgotten Daughter,'* by Gerard Noel.

'I might have something for you. One moment please,' I repeat and walk over to the first edition section at the back of the store, find the book and bring it and place it in Mrs Addington's hands.

'This is a first edition 1974 hardcover in excellent condition as you can see by the dust jacket. A genuinely nice copy with several illustrated black and white photographs. If you gently open the book, you will see it includes a fold-out family tree at the rear,' I say.

'Oh, that is interesting. What else can you tell me about the book or the individuals in the book?' Mrs Addington asked.

'Well Mrs Addington, Princess Alice, was born in 1843 and was the third of Queen Victoria's children. She inherited her father's brains and ideals to the fullest, and in her close relationship with Bertie, the future King Edward VII. She was a dutiful daughter. In 1861 she heroically endured her mother's almost demented grief on the Prince Consort's death. Quite an interesting woman,' I answered.

'Well Daniel, you know your history!'

'No, Mrs Addington, I know my books. Are you interested in this one? It is on sale for $220.'

'It seems a reasonable price for a first edition, yes, I will take it,' as she hands me the book back and reaches for her purse and pulls a wad of Sir John Monash's notes and wipes one and then a second one and then a $20 and places them on the countertop.

Taking the book, I grab a bag and I add the flyer that Peter Bozeman left me when Mrs Addington says: 'Hold on there. What are you adding to the bag?'

I reach and take the flyer out and hand it to Mrs Addington who skims it and says: 'What a wonderful idea. I do not live around here but I have heard of the *Northport Sunrise Centre* through some of my charity work. Here, please continue placing the flyer in the bag and a few extra. I will see if my husband and I can attend after I check with him and I will pass the extra flyers to my friends. Maybe they can also attend. It should be fun.'

'Oh, that is wonderful Mrs Addington. I am sure all the support that you can provide will be appreciated by the *Northport Sunrise Centre*.' I handed her the bag containing the book, receipt, and a small stack of flyers.

'Until next time, Daniel. You are a darling indeed, just like Miguel said,' and as she turns, she notices the poster that Peter placed on the window, points to it, and giggles to herself on the way out.

OK, if this was a setup it did not work because there was no insinuation about the break-in or anything about the stolen baseball cards so chuck it down to one of those chances in life. She did just come from Albert's place with Miguel doing her hair, so that was that, just a coincidence. It only took twenty-two minutes for the first sale, so I hope that the rest of the day goes as smoothly as this early sale and to my surprise it did.

Until lunchtime, the store had a multitude of visitors and plenty of sales, mostly small, and in most the categories in the store especially there was a sale flurry in the bestseller book section making this section the overall winner before 12 PM.

A little after 1 PM, the parade of customers continued to stroll in, and some more sales continued ringing in my cash register. As I handle the last sale, a birthday card, and I place it in a small bag along with another flyer, the light bulb goes off in my head.

Maybe Mr Addington has replenished his baseball collection with the insurance money? I need to remember to have Albert do his thing and try to find out.

The reaction must have startled the customer, for he said, 'Mate, are you OK?'

I smile and then say, 'I am good, thanks. Just remember something I need someone to check on,' so he takes his bag and walks out leaving me in an empty store. My instant reaction is to do a quick search on the surname. The *Who's Who in Australia* volume I pick shows me fifty individuals with the surname Addington in all of Australia so the probability that this Addington is the spouse of Michael Addington is, well, huge!

Now my mind shifts into high gear. We 'acquired' the baseball card collection, but could there be another possibility for something as valuable? Maybe it is coins? A painting, perhaps? Some type of manuscript? My little bell disrupts again my mind tingling; a potential new customer is walking in. A middle-aged man and a boy, maybe seven or eight, walk up to me.

'Good afternoon. I was wondering do you perchance have any collectables for young boys specifically the 1974 Scanlens Rugby League Sticker Card for the Balmain Tigers?' asks the man.

'Sorry, you are asking if I carry sticker cards?' I repeat.

'Yes, sir,' answered the boy.

'No, sorry I do not sell sticker cards.'

'By chance,' asked the father, 'do you know who might be in Northport?'

'Sorry, I do not.' I respond to which a sadness fell over the boy and they turn around and leave the store the way they came in.

As I watch them go by my display window, a second light bulb lights up; jewellery! Specifically, something easy to get and worth a small fortune to increase our 'shadow super.' How has fate created a path for the Addingtons and the Monks to cross again?

'The Monks,' I said with a smile. There is only one Monk, me. Fate sometimes throws a curve (another baseball thing) at you when you least expect it. I must tell Albert to look into it.

Glancing at the wall clock I see that I have less than forty minutes till closing time and hold and behold, guess who walks in, making sure my little doorbell gets a workout today; Albert Matthew Guzman.

'Danny, darling, how are you today?'

Albert walked in looking mighty spiffy wearing a total purple suit. That is correct, pants, vest, jacket with an open collar white shirt and a purple cravat and tan Cuban shoes. I swear he looked like a miniature Matt Preston. 'Was that Mrs Hermione Addington I shortly saw come into your store before lunch? I went to get myself a delightful coffee today at the *Java Hutt* and tried their 'unicorn latte,' which by the way, does not have coffee in it. Is that not a riot? It contains coconut milk with ginger, honey, lemon, and blue-green algae and it tasted delicious!'

Wow, I think to myself; coconut milk with ginger, honey, lemon, and blue-green algae, yeah, really delicious, not! If Albert spills any of it on his suit, he will go bananas. 'What brings you in so late in the day?' I asked.

Albert looks around to make sure no one else is in the store and before he speaks, I disturb him: 'Albert, why is it you always glance around the store to look for anyone that might be in it when you can clearly see from here, we are the only two souls here?'

'Drama, darling, drama. Nothing builds suspense up like a bit of drama. Obviously, you have never acted before,' Albert stated.

'No Albert, I never acted, so tell me, now that you have made your dramatic scene, what gives?'

'I am the bearer of glorious news.' He picked up one of Peter Bozeman's flyers and started fanning himself with it. I have contacted our 'distributor' (Albert calls our fence, 'our distributor'); he says it is most demeaning to call someone who deals in stolen things 'a fence.' Hence that is why since I have met Albert we do not 'steal,' we 'acquire.'

'Our distributor has several individuals who are interested in all the coins and they are ready to move fast in the purchase of our acquisitions but…'

There is always a but… I thought to myself. 'What is the but? Albert?' I asked.

'We have not one but four different prospective buyers so our distributor has more work to do and is upping his commission from us. So, one buyer is interested in the Hawaiian stamps, another the United Kingdom Edward III Florin 1343 or 1344 gold coin, whichever year it is, followed by someone else interested in the 1870-S Seated Liberty Silver Dollar and finally, the 'Misc. Find$$$ coin also has a buyer,' Albert said sadly.

'Well, it does not matter whether there is one potential buyer or fifteen potential buyers as long as the items sell, right?'

'Sweetie, are you not curious why there are four different buyers at all?' asked a quizzically smiling Albert.

I glanced at the wall clock, ten minutes to closing time, so I walked past Albert, turned the 'We Are Open' sign to the reverse, locked the door, walked back to Albert and as dramatically as I could speak, I asked, 'What do you know that you are dying to tell me, Albert?'

'Oh Danny, I love it when you are forceful. Here, sit down in this nice lounge.' He sat in the one across from me.

'First, we sold the Hawaiian missionary stamps. The United Kingdom Edward III Florin 1343, it was not 1344, is also sold. The 1870-S Seated Liberty Silver Dollar is 'finito' as Albert snaps his finger. Finally, the pièce de résistance, our 'Misc. Find$$$' is also ready to walk out the door.' A delightful Albert finishes his announcement while using Peter's flyer to fan himself.

I take a minute and wait for Albert to continue. A minute passes and I am still waiting so I almost scream: 'Albert, finish the conversation!'

'See Danny, that is how you make a dramatic moment I will let you know.' He got up, moved to the counter, ruffled into the bottom drawer, and comes up with a handheld calculator.

He is driving me crazy; I think to myself. Albert now stands in front of me and starts speaking and punching numbers into the calculator as he looks down on me sitting comfortably on my lounge: 'First, the Hawaiian missionary stamps went for $52,000. Then the United Kingdom Edward III Florin 1343 came in at $356,000. So, this is not too bad since after our distributor's commission we will receive $249,000 for these two items Not bad for one night's work in the kitchen if I say so myself.' A grinning Albert states. He picks up the conversation before I can ask him about the two other coins.

'Danny, you are one of the most blessed human beings I have ever met. Grabbing the two other coins was a stroke of fate or lady luck has it for you, my boy.'

'Our distributor could determine the retail value of both coins. The first one, the 1870-S Seated Liberty Silver Dollar is indeed uncirculated as its casing detailed, and it has a value of, hold on to your pantyhose dear, $2,142,000.'

'What do you think of that?' Albert says as he continues to smile.

'And?'

'Well muffins, it seems that the 'Misc. Find$$$' coin has a name and most importantly a '$$$' behind it after all.' Now Albert is beaming.

'The 'Misc. Find$$$' is actually called the 'Flowing Hair Dollar' minted in 1794. They based its size and weight on the Spanish dollar which was popular in trade throughout the Americas at that time. It is in impeccable condition and it was bought by, are you ready for this, by our dear Mr A. G. Michael in January 2013 at the Walter Stacks Gallery in New York USA for $12,340,000! Our distributor has found someone who will give him $7M for the coin. Now minus his 'commission' of 30%, you add our profit of $285,600, the $1,499,000 for the 1870-S Seated Liberty Silver Dollar and you add the wonderful pièce de résistance the 'Flowing Hair Dollar" at $4,900,000 and you split that like we always do 50/50, we each will walk away with $3,342,000. After we provide Timothée and Marta with the $1,000,000 each we end up with $2,342,000 in our hands. Not bad sweetie, not bad at all.'

With that statement, Albert just flops down on the lounge next to me and continues to fan himself with Peter's flyer.

I am stunned. Here I was thinking of asking Albert to look at a possible 'acquisition' from the Addington's and he comes up with this amazing news. No need to take any additional risk so no need to get greedy so I decide not to bring up the Addingtons' to Albert.

As I continue to indeed ponder why lady luck has been so good to me, I see Albert glancing at the flyer for the first time. He looks at me and says:

'Danny, you and I are going to this soiree and you will not be wearing jeans. I will make sure of that. And I will bring you a date, as I will, and we will have some fun for once outside of our 'acquisition' moments. Call it our first double date. It will be fun!'

Great - a double date with Albert. What could go wrong?

HUMAN PSYCHOLOGY

Last week Albert, Tim, Marta, and I met, signed additional paperwork to complete our partnership, cementing our new restaurant in Northport and enabling both Tim and Marta to take a twenty-one-day holiday to New Caledonia before returning and looking for a locale to establish our new restaurant, yet to be named.

So, a few weeks have passed, and life goes as customary as it does in our little hamlet of Northport. The days have that stronger breeze that lets us know we are slowly migrating out of the sweltering summer months into those breezy autumn days when you are not sure of what to wear since the climate changes into all four seasons in one day. I am so lucky I do not have to commute for work.

Turning over my little sign to the 'We Are Open' side, I am ready to take on the world and all that it brings for today is Saturday and it is always a short workday for me. I hope I can call Alessia later this afternoon and see if she wants to catch a movie or something.

This morning brings in a familiar face accompanied with an unfamiliar face as I hear the little doorbell tingle welcoming none other than Detective Malcolm Cassell and another well-dressed individual of the female persuasion.

'Good morning, Detective Cassell. What brings you into my store this morning?' I gleefully greet the men.

Without acknowledging my cheerful greeting, Detective Cassell introduces the well-dressed lady. 'Monk, this is Chief Inspector Wendy Montague of the Sydney City Area Command. She has some questions for you,' brusquely states Cassell as he nods to the Chief Inspector.

'Mr Monk, are you familiar with the *Royal @ Bondi* restaurant?' asks the Chief Inspector.

'The *Royal @ Bondi*? You mean the fancy French restaurant in the Majestic Towers and popular with everyone who is anyone in Bondi?' I merrily answer.

Detective Cassell jumped into the conversation: 'Listen, Monk, quit being a smartass here. We know you were there several Saturdays ago.'

'Detective Cassell, please let Mr Monk answer. Do not interrupt again!' a strong rebuttal to Cassell by the Chief Inspector. I am beginning to like the Chief; I think to myself.

'As a matter of fact, Chief Inspector, I was and so was my new business partners Timothée and Marta Bené formerly of the *Royal @ Bondi* for now we have formed a partnership to open a new restaurant in Northport. The owners of the *Royal @ Bondi* are not so upset that Timothée and Marta jumped ship and left their employment that they went and asked for police assistance.' I smiled as I said all that.

As I finished my small repertoire, I could see smoke coming out Cassell's ears while the Chief Inspector was cool as a cucumber.

'No Mr Monk. That is not the reason for our visit. A very sophisticated break-in occurred at the Majestic Towers and we are asking as many individuals as possible who might have been in the vicinity if they noticed something strange when they visited the restaurant. I was told by the Lord Mayor of Bondi that she met you there that night.'

'I remember meeting the Lord Mayor, a lovely lady indeed. We made comments why I was there trying to understand the business a little more before deciding if a mutually beneficial proposition could develop between the Bené's and I.' I smile. I do a lot of smiling when I am in front of law enforcement.

'Did you see anything strange that evening, Mr Monk? Did you go out the front of the building and notice something different by any chance?' the Chief Inspector asked.

'No, not a thing, Chief Inspector,' I responded.

'So, when you took a little under an hour away from your shadowing Mrs Bené as a maitre d' you did not wander off to areas you were not supposed to be in?'

This time the Chief Inspector's tone of voice took a turn and was not as nice.

I studied the Chief Inspector a little closer. Wendy Montague is in her late thirties. Fit, attractive, long auburn hair well-groomed with just the right amount of makeup to be feminine but at the same time be able to get things done in a male-dominated police force and by her voice and tone a highly educated individual. Nothing like Detective Malcolm Cassell for these two seemed like chalk and cheese by comparison. I bypassed my answer and go on the offensive.

'Chief Inspector, I can understand you coming here today and asking me questions about a matter that occurred in what I imagine being, shall we say, your neck of the woods, but I do not understand why Detective Cassell is tagging along.' I smiled again.

Without skipping a beat, the Chief Inspector replied, 'Mr Monk, if you would be so kind as to answer my question.' A polite approach the Chief took. I played along.

'Sorry Chief Inspector, I thought I had answered that question. A lapse of concentration on my part, I guess.' And I hear an 'ahem,' from Cassell but continue. 'I took a few minutes outside in the back to take a personal call from a lady friend and then I walked to the main street and watched the ocean for a while. Why?' I seem to beam when I answer this question for the Chief Inspector.

'Now listen here Monk,' interjected Detective Cassell. 'You somehow pull this job and you and I know it.'

'Detective Cassell, please step outside the store and wait for me there. Now!' a much-agitated Chief Inspector almost shouted to the now humbled Cassell.

With his tail between his legs Cassell leaves, leaving behind my little doorbell tingling and a much anxious Chief Inspector. Again, I jumped on the offensive.

'Chief Inspector, you believe Detective Cassell's insinuations that I am now, what a burglar, and not your regular everyday shopkeeper? I feel quite defamed by these unfounded accusations.' I think of Albert and his performances and I felt inspired with my own.

'Mr Monk, I find Detective Cassell an old uncouth police officer who has a keen knowledge of his territory and if he feels you had something to do with this break-in, I will follow any lead he may provide but ultimately I make my own decisions as to whom to investigate and at this moment unless you come up with a possible and solid alibi you are one individual of interest. Do I make myself understood?'

Again, why does law enforcement individuals use 'understood' all the time?

'Like what kind of alibi do you want me to provide? Who I was speaking to on the phone, for example, and for how long?' I offered.

'Yes, that would be a good start, Mr Monk. Who were you on the phone with and for how long?' the Chief Inspector enquired.

'Okay. I have not contacted the individual I am about to provide you with her name so when you speak with her, I ask you to do it in a manner that will not cause her stress. Agree?'

'Mr Monk, the Sydney police department is not accustomed to making deals during an investigation, so what is the name? Now!'

'The lady's name is Laura M Burton,' I answered.

You know when suddenly you hear something that completely takes you by surprise and you feel a tremendous knot in your stomach, and you get queasy and you go pale. Well, that was happening right now to Chief Inspector Wendy Montague.

'Laura M Burton, you say?' almost stuttering, the Chief Inspector repeats.

'The one and only. She came into my store about a month and a bit ago and purchased a book for her father, from memory I believe it was *Purple and Blue. The History of the 2/10th Battalion, A.I.F. [The Adelaide Rifles] 1939-1945,* which I believe I sold to her for $550. We got to talking, and well you know nature took its course over the next few weeks. She was on her way overseas when she called, and we must have spoken for say twenty minutes to twenty-five minutes or so.' I know you can see the smile on my face as I laid my somewhat stretched 'alibi,' on the Chief Inspector.

Suddenly the Chief Inspector's shoulders seem to lose their tension. She also seems to relax her face because the redness in her cheeks softens as it happens when you do meditation exercises.

'So, you and Laura are friends. Is this friendship going anywhere?' the Chief Inspector asks.

Well, that is an interesting turn of events. Where is this line of questioning leading towards for it did not sound too 'official' now, I wonder? Hey, when in Rome, you know what to do.

'Very early stages I believe. We only had one dinner, in fact, at the *Royal @ Bondi*, which seems to be the 'in' place in Bondi and now I wait for her return to continue our 'friendship.' Why do you ask?' I questioned the Chief Inspector.

'Well Danny, do you mind if I call you Danny? Laura and I went to university together and had two courses together: *Human Psychology* and *Effective Execution of Organisational Strategy.* We were, you could say, study buddies.' A very much relaxed Chief Inspector shared.

'Yes, Chief Inspector, you can call me Danny,' I said. My, oh, my I think.

'That is nice. That is all I have for the moment. I will be in touch if I need further information.' She quickly turned, opened the door, and are you ready for this surprise, winked at me as she left the store.

Standing outside the window display, I saw both the Chief Inspector and Cassell in a short and what seemed like an intense argument. But then a smile came over Detective Cassell and they both walked away. If there is one thing, I believe I know, that is to never trust a semi-corrupted smiling copper to which Cassell falls into this category. The next thing I know is to never fall into a self-confidence mode with a female police officer for they have a higher moral compass and yet, Chief Inspector Wendy Montague presents an interesting study in contradiction.

Taking the phone out of my pocket I ring Alessia.

'Daniel, so lovely you call. I am about to leave the library for the day. How are you doing today, sweetie?'

'I am doing great, and I was wondering if tonight you might want to catch a movie. The Aretha Franklin movie with Jennifer Hudson playing the Queen of Soul is on. I thought we would watch a girl movie this time. You up for it? We can have a quick dinner and then catch the late show.'

'Oh, Danny that sounds so good but I have some plans already for tonight. I am going over to Mosman to a girlfriend's house for a baby shower. Let's catch up next Saturday. Are we good with that?'

'Yes, sure. That is okay. A baby shower, you say. Normally they are done in the afternoon. Why tonight?'

'My you are one curious one. She works just like I do and evenings are the only times for us, and of course the rest of the girls. It seems you do not trust me with that question Danny. Do you trust me or not?'

'Of course, I trust you. It is just so strange that I could not help myself asking the question. I am sorry if I hurt you with the question. It was not my intention Alessia. You know I care heaps for you.'

'I know you do Danny. I know you do. It was just how you asked the question. The tone of your voice sounded distrusting. That is all. Catch you later, okay?'

'Of course. I will see you later.'

Alessia hangs up and I do not get my customary kiss blown at me.

Between Chief Inspector Wendy Montague and Alessia, I wonder how much *Human Psychology* I came under today.

NOT MY LUCKY NIGHT

This morning's meeting with Detective Cassell and Chief Inspector Wendy Montague, especially the Chief Inspector, gave me a lot to think about so I decided nothing clears a mind like a nice cold drink after closing time. Right before I close the store for the day, my little doorbell rang announcing the last sale of the day. I saw Mr Ewan Carmichael walk in.

'Good afternoon, Mr Carmichael. Is there anything I can help with?'

'Yes, young man you can. Have you decided to carry *Newport News* yet?'

Well, Mr Carmichael either is forgetful or stubborn and will not accept my explanation why I will not carry the local newspaper, or any newspaper, since we have a nice news agency just down the street.

'No Mr Carmichael, I still do not carry the *Newport News* or any other newspaper for that matter since we have a nice newsagent just down the road already.'

'Well, you should since it would certainly make it so much easier for me not having to walk all those extra steps to get the local news. Think about it and I will come back to see if you have changed your mind. Have a delightful afternoon.'

'You have a pleasant afternoon as well Mr Carmichael.' I answer as I escort him out the front door and lock the door concluding the business day.

Well, that made closing on a Friday more interesting for sure. So, I packed up the little money I collected in notes and coins and placed them in my secure money bag that I dropped into one of the last remaining night deposit machines in all of New South Wales, (I have yet to try the new money taking deposit ATM).

I return home and climb into bed for a well-deserved nap. Sleeping until 8PM or so I get up and shower and get ready for a night out.

A night out for me comprises going to the *White Sheep,* our local watering hole in Northport and deciding on what to have. The *White Sheep* might be a pub, but we do not have a cook, we have a chef by the name of Chuck that will give Tim and Marta a run for their money. Tonight, I want something special and something different. The special was my drink. I asked the server to bring me a 'breakfast margarita' which has turned into my second most favourite drink. A breakfast margarita comprises tequila, Cointreau, dry orange marmalade, fresh lime juice and Agave syrup and it is quite tasty.

As I waited for the drink to arrive the Friday night crowd poured in. A few but enough individuals are present to give the place a lively feel for the early evening, consisting of mostly couples and a few loners at the bar the place has a nice ambiance which is one reason I return, that and the quirky food the chef concocts up.

The server, Maire, delivers my drink and said, 'Here Danny, tonight you should try the entrée bruschetta which Chuck has made with peach and goat's cheese with pickled garlic shoots and a drizzle of honey. Just delicious, you get three and they will go well with your drink.'

'Well, Chuck always has a surprise. Okay, bring the entrée and I will peruse the menu and give you my order when you return, how is that?'

'Great,' said Maire as she turned to put my entrée order in.

Looking at the menu I realise that the menu has something I have not had in a long time and definitely is something one rarely finds in a local pub, confit duck with sautéed king brown mushrooms with fennel and rhubarb and a mixed green bean salad with nectarines and roasted almonds. Different, I thought and reasonably priced. Well, I had already chosen something special and this concoction will be something different.

The entrée arrives and I give Maire my order to which she says, 'Excellent choice Danny, Chuck will be pleased,' and walks away to place the order. Why Chuck would be pleased is not important, but I am glad I can bring him some happiness. What is important is that food is well prepared, which I am sure it will be as I savour the bruschetta.

Munching on my bruschetta, I think of the conversation with the Chief Inspector and how it ended. I just did not like the way she and Detective Cassell were handling themselves outside my display window and as I crunched my last bruschetta, I thought to ring Albert.

The phone rang and rang and just as I was about to hang up Albert picks up: 'Danny, sweetheart, I was in the hot tub and I forgot to have my mobile phone handy, and I just rushed out to answer it and saw it was you and it brought happiness to my soul that you would ring. What is going down with you tonight?' Albert cheerfully asks.

'Albert, I need to discuss something with you, and I do not want to do it over the phone. How about you come down to the *White Sheep* and meet me for a drink or two or even dinner if you had not eaten yet?' I asked.

'Okay, it sounds lovely, and I am bringing some friends that I would like you to meet. See you in an hour. Bye. Ciao!' and Albert hangs up before I tell him I just wanted him alone, to go over my thoughts. Oh, well, I am sure I can wait until his friends leave and then I can have my conversation with him.

Just then Maire brings out my dinner in a beautiful layout presentation that, honestly, it was a shame to eat, but eat, I did and did not leave a single speck on the plate. Unbelievably, I still had room for dessert and while Maire cleaned up after me, she suggested I try the special; a mango and coconut strudel and to top it off with a glass of Alsace wine whose tingle of acidity makes it a perfect match for the dessert. I could not find an objection to Maire's choice of dessert or wine, so I smiled and nodded and acknowledged her brilliance as well.

The dessert came out and not only did it contain the mango but also papaya, coconut and pine nuts and a bit of apricot jam on the side. Taking small forkfuls of the dessert amidst a small wine sip, I thought that Tim and Marta will have to bring their best to the table because Chuck was smashing it tonight.

As I finish the last sip of wine, the entire pub goes into silent mode. I look and I see Albert walk in with the two most gorgeous women I have ever seen. One each hanging off his arms and I see the men ogled them, while the women must have gone into jealousy overdrive.

Albert, as always, dressed to the nines and this evening he wore a Hawaiian suit with an orange background and a floral assortment of pineapples and green palm leaves and a few tropical birds to boot! He added an open white shirt that showed off his hairless chest and only Albert could walk around Northport looking that 'loud' and get away with it.

'Danny darling. Let me introduce you to Gabriela and Mandy. They are our dates for the night!'

Gabriela was the first to extend her hand to me, which I took and pecked. She was wearing a strapless neon blue and green dress featuring whimsical and tropical leaves, which gave her a perfect blend to Albert's suit. Her long brunette hair fell over her shoulder and made her look quite alluring.

Mandy was next and as I also placed a peck on her extended hand, she giggled a little which made her even more attractive in her pastel plaid sleeveless dress which made her look just like the girl next door in a South Georgia USA small town. It made me want to say aloud: 'Bless her heart.' She was just yummy. This might be an interesting night after all since I never thought that Albert played on my team, but you never know these days.

Albert took over and immediately started ordering drinks for the ladies and himself and noting that I had already had dinner he offered me a Harveys Bristol Cream sherry which I gladly took. Gabriela sat to my left and Mandy to my right and Albert across from me and before you know it, the first hour passed and then the second and then the third. I for one was getting tipsy while my Harveys came in a small glass they still had a punch in alcohol content, but I was not worried. I can walk home but I noticed that both Gabriela and Mandy were holding their liquor well while Albert was already flaking out on me.

Suddenly, I felt Mandy's hand on my leg and reaching for the holy grail. It took me by surprise, and I jumped a bit, which made Mandy laugh aloud and she looked over to Gabriela. Mandy then said, 'Come Gabby, let's go to the powder room to freshen up and let the boys talk a bit.' I got up to acknowledge their departure, and they laughed and smiled as they head to the loo.

I told Albert what Mandy was searching for under the table and said to him: 'Albert, my friend, you have outdone yourself with these two beautiful ladies. I think that your Danny boy will have a good time in Northport tonight!' as I drank the last of my Harveys.

'Danny my dear. You do know that these two 'ladies' are guys, do you not?' says a tipsy Albert.

'What? No, it cannot be. Mandy just made a pass at me!' I almost yelled at Albert.

'Why yes Danny dearest, they are two female impersonators from the *Little Parrot* show over at the Cross. They are great fun, are they not?'

'Albert, Mandy is hitting on me, you know that, right?' I exclaimed.

'What can I say, Danny, you are a good-looking man. Of course, Mandy would hit on you. I do not blame her. Now I have to go to the loo because I am about to explode!' as he pushes himself off the table and staggers to the toilet door.

Just then both Gabriela and Mandy return. I need to understand what is happening and put a stop to any misconception, so I ask Mandy: 'Mandy, Albert just told me that you and Gabriela are female impersonators from the *Little Parrot* over at the Cross. Why in the world are you hitting on me? I do not swing that way.' I sounded strong, confident, and sure of myself.

Mandy simply takes my hand and says: 'Danny, does it really matter?' and she had the most radiant smile I have ever seen on a woman, I mean man.

'Yes, it matters Mandy. I am into genuine women, so I am sorry if you got the wrong impression during the evening. I just did not realise you were not really, well, a woman. Or you Gabriela, you are sure beautiful but sorry it is not who I am.'

'That is okay Danny, we both understand. Gabriela and I thought we might get lucky tonight, but it was not to be.' So, they both quickly get up, plant a big, wet kiss on each of my cheeks and walk out of the *White Sheep* leaving a lot of men wondering why I was not leaving with them and the 'real' women in the place happy to see them go.

Albert returned from the loo and he is sozzled and plants himself on the chair, looks around and says, 'Where is Gabriela and Mandy, I thought we were going to get lucky tonight!'

I motion over to Marie with the international signal for the bill and give her my credit card to pay for my meal and all the drinks that Albert ordered and help Albert up.

'Hey, Danny, cariño, are you walking me to my car? It is just out the back-car park.'

'No, I am walking you to my place and letting you sleep on the couch tonight. You are in no condition to get behind the wheel of a car,' I said.

'But Danny, I am fine, really I am. Just had one too many, or was it two too many? I forget. Where are Gabriela and Mandy? I thought we were going to get lucky tonight?'

As I prop up Albert and walk down Main Street towards my place, I think I never got to share my concerns about Chief Inspector Wendy Montague with Albert and I 'did not get lucky' either as Albert kept pointing out so I guess it was not my lucky night.

DOUBLE DATE!

O n Saturday mornings, as usual, I generally get up at 7 AM and have a leisurely morning with a hot breakfast, while listening to another oldies station in Northport, Vintage 99 and then get ready to open my store and have a profitable day.

This Saturday morning was a little different for when I woke up and went into the kitchen and I saw Albert making breakfast for us, or so he said. Last night I had asked Albert to meet me at the *White Sheep* to discuss some thoughts I had, and Albert showed up with two of the most gorgeous looking female impersonators I have ever seen and well, the evening transpired in a manner I had not expected. Albert had drunk enough for the entire *Southwestern Crocodiles* team in one night, and I just could not let him drive himself home, so he stayed with me. I was not expecting him to be awake and alert so early in the morning.

'Good morning, Danny sweetheart. I am making us breakfast with the limited condiments you have in this small place you call home. I hope you like the basics. I am making scrambled eggs, bacon, and toast. I also made a coffee for myself with that awful instant stuff you call coffee. Why don't you go and buy yourself a real coffee machine? You can afford it, I know. Would you like me to make one for you? Please sit at the counter since it will be easier to deliver your breakfast and pour you a cuppa,' a smiling Albert asks.

'Good morning, Albert. No, what you are making is fine and yes, a coffee would be great with cream and three sugars.' I say as I sit on the breakfast counter and notice Albert is in his underwear (pink shorts at that).

'Excellent. They will be ready in a jiffy. Thank you so much for inviting me to stay last night. I am sure I would have made it home, but it was nice that you cared enough for me to stay with you. However, I am not sure what happened to Mandy and Gabriella. Did I upset them?'

'No, you did not upset them, Albert. I spoke with Mandy and after she realised I was not into her, she and Gabriella left. I hope it does not upset you for spoiling your evening.'

'No, no. I am not upset, to be honest. The evening is blurry and I am not sure what was going to happen, anyway. Here is our breakfast anyway.' As Albert places the plates on the counter and walks around to sit next to me to enjoy his creative breakfast.

It turned out that Albert's scrambled eggs were kind of a gourmet treat. While he said that my kitchen was limited since my pantry is not much to speak about, he could still find mayonnaise, parmesan cheese, butter and fresh basil and make one delicious breakfast which we both devoured.

We both finish our plates and Albert goes around the counter and pours us both another cup of coffee and stands there and says, 'Now what did you call me about last night when you asked me to come down to the *White Sheep?*'

Intoxicated or not, Albert at least remembered that I had called him down to speak about something, so I decided now was as good a time as any since I did not have to open the store today until 10 AM.

Diving straight into the topic I explained to Albert what had happened starting with the introduction of Chief Inspector Wendy Montague by Detective Cassell and how the Chief Inspector is well acquainted with Laura Burton and how they were investigating a break-in at the Majestic Towers when we were there at the *Royal @ Bondi*. I also explained how agitated they both got outside my front window, but how at the end Detective Cassell was smiling, which gave me pause for caution.

While I shared all this information Albert stood there in his pink underwear, holding his cup of coffee in both hands, and just staring at me like a wombat in front of the proverbial headlights. He did not say a word, move, sigh, or make a sound while I described what had happened. The most unusual thing about Albert is that he does not get agitated when things flare up around him. So, when I finished, I waited for a response.

Albert takes a small sip of his coffee, lays the cup on the countertop, comes around the counter and gives me a hug and says, 'Danny, we are screwed. Cassell is on to us and we are going to jail!'

'Albert, is that what you got out of the information I shared with you? You did not see the possibility that the Chief Inspector may be a reasonable person and will only act if she sees good cause for an arrest. She is nothing like Detective Cassell, who I believe is on a mission to find something linking us to the crimes that he can use to his benefit, not for the benefit of the community.'

'No Danny, we are screwed and going to jail. What am I going to do with my business? I will never survive in jail! Have you seen the outfits they make people wear? Ghastly, just ghastly outfits.'

Now Albert was picking up pace basically being Albert which was a lot easier to take than a 'calmed Albert.'

'Albert, I think the Chief Inspector is fishing for any possibility she can find that might lead to the individuals responsible for the break-in.' I say to Albert in a sure tone of voice.

'The individuals responsible for the break-in are us. We are screwed. We are going to jail.' Albert now goes into a bit of a frenzy and starts walking around the room as if that will help calm himself down, which I know it will not.

'Albert, go back in your mind the evening of the break-in. You were in the kitchen the entire evening. You had witnesses that saw you working hard all evening scrubbing pots and pans. You have nothing to worry about.' I reassure Albert the best I can.

As if I have lifted a weight from his shoulders Albert says, 'You are right Danny darling. I am OK. I will not go to jail for this. If someone goes, it will be you! But wait, you said you gave the Chief Inspector Laura as an alibi and the Chief Inspector seemed okay with that, right?'

There was no way I would go to jail for this break-in. The police were now searching for suspects and it seems I am one of the usual suspects according to Detective Cassell who has joined forces with Chief Inspector Montague. Where this may lead, I am not sure, and the connection between the Chief Inspector and Laura and me might prove tricky.

Looking at my watch, I tell Albert; 'You need not worry about a thing. I will handle it all. I need to get ready to open my shop. Stay as long as you like. I will speak to you later if I hear from the Chief Inspector or Cassell. OK? You know how to lock up and find your car, right?'

I quickly dress and finished a little before 10:00 AM, I walked downstairs to open my store and as I unlocked the door to go downstairs, Albert has also dressed and comes toward the front door and says, 'Again, Dany sweetie, thanks for last night. I finished washing up breakfast and straighten out the place a bit. Ciao Danny!'

After Albert leaves to get his car and then go to his hair salon, I turn my little sign to the 'We Are Open' side and hope to receive some customers which will make the day a profitable one.

From the moment I opened the store's door till 1 PM, not one soul came in, which is not typical for a Saturday, but then slowly people came in and browsed and made a few small purchases. As I sat behind my counter, my day was made when no other than Laura M Burton walks in the arms of Chief Inspector Wendy Montague.

'Danny, hi, handsome. Give me a kiss.' Laura leans over the counter as she steals a quick peck from me.

'I hear you have met Wendy, or do I call you by your formal title Wendy?' The Chief Inspector just smiled and said, 'Between us three, you can call me anything you like,' with a big broad smile on her face. Laura continues, 'Anyway Danny because of the really dreadful break-in at the Majestic Towers which affected my father terribly I have been incredibly upset and busy as you can imagine.'

'Yes, the Chief Inspector, I mean Wendy, told me all about it the other day. So sorry to hear that this terrible crime has impacted your family. There are awful people out there. When did you return from your business trip? It is so good of you to come by.' I say, hoping the conversation does not go into the break-in anymore.

'Yes, I missed you and while I have been in town for a few days, I was busy with the insurance company going over what had been stolen and filling out a ton of paperwork for them, providing them valuations and appraisal forms and then I had to speak with the Sydney police. I am so glad I knew Wendy; she has been so helpful during this troublesome time. My father should have been doing all this but he came in, went to the safe to put something away and found the items missing, and left me to handle it all since he had to leave again for Europe for a couple of business meetings.'

While Laura has been relegating me with all the insurance issues, I notice that the Chief Inspector picks up the flyer for the *Northport Sunrise Centre* and is having a look.

'Laura, look,' as she hands her the flyer, 'maybe this is something we both can do in the next few weeks?' the Chief Inspector says in a very smoothing manner trying to calm Laura. I cannot bring myself to call her Wendy, not just yet.

Laura reads the flyer as an enormous smile appears on her face showing off her beautiful teeth and she immediately changes her dreary attitude to a much more pleasant one.

'Wendy, what a marvellous idea. Yes, I agree we should come to this event. Not only will it help a worthy cause, but it will help get my mind off this dreadful insurance and robbery. Now, who do you think of bringing?' Laura states.

Without missing a beat, the Chief Inspector looks at me and says, 'Well I thought you and I could walk in the arms of this handsome shop owner who I am presuming is going to the event since he is offering free advertising to the event. Are you going to the event, Danny?' a grinning Chief Inspector asks.

'Oh, Danny, how wonderful if you come to the event with us. Imagine us walking in your arms ME on one side and WENDY on the other. You would be the centre of attraction, I am sure. Please, Danny, say yes!' a very enthusiastic Laura exclaims.

What a dilemma! Or is it a dilemma? What man would not love to amble into an establishment of any kind with two beautiful women, one in each arm, and make every man stare at him and be amazed while every woman in the place wonders what does he have to attract such women! What could I say?

'It will be my honour to escort you ladies to the *Northport Sunrise Centre* event.' As I take a small bow behind my counter.

'Excellent,' a delighted Laura exclaims and gives the Chief Inspector a quick wink and again leaning over my counter gives me a quick peck on the cheek.

'Wonderful Danny and thanks for accepting even though it was my idea. I think it will be fun,' a chuckling Chief Inspector says.

'Yes, a double date, Danny, a double date. What could be more perfect! What will you be wearing, Wendy?' ask Laura.

'We got time to work that out. Let us grab lunch and let this honest shopkeeper make a living,' the Chief Inspector said with a beaming smile.

'Great. Let us go to the *White Sheep*. The food is good there.'

With that Laura grabs Wendy's arm (see I finally got comfortable enough to call the Chief Inspector by her first name), turns and walks off in search of food, both women just laughing to themselves as if it had been all planned.

Great, I think to myself, a double date, how am I going to handle this situation. I know that Laura sometimes acts like a sixteen-year-old, even in the way she speaks but the Chief Inspector, well she is another kettle of fish.

Also, why is the Chief Inspector, Wendy I mean, so chummy with me? She even said *'honest shopkeeper'* in front of me. Am I off her list or is this a trap? Maybe I need to call later an make an excuse to not attend. Maybe I need to research more this Wendy, or maybe it will be a good night after all and nothing crazy will happen. I mean, it is a charity event. Again, I think to myself, 'What could go wrong!'

THE NORTHPORT SUNRISE CENTRE BALL

A few weeks pass and the big day arrives. Yes, the *Northport Sunrise Centre Ball* is tonight, and I made a mess of things.

First Albert suggested I double date with him and before I could answer he presumed I had accepted his offer.

Second, Laura Barton and Wendy Montague, make a date as well. I decided that while they seem more relaxed with our new 'relationship' I do not trust either of the women and they bamboozled me into a double date with them so I need to call Albert, try to explain, and let him down easy.

After many attempts to call him at his place of business and leaving him more than a dozen messages on his mobile phone, Albert has yet to return my calls. I guess I will have to face him at the ball.

Having agreed to meet both Laura and the Chief Inspector at the ball, I locked up for the day. Luckily, the ball is on a Saturday which means my shop closes at 3 PM thus giving me plenty of time to rest, freshen up and get to the ball which is supposed to start at 7 PM until late.

The *Northport Sunrise Centre Ball* is being held right at the centre. The centre is a gingerly 10-minute walk from my shop so I figure I need not worry about having a few drinks tonight, but not too many, since I am not sure where my 'double date' with both Laura and the Inspector might lead to. Then there is Albert showing up and going ballistic since I left him up in the air with our 'double date' which is very possible.

Having had a few weeks to get ready, I spent a few dollars on a new tuxedo, which Albert insisted I do and even made an appointment with a tailor for me. I hope I will impress anyone who attends the ball. I never mentioned the ball to Alessia since I believe it would have been a catastrophe for me to walk in with Alessia and then Laura and the Inspector walk in and see me with Alessia. Add Albert and our double date and, well I cannot envision what it would be like.

My relationship with Laura is strange. Albert and I kind of 'acquired' some priceless coins from Laura's father's vault at the Majestic Towers and from that moment on I come to know that Laura and the Chief Inspector, through an introduction by Detective Cassell, have 'known' one another. Since my introduction, I have also come upon the fact that Laura and the Inspector were students at the same university during the same period and knew each other and developed a very intimate friendship. I have seen some of this nuance frequently and during one conversation with the Inspector, her tone of voice and approach towards me transformed once I mentioned I knew Laura. Well, that is at least what I have seen and sensed.

A quick look in the mirror and I have to admit, I look good. I exit through the front/back door to my unit above my store and into the car park and I walk around the block and head toward the *Newport Sunrise Centre.*

A few weeks ago, a young man named Peter Bozeman came into my shop and dropped off a handful of leaflets about the ball, and since that moment every customer coming into the shop has picked up a flyer and made comments. That is how Albert, Laura and the Inspector became aware of the event. Originally, I was planning to attend in a very low-key manner by providing an item for the auction and maybe grabbing a quick nibble and a drink, maybe donate or bid on an auction item and skedaddle out of there but now, it seems it is going to be a big evening and I will be at the mercy of Laura, the Inspector and Albert.

Arriving at the centre, I take a quick overall inspection of the building. The purpose of the ball is to raise funds to purchase the building and upgrade it so more services can be done to the needy, runaway children during a troublesome time in their lives. My thought of a donation was going to be a small donation but looking at the building and after researching what the centre does, I feel that a 6-figure donation and that includes the decimal point, might be more forthwith and that is on top of my offering of the auction item valued at $24,500.

Walking in and registering, I see the centre volunteers have decked out the centre in a very festive way. There are balloons all over the place. It does not look gaudy or infantile and flowers in beautiful vases are laid throughout the entire hall. Tables staffed by volunteers in tuxedos and long dresses are serving up punch and soft drinks while a solitary bar stand is currently flooded with both men and women gathering a bit of the hard stuff which I can see is a 'pay-as-you-go' bar. Makes sense. Why spend extra on liquor when folks will drink anyway if allowed.

Grabbing and paying for my favourite beer, a Great Northern Super Crisp, I mingled around and looked at the individuals already present while keeping an eye for both Albert and our double dates and Laura and the Chief Inspector. I pass one table with a beautiful vase featuring two etched intertwined hearts and hand-applied Swarovski crystals, with pink roses I pick up the card and see the inscription and name: 'Donated by *Ophelia's Pink Petals Flower Shop*' and it gives me a big smile. Marcelo and Allison are really getting into the advertising of the business.

'Danny! You made it! So glad you could come.' I turn as I hear Peter Bozeman say.

'Hi, Peter. I told you I would be here and so I am,' I proclaim.

'Danny, let me introduce my mother, Mrs Phyllis Bozeman and Director of the *Northport Sunrise Centre*. Mother, this is Daniel Monk, owner of the *Village Books & Stuff* and the first establishment that allowed me to place the centre's flyers in his shop.'

Mrs Bozeman is a very attractive woman in her early forties. She looks a woman of confidence, strong, purpose, a good degree of self-possession and a sharp intellect and she has not even spoken. She oozes success and power. I like that in a woman. Peter did not look at all like her so he must have received all his genes from his father side.

Taking Mrs Bozeman's hand, I declared, 'A pleasure, Mrs Bozeman. You decked out the place for this ball. I saw the small band and the dance floor. I believe you are expecting a good crowd and a fun night.'

'We are, Mr Monk. I received over 100 RSVP's and most of them are from wealthy individuals from all over Sydney. It seems that your shop is well frequented by some of the high and mighty in Sydney,' a delighted Mrs Bozeman said.

'Oh, I would not say that. It just so happens that I have been able to establish myself in Northport as the good office supply, gift cards, a superb assortment of the best writing pens and a great offering of the current bestsellers books. Add to this mixture the extensive array of antiquarian books makes my store a kettle of wonderful items. So, I can cover a lot of bases. The clientele is both local and, like you said Mrs Bozeman, from all over Sydney. Each with their own unique need, which I try to serve,' I replied, taking a quick sip of my beer.

'Well, I am glad you made it. Please mingle and have fun. See you,' Mrs Bozeman said as she glided off into the crowd.

'She is a blast, right Danny?' asks Peter.

'Oh, yes,' I say.

'Well, I am going to also mingle and keep making the introduction. I will see you around. It should be a great evening.' And as his mother did, Peter also glided away.

I continue to watch folks drift in, and I cannot recognise many of them, but I can tell by their facial expression, their overall demeanour, and the way they sashay into the centre that these folks all have money. Lots and lots of money.

Now a few familiar faces come in. First are Timothée and Marta Bene' who see me and rush over.

'Hi Danny, so lovely to see you here. How are you? Are you bidding on any item?' says Marta.

'Hi, Marta,' I say as I shake Timothée's hand. 'No, I have donated a first edition signed book by Fidel Castro. Are you guys thinking of bidding also?'

'No,' said Timothée. 'We thought the ball would bring in a few important folks, so we thought we would attend, introduce ourselves and mingle and let folks know we are doing our grand opening next Friday of *Petite Maison*. You should come, Danny.'

'If I had a date, I would but this way you have one more table available to seat folks. Good luck on Friday by the way. Albert and I will stop by the week after the grand opening and you can tell us all about it, OK?'

'Of course, Danny, see you soon,' said Marta as I got a quick little kiss on the cheek.

As Timothée and Marta Bene' start mingling I see Frederick Holloway, owner of the *White Sheep*. There is also Barry and Michelle Carmichael of *River City Diamonds* and Arnie Kimball from the *Northport Stamp and Coin Shop* and I even see Mr Ewan Carmichael accompanied by a younger man and both walk over. Mr Carmichael said, 'Still thinking about getting the *Newport News* into your store?'

'No Mr Carmichael. As I mentioned to you before on several occasions there is no need for me to carry *Newport News* when we have a perfectly good newsagent down the street.'

'Okay, I will give you more time. Enjoy the ball.'

I could not believe the audacity of the man, but I really admired his persistence. So, I continued to watch the crowd, which seemed to fill up the centre. I was yet to find Albert or Laura and the Chief Inspector. A quick glance at my watch and I see it is 8:40 PM and I see Mrs Bozeman heading to the stage to make an announcement and just before she speaks there walks in Albert in all his glory with our 'dates' in his arms.

Wow, I think to myself. Albert has really gone over the top, but first, our 'double dates' are hanging on his arms and those faces I also recognise. Wearing long evening gowns, our double dates look stunning.

First, Gabriella entered with a tinted ever-so-light shade of blush gown that made her look smashing. It looked like they made it of stretch crêpe. It has a one-shoulder neckline with artful gathering and beaded embroidery. It is a full A-line skirt falling to a floor-sweeping hem with a slight train at the back.

Second, Mandy looked as ravishing as Gabriela in her sultry yet vibrant body-sculpting gown that also featured an asymmetrical neckline and offered Mandy its full-length silhouette, which added a floor-sweeping trail for added drama.

Albert, oh yes Albert. Albert walks in wearing a new tuxedo that I can tell is in the style of Versace. The eye-catching red and black print is crafted in cotton and silk and is emblazoned with Versace's signature gold-tone baroque print. With notched lapels, long sleeves, button cuffs, a front button fastening and side slit pockets, Albert looks completely at ease in the more subdued atmosphere of black tuxedos that seem to float around the centre.

'Danny, dearest, we found you. You look smashingly bland in your new tuxedo. Nice!'

'Well Albert, you look bland but stellar! Gabriella, Mandy, so nice to see you again.'

In a split second, both Gabriella and Mandy corralled me and each landed a soft kiss on my cheeks.

'Wonderful to see you Danny,' both of the 'ladies' said simultaneously.

'Albert, may I speak with you for a second privately?' as I grab one of Albert's arms and steer him away as Gabriella and Mandy head over to the bar.

'Sure Danny, my boy, what is up?'

'What is up Albert is that you never returned my many calls and now I am in a fix.'

'How, Danny? How are you in a fix?'

'Well, I have a double book for tonight. Laura Barton and the Chief Inspector are also coming to the ball tonight and they made me their 'date' so you see if you had answered my phone calls I would not be in this predicament.'

'Oh, do not fret darling. I am sure that I can handle both 'ladies' especially after they had a couple of drinks tonight. Besides, I asked them to come for me, not you. They know where you stand,' said Albert with a little smirk on his face.

As if by providence the centre seems to quiet down, and Laura and the Chief Inspector walk in and my jaw drops.

Laura strolls in, looking fabulous with what has to be an Alex Perry maximalism meets minimalism gown. Scores of purple and gold sequins countered Laura's silhouette and with a strapless fitted bodice, a nipped-in waist, and a column skirt, Laura becomes the centre of attention immediately.

Not far behind is the Inspector. Chief Inspector Montague is dressed in what has to be described as refined elegance in her black gown. The long column outline of the Chief Inspector's body is accented with chain-link straps and cream panels, which draw attention to her small waist.

'I got to go, Albert. There are my dates', as I hurry over to meet Laura and the Inspector.

'Go on, darling. I will take care of Gabriella and Mandy. Have fun. Stay out of trouble. I will see you as I mingle around. Love you,' Albert exclaims as he also walks over to the bar to get into the mood of the evening.

'Wow Laura, you look amazing,' as I get closer.

'You look spiffy as well, Danny,' she responds.

'Hi, Danny,' says the Inspector.

'Good evening, Chief Inspector. You also look dazzling!'

'Now Danny, I told you when not on police business you call me Wendy and tonight is not police business, OK?'

'Right, OK, Wendy, it is. May I get you some drinks?'

'No, Laura and I will get ourselves something. You hang back and just watch us a bit, OK?' a smiling Wendy says as she grabs Laura by her arm and heads over to the bar.

I stand there watching them head over to the bar and start wondering what those two are up to this evening. The evening seems to progress very well because I hear Mrs Bozeman's voice rattling off the names of the many organisations and individuals that have contributed to the night's festivities in the way of donations for the auction and the fact that the auction is going to start in just ten minutes. As I hear Mrs Bozeman, the crowd gathers in front of the stage to get a better view of what is going to be auctioned off, so I also meander to the front when a tap on my shoulder makes me stop.

'Good evening, Monk. Fancy seeing you here.'

I turn around and there in his scruffy grey suit is Detective Malcolm Cassell. Damn, what is he doing here?

'Detective Cassell. Yes, fancy meeting you here as well. What brings you to tonight's festivities? Are you on a case or here to offer a bid?'

A soft laugh comes out of his mouth. 'No, the Chief Inspector asked me to come along and just make sure you behave tonight.'

'Really. The Chief Inspector thinks I will misbehave tonight?'

'Okay, she really did not actually say that, but she thought I should be around since there are a lot of influential individuals here tonight and a few of them live in the Sydney council area which is where the Chief Inspector works in and she just wanted to be sure she had a backup in case something happens.'

'What do you think will happen tonight, Detective? It is a friendly gathering for a worthy cause, and while all the individuals here appear to have a good financial standing in the community, they are not bringing suitcases of money with them to bid on any of the articles in the auction. I am sure they are good for their bid should they win. I do not expect an armed robbery tonight. Do you?'

'No, I do not. Just shut up. Sometimes you talk too much Monk. Well, I will be just hanging back during the evening. See you around, Monk. Got my eyes on you!' laughing as he steps away toward the punch bowl.

Great, I think to myself. Someone else to watch out for tonight.

Again, I get a tap on my shoulder and Albert is holding two drinks.

'Here, Danny. I brought you a drink for you.'

Looking at the strange concoction I ask: 'What did you get me, Albert?'

'The bartender said that it has a very sexy name, the 'Porn Star' martini. It is a passionfruit and vanilla vodka cocktail served with a shot of Prosecco. I am sure it will fit tonight's festivities and its aftermath for you perfectly. While I am having an 'Aviation' which is a lavender-coloured cocktail made with Crème de Violette, maraschino liqueur, gin and lemon juice.' again Albert smiles smirky.

I took a quick sip and found the 'Porn Star' to be lovely, but I also thought that while it might not seem dangerous, I am sure after downing a few of these during the evening they will impair my senses. I hear Albert continue his conversation; 'Danny, do you see all these wealthy and important people here? I picked up some goss on some of the attendees. What to hear?'

Before I could say yes or no, Albert started.

'Oh, I have spoken to or know a lot of individuals here tonight. To start, there is a Mr Steven Kelly and Mrs Elizabeth Kelly. They own 90% of the common shares in Albion Mining and are said to be worth over $9 billion each. I also heard that Mr Kelly has an extensive coin collection. Then there is Mr Jack Nguyen, owner of Lorraine Farms, also an avid coin collector. Finally, there is Ms Jacqueline Barrett, heiress to the fortune of Ascot Gold who owns an extensive jewellery ensemble in her repertoire of gems and bubbles. They innocently drop the fact that after the ball tonight they will leave to various places around the globe to spend the next couple of weeks. Mr Nguyen will return to Vietnam to visit family and the Kelly's are to join Ms Barrett on her jet flying back to Perth also to visit family. These folks seem to know each other well,' a smiling Albert declares. 'It is my opinion that the next couple of weeks will be an excellent opportunity for us to increase our 'shadow super.' What do you think, Danny?'

'Albert, you have been here for about 45 minutes and you already have a scheme up your sleeve. Let us talk about this opportunity next week since we seem to have time, at least like you said, a couple of weeks if you heard correctly. Did you not see Detective Cassell in the crowd?' I stated.

Suddenly Albert's face goes solemn. 'No, I have not seen that nasty man. Why is he here?'

'He said the Chief Inspector asked him to be here to make sure I do not misbehave,' I responded. 'By the way, I loved the martini you got me.'

'You do not seem concerned that the Chief Inspector and Detective Cassell are here tonight, Danny. Do you know something I do not know?'

'Albert, my friend, you worry too much. We have been lying low since our last 'acquisition' from the Majestic Towers and working on our legit businesses and our future law-abiding projects. We are two citizens going about their business. Stop worrying and enjoy the night. Are you planning on bidding on anything tonight?

Before Albert could answer Mrs Bozeman's voice again resonated throughout the centre. 'Ladies and gentlemen, the auction is about to start. Please gather your auction number and come closer to the stage so you may see what you are bidding on better. Please remember why you are here and bid handsomely for these wonderful items donated by many well-known establishments throughout Sydney. Please remember why you are here and be sure to know that I will personally be asking you for your own personal donation in addition to your bid' Many clapped and laughed when she said that. Then Mrs Bozeman says: 'Let us get started.'

As the auction starts I wait around to see if I could see Laura and Wendy but they were not to be seen. The auction was brisk with items presented and scooped up by the attendees who did not seem to even blink as the bid dollars went up. Okay, I know it was for a worthy cause and the items being auctioned were exquisite and unique, but goodness, being rich blurs your sense of the value of money.

Having my third 'Porn Star' martini and luckily not feeling the effects of the vodka I see Albert in a giddy mood hold on to both Gabriella and Mandy as if they were a pair of crutches, so I am sure he is going to have a short evening. I also notice Detective Cassell in the corner leaning on the side of a cabinet standing next to one of the beautiful flower arrangements from Marcelo and Allison. His eyes darting around the room, looking for trouble or looking for me? I do not know.

A sweet voice interrupts my thoughts; 'Hi there, stranger. Missed us?'

I turn and there is Laura and Wendy, looking as incredible as the moment they walked in and looking a bit inebriated.

'Hi, ladies. Where have you been up to? I lost sight of you.'

'We went into the powder room to freshen up a bit and then we headed backstage to look at some items before the auction. The printed catalogue just did not do any justice to the items we saw. We saw your contribution. The Fidel Castro collection seems fascinating. I might just bid on that for my father's collection,' said Laura.

'Oh. That is great. And you Chief…, I mean, Wendy, do you have your eyes on anything here?'

'Not on my civil servant salary. I came to watch, learn, and see how the rich live and spend their money and to be with Laura and see you again, Danny. Are you having fun?'

Before I could answer Laura raises her bidding number fan. It seems my collection is on bid. The bidding apparently started at $24,000 and now stands at $29,000 with the bidding going up in lots of $1,000. I watch the intensity in Laura's face as the bidding continues to go up slowly. She seemed determined to stay on the hunt, and I wondered what her limit would be. Suddenly she raised her bidding fan one more time and screamed out, '$39,000.' And if by magic Mrs Bozeman asked if there are any more bids. Going once, twice and bangs the gavel and now Laura owns my Fidel Castro collection for $39,000. Following the bid's soaring panegyric, the auction participants fall into sudden thunderous applause, showing appreciation for the winning bid. Glad I thought of donating the collection to the centre.

'How wonderful and exciting Laura,' said Wendy while I smiled and mouthed a silent 'congratulations.'

Laura seems happy and goes towards the auction registration table to handle the proceedings of the payment for the item. The Chief Inspector leans over to me and says, 'Well Danny, what are we doing the rest of this evening now that Laura came and accomplished everything she wanted to do. Got any ideas? Because if you do not, Laura and I do.'

As I was getting ready to answer Wendy's question Laura walks up to us.

'That was fantastic! What a rush! I love auctions! They are delivering the collection to my father's place next week. I cannot wait to tell him I got it for him. He will be pleased.'

'I am sure he will be,' I said. 'Why did he not come himself?'

'He is in London for the next two weeks, so I have the penthouse all to myself. I was wondering if we all should go there right now before the festivities get slowed down by the impact of the drinks. How about it, Danny? You up to it?' Laura glanced at Wendy with an expression of sultriness in her eyes.

I have known Laura for a while now and I have a good idea of what she, and the Chief Inspector, might have in mind to spend the night away and being a full-blooded Aussie bloke, I felt I was up to the challenge, three 'Porn Martinis' or not.

'Yes, let us go. I remember the view from the penthouse of Bondi Beach is lovely.'

'Oh, you will not be seeing much of the view tonight, Danny,' said the Chief Inspector as she grabs one arm and Laura the other and we march toward the door.

Oh boy, Danny. What have you got yourself into?

FIRST SALE OF THE DAY

This Monday morning the wake-up sounds emitting from the alarm clock sounded extremely loud even though I knew it was not. Even after 24-hours from the festivities from the *Northport Sunrise Centre Ball* on the previous Saturday evening the effects of the drinks still were throbbing a bit in my head. I guess I am not as young as I thought I am. Also, the additional 'activities' with both Laura and the Chief Inspector further impacted how I felt this morning.

Taking a second look at the alarm clock the time said 6:35 AM, yes it was time to get up and start another day at the store. Completing all the necessities and grabbing a cup of coffee I went downstairs, keyed in the security code to cancel the security alarm, and turned on the lights of the store. I shielded my eyes a bit until they recovered from the shock of the cool white lights in the store. I checked around and noticed that I did not need to tidy up and walked to my counter and sat down and took a long sip of my coffee. Looking at the wall clock the time showed I had a good 15-minutes before I had to walk over and open the front door and turn my 'We Are Closed' to the 'We Are Open' position which gave me some more time to reflect on what had happened after I left the *Northport Sunrise Centre Ball* with Laura and the Chief Inspector.

Thinking back to the evening, it was one strange night. I am not sure if I was used as a toy by Laura and the Inspector or it was the other way around. All I know is after we left the event, we arrived at Laura's fathers' penthouse at the Majestic Towers and the evening progressed in a direction which, while not taking me by surprise, gives me a feeling that maybe this three-way relationship may prove to be a dangerous one.

At this point, I believe I need to get out of this strange relationship, but I have no reason to do so. I needed a quick analysis to see if the advantages outweighed the disadvantages. I immediately ran a pro and con scorecard in my mind.

Pros: Well Laura is Laura, and she provides me with superb entertainment, in all ways. While the Chief Inspector, I should just call her by her first name, Wendy, since last night we really got to know each other much more and this new 'friendship' has distracted her from my other 'ventures' and has kept Detective Cassell off Albert's and my back for a long while now although he is still around like an unpleasant smell.

Cons: This relationship with these two women is way too sensational to me. They bring together a shocking and dangerous atmosphere which I do not want to continue. I have realised that I am an old-fashioned kind of a guy when it comes to my female relationship. I am a one-woman man if I have a relationship with both Laura and Wendy, this does not qualify me as a 'one-woman' man. Besides, I already have one woman, Alessia and when I think hard on this, she completely outweighs both Laura and Wendy. It is time to cancel these two. The question is, how?

So, as I glance at my wall clock, I see it has hit the magic moment to open the store and I waltz over and turn my little sign to the 'We Are Open' position, unlock the door and head back behind the counter.

No sooner than placing my mug of instant coffee under the counter, Albert made my security bell tingle.

'Buongiorno tesoro,' said Albert as he quickly locked my door and turned my little sign to the 'We Are Closed' position. Why does he do this every time? More importantly, why do I let him?

'Good morning, Albert. We are now in Italian mode?'

'Darling, I am a man with many talents. You know that and languages, all languages are the languages of love, some more than others, for sure.'

'So, what brings you here this morning?'

'Have you heard the name of Miss Wang Xiu Ying Danny darling?'

'Not really. Where are you headed with this Albert?'

'Danny, my darling, Miss Wang Xiu Ying, is the sole heiress of the Hulan Industrial empire.' 'You ever heard of Hulan Industrial?'

Gosh, this is going to be a long dissertation, I can feel it. 'No Albert I never heard of Hulan Industrial.'

'Darling, darling. Let me make it clearer for you. You heard of the brands: Yuki, Amazonian, Dulcimo, Palomino, Panthers among a few?'

'Of course, those are shoe brands, women's shoes, runners, that sort of thing. What does it have to do with Hulan Industrial and Miss Wang Xiu Ying?'

'Well, Miss Wang Xiu Ying's father Zhang founded Hulan Industrial in 1999. Hulan Industrial has factories in China, the

Philippines, Vietnam, Santo Domingo, and manufactures all these brands and fourteen other brands.'

'Okay, thanks for the Dun and Bradstreet update. What is your point, Albert?'

'Well Miss Wang Xiu Ying was in Sydney and spent the entire morning at Barry and Michelle Carmichael's store, you know the jewellers.'

'You mean over at *River City Diamonds*? What is so unusual about that? A lot of folks go there.'

'Yes, they do but do they drop $29,500,000 million in one morning?'

'$29.5 million. What in the world did they buy?'

'Well, Miss Wang Xiu Ying decided that daddy's billions need to be spent and bought herself several beautiful necklaces. First on the list was a 55.36ct briolette diamond necklace known as The Star of Malta, for which she paid $11.1 million for. Next, she went and also purchased another necklace set with a 47.12ct vivid yellow diamond. This one is also attached to a diamond-studded chain with the price of $10 million. Finally, trying to make a trifecta, Miss Wang Xiu Ying laid her eyes on a set of flawless-circular diamond oblong necklace priced at an impressive $8.4 million. So, the Carmichaels' had a $29.5 million sale, and it was not even lunchtime!'

'Not a bad day's worth of sales.'

'Indeed Danny, indeed. You know where Miss Wang Xiu Ying is going to keep the necklaces until she returns to Taiwan in eight or nine months according to the gossip?'

'In her back pocket? How should I know Albert?'

'The necklaces will be placed in a safe deposit box at the Protector Vaults in Sydney. Mr Carmichael is going to do all the paperwork for an official appraisal so Miss Wang Xiu Ying can have them insured before she takes them out in public. She has already arranged for said safe deposit box. Once the paperwork is done Mr Carmichael will take and place the necklaces in the safe deposit box for her and then get her the key so she can use them to her heart's delight. This is supposed to take about two to three weeks or a bit more. The gossip columns are buzzing with rumours of Miss Wang Xiu Ying remaining in Sydney for close to a year so the necklaces will be out and about because I am sure Miss Wang Xiu Ying will have various galas and functions to attend and the necklaces will be on her lovely neck. Thanks, goodness, for the print press and the celebrity sections you can get a wealth of information these days. Then there is the vanity social media which people contribute to every day. I see an opportunity Danny, my boy!'

'Really? How Albert. How are you seeing this opportunity and how are you going to seize the opportunity?'

'Sweetness, for once this time it will be my plan and your execution, not your plan and execution.'

'How is that?'

'Simple when Mr Carmichael comes out of the Protector Vault you get the key. Then you give the 'new' Alessia the key and she goes in, gets the necklaces, returns them to me for disposal.'

'Wait, Albert what do you mean by the 'new' Alessia?'

'Easy sweetie. I am going to treat Alessia to a complete makeover, I am thinking of getting her a fine black, long flowing wig and changing her eyes to a moon green hue. I will give her a fresh look, eyebrows, foundation and concealer, eye makeup, and blush and lip colours. You will not recognise her and neither will anyone if they catch her on the CCTV cameras.'

'So, once she has returned, I will get rid of the wig and take off all the makeup. Then I will transform her again to a brand 'newer' Alessia for a second time. This time she will get a cut and styling with a short blonde layered cut, a change of eye colour using some contacts to blue and a good colouring using a neutral palette that may include peach, rosy pinks, copper, or light brown which will work to highlight her new blue eyes, which she and I can decide at the time.'

Albert continues; 'Once finished I will contact our 'distributor,' sell the necklaces and split the sale, which by the way should be around $15 million or a cool $5 million each. Now that is a plan! All you have to do is convince Alessia to take part. Easy, right?'

'You have already contacted our 'distributor' have you not? This why you know the 'acquisition' will net us $15 million. Am I correct in my assumption Albert?'

A sly smile grows on his face and shyly he says: 'Yes, darling. I have.'

You know the simplicity of Albert's plan is, well, simple, and it should work. The only problem is that there is no way I am going to get Alessia involved. What would she think of the shenanigans Albert and I have been in? I never told her of our extracurricular activities. How will she react? No, I do not think I will ask her but if not Alessia who? Is not like I can go to www.seek.com and put in an ad; 'Female criminal needed for heist help. References required!'

'Albert I am not comfortable getting Alessia involved.'

'Mi cariño, Danny. There is no other choice. There is no one else we can trust. The woman loves you. You can just see it in her eyes. At least approach her. Imagine another $5 million in our 'shadow super' and you could even retire and take her somewhere and live happily ever after, like in the fairy tales!'

Without waiting for an answer Albert blows me a kiss, turns, and unlocks the door, flips my sign, and walks out.

Fifteen-minute pass. I am sitting on my stool, in a daze still, and my security system tingles again showing the first customer of the day has arrived. Suddenly my heart stops.

In walks Alessia. As always, she looks just stunning. Her silky auburn hair is just flowing over her shoulders and she is dressed in a simple black skirt and a remarkable long sleeve silk blouse and mid-size heels. Wearing just a little makeup for she almost needed none she walks over to the counter and her voice flows out like honey.

'Hi, Danny. How are you today?'

'Well good morning Alessia. How can I assist you this wonderful morning?'

'At last night's *Northport Sunrise Centre Ball*, there was Fidel Castro's collection on auction. Did someone win the auction? I wanted to attend and bid on it but could not attend. I tried calling the *Northport Sunrise Centre*, but all I got was that the number had been disconnected which I found strange. So, I dropped by this morning and all the doors were locked. Very strange, so I dropped in on you since the catalogue said you had been the donor stated,' Alessia with an adorable voice.

Oh, my goodness. Alessia wanted to come to the *Northport Sunrise Centre Ball* auction and did not make it. Thanks, Momma, for watching out for me!

'That does sound strange, Alessia, and yes, the Fidel Castro collection sold at the auction for $39,000 - far over the cost had someone walked into my shop and bought it. It was for a noble cause, so I did not mind donating the collection. Sad that you could not go to the auction,' I said as gently as possible, for I wanted nothing to increase the conversation about the ball and me, being a man, saying the wrong thing.

'There are always complications in life, but I would probably not have been able to bid that high. Maybe $30,000 would have been my top bid. While I enjoy collecting, I also stick to a budget,' again, the angelic voice responded.

'Alessia you are in luck for as you know I have plenty of excellent antiquarian books here for you to browse and purchase. Please look around at the rear of the store and take your time. PS, special customers get special discounts in this store,' winking at her I say.

'Thank you, Danny, I will do just that.'

As she turns and she goes to the rear of the store, I cannot help but enjoy her form as she slowly floats to the rear of the store and just then my little door alarm sounds again and in walks Albert again. Now what?

'Danny dearest the world is smiling at us. Do I have news for you!'

Oh boy.

'Albert, you have been gone fifteen, twenty minutes tops, what could you have found out about? Speak softly for Alessia at the back of the store.'

'There is basically no order as to what I have said since both pieces of news are dynamite information. First, I got a visit from Detective Cassell, which I am surprised he is not here already speaking with you about it.'

'Speaking to me about what, Albert?'

'The disappearance of both Peter and Phyllis Bozeman. It turns out Peter was not Phyllis's son but her lover and they are professional cons artists and burglars, or so said Detective Cassell and it seems they skedaddle with all the items that they auctioned and even the ones that were not auctioned. Everything has disappeared. Including the money and all the articles. The police are calculating the theft at over $4 million dollars, and that is a conservative estimated for some of the wealthy individuals at the ball actually transferred additional donations to the account that Phyllis Bozeman told them to as a charitable contribution. The police were notified of several break-ins this morning when the servants of the Kelly's and Ms Barrett's called to say they were burglarised. Coincidence, I say no way! For once I believe Detective Cassell has his sights on someone else instead of us both. Cassell even hinted, ever so slightly, that they might be the culprits for all of those other burglaries which he always thought you and I did. My oh my, who is that young goddess at the rear of the store Danny? Is that Alessia? How come I have yet to meet her?' an exhausted Albert says.

'That my dear Albert is going to be the future Mrs Danny Monk if I have anything to do with it. Yes, that is indeed Alessia. You have never met her because you never go to the library. Also, you said you had two pieces of information, what is the second piece?'

'You know how I have shared with you the fact that I am getting too old to still be in the hair business and I have been thinking of retirement, remember?'

'Yes, Albert, I remember you saying that to me. Especially the part that you are 'old' which makes me wonder how 'old' since I am years younger than you.'

'Semantics darling, just semantics. Let me finish, well, I spoke to my accountant, and he put out some feelers and guess what, Tommy Wynn's has come back with an offer to buy my little salon!' a smiling Albert admits.

'Albert let us be clear. Your 'little salon' is the premier hair salon in Sydney if not all New South Wales, so I am not surprised that some companies would be interested. My first question is who in the world is Tommy Wynn and are you happy with the offer and are you thinking about it?' a very shocked Mrs Monk's son also thinks.

'Oh darling, how little you know of the hair business! Tommy Wynn is the largest hair salon owner in all of Australia. He came to Australia in 1998 and opened his first salon and has expanded his name and empire to over 400 salons all over the country. He is a billionaire! Well, maybe not a billionaire but certainly in the high hundreds of millions are lying in his bank account. And yes, the offer was extraordinarily attractive which made me thrilled and I accepted it. He wants me to stay on for three to six months to help in the transition and then I plan to retire after that.'

'Wow! I am so happy for you. Where are you retiring to? Mosman? Byron Bay?' I ask.

'Oh, Danny you are so domestic! I am thinking of either Vietnam, Cambodia, or Portugal. All three countries offer a glorious return of the Australian dollar exchange or have a low cost of living, or both, so as soon as I decide, I will let you know.'

'Damn, Albert, you are going to be living outside of the country. Why?'

'It is time to explore other adventures and with the sale of the business and our 'shadow super fund' that we have built over the years, I will be exceedingly comfortable.'

Saddened to hear his answer, I asked one more question: 'Will you not miss your friends?'

'Of course, I will miss you my sweet boy but you, and maybe the future Mrs Monk,' nodding to Alessia still looking at the books, 'can come to visit me. Besides, Gabriella and Mandy are coming with me.'

Surprised at that statement I say: 'Albert, they might take advantage of you, my friend.'

'No Danny, they are not. They agreed to come only on the condition that they both take care of the house maintenance, cleaning, cooking, and the rest so I will do nothing around the house and they get room and board, sort off, out of the deal and besides, they are a lot of fun in many, many ways.' a smirking Albert shares.

I lost Albert, at least I will visit since I too have ample funds in my own 'shadow super fund' which we both built over the years.

'Albert my friend I wish nothing but the best for you. You will come by before you leave so we can celebrate.' I state.

'Of course, Danny, of course,' and nodding to the back of the store, 'be sure to introduce me to her. At least mention me, will you cariño, and please, pretty please, speak to her as soon as possible about the opportunity we spoke about earlier.' Albert lands a long kiss on my lips which takes me by surprise, but I did not mind because Albert is Albert and he is my best and loyal friend and I will miss him.

As Albert leaves the store Alessia comes up to me with a signed, first edition hard copy of *'Havana Dreams a Story of Cuba'* by Wendy Gimbel. I do not believe I remember its price. I would have to check it in my inventory software.

'Danny, who was that man that I saw kiss you?'

'That my dear is my best and loyal friend Albert Matthew Guzman, owner of the *Cut Me Crazy* hair salon. I got to get you to meet him at some point. Now how can I help you?'

'Danny, none of your antiquarian books are labelled with a price. I am interested in this one. How much is it?'

'Let me check my computer. Alessia, give me a moment.' I input the title into my computer and yes, the price is a very reasonable $50. I said, 'Alessia, today it is on special! The prize is zero because you missed the auction.'

'Oh Danny, no you cannot do that. Please let me pay for it or tell me how I can make this up to you for such a lovely gesture?'

'Alessia, how about having dinner with me at the new restaurant that is having its grand opening tonight, the *Petite Maison*, owned by the husband-and-wife team Timothée and Marta Bene' and some investors right here in Northport. Would you do me the honour of attending this grand opening with me? The grand opening is at 8 PM. Besides, there is something rather important and controversial I wish to speak to you about.'

'Goodness. Something rather important and controversial! Sounds intriguing and dangerous. I am indeed fascinated. Yes, Danny, I will. I will meet you there if it is okay with you.'

'That is fine,' I said, bagging the book for Alessia and as always, she quickly gave me a long and soft kiss that got my heart fluttering! Maybe, just maybe she will go for this crazy stunt.

As soon as Alessia left, I picked up my landline because I realised, I had not checked with Timothée or Marta and hoped that there was still room for me and when Timothée answered. I explained my situation and I could almost sense Timothée's smile and he assured me that there would be the finest table available for me at 8 PM at *Petite Maison*.

'Danny, remember our partnership agreement. Both you and Albert have a lifetime reservation guarantee at *Petite Maison*. No need for explanations. Just call and you are in. See you tonight.'

Ah, I had forgotten the proviso of the partnership agreement. Maybe I am getting old after all. Checking the time, I notice it is only 11:30 AM and I have yet to make a sale but receiving news about Detective Cassell, Albert's upcoming sale of his business and soon retirement and topping this list I get my umpteen date with Alessia. Well, I have already made my day, sales, or no sales.

Knowing that this date is not my first since we have been together for a while now and especially after our lengthy conversation at the *Java Hutt* and Alessia spending the entire night with me in long deep conversations I know she is not someone I am just having a 'fun relationship' with. Alessia is not Laura or Chief Inspector Wendy or Mary or some of the others. Alessia is special, incredibly special for I think I knew that when I told her I love her. Yeah, I fell head over heels as the old cliché goes.

So, there are two things I had to do. First, I needed to think about what to wear tonight because I wanted this to be a great evening; and second, all I have to do is wait for the first sale of the day.

MUM YOUR DANNY IS IN LOVE!

Getting ready for a date is an art I believe. The first thing in getting started is the shower. Here the water temperature is especially important. In the morning I usually do a quick cold shower which charges me up to start the day but, in the evening, a hot shower is best. Second, since I do not have a beard, I concentrate on my hair. I shampoo and condition every other day and today is a shampoo and condition day which I love doing. Now I am not a vain man but now that I have completely fallen for this woman a little more care will go far, I believe after all I am courting (yes, I know an old word) this woman and what woman does not like to be wooed by a clean and good-looking guy. Oh stop it Danny, like Carol said; you are so vain.

Then for my wash, I use a high-quality body wash which I follow up with my loofah which I replace every three months thus ensuring it is always clean thus helping it remove my old skin better and any body odour as well.

The next step in the shower is onto that charming face of mine. The skin on my face, like most men, is less tough than on my body, so I use a more formulated and less intense face cleanser.

In the last step, I dry myself. First, I pat my face with the towel to dry it then without rushing the towel back and forth I do my hair. All men should know that the hair is fragile after a shower, and that is the quickest route to hair loss.

Once out of the shower, it is time to shave. My skin is relaxed, the hair follicles are soft and the pores are open after a hot shower thus making this the perfect time to shave because it makes it easier for a razor to glide over my skin. Again, all men should know this, but most do not practice it because all of this takes time. Being single, I have time. I wonder if this changes after you get married. Probably not, I guess.

So now I performed just the last additions. A bit of moisturiser, a quick check to make sure my nails are trimmed and then I get the hairdryer and comb and dry my hair to my desired style. Done. Now to choose the clothes.

Tonight, I am going to be casual, so I decide on a slim stretch sage colour Chino pants which I top with an Australian lambswool black Pima crew t-shirt and leather sneakers and no socks. I look in the mirror and I approve.

Taking my keys, I go out the front/back door and start walking towards *Petite Maison* for my rendezvous with Alessia.

Arriving about ten minutes early Marta greets me.

'Danny, so good to see you. Timothée told me you wanted a table for tonight. Am I finally going to meet Alessia tonight?'

'Albert has obviously been blabbering about her even here.'

'Timothée mentioned something about a woman when I spoke with him so I assumed it would Alessia. Yes, Albert was here last night with Gabriella and Mandy and had a wonderful time and stayed even after we closed up, so he also might have mentioned her. Timothée and I grabbed a couple bottles of wine and joined them. Such fun people! We must have stayed up till 3 AM when we had to push him and the girls out the door. We had to get some sleep. Albert never seemed fazed for sleep.'

'Yes, that is Albert all right. So where do you want me tonight?'

'How about I get you by the big window overlooking the outside patio that way you and Alessia can see all the lights streaming through the trees?'

'Sounds perfect. Bring us the menu when she comes in and how about my favourite beer while I wait for her.'

'You got it. back soon.'

Glancing at my watch I notice it is a little after 8 PM so Alessia is running late. This time of the year the library stays open late just about every night with guest Australian writers talking about his or her recent publication. Sometimes the library would show a short documentary or movie that would go past the 8 PM closing time and tonight was probably one of those nights.

Looking around *Petite Maison* the establishment was not full but comfortably spaced so that everyone was close but not so close as to hear a conversation. When Albert and I approached Marta and Timothée about opening in Northport, we gave them an offer they could not refuse and while we will lose nothing financially since we knew that both of them were excellent chefs the proviso of opening in Northport over Bondi or Leichhardt was a brilliant point, which I thought of by the way, because it gave both Albert and me the ability to book a table on short notice at a restaurant that has superb cuisine. Yes, I know I forgot this time. Please reader do not remind me of my ever-getting older grey cells.

Hearing Marta's voice I notice her walking Alessia over to the table. I stand and wait for her to arrive.

'Hi, Danny. Marta was telling me you arrived early and here I am making you wait for me. So sorry but the movie ran a little longer than we expected and then we had to usher the people out and close up. Hope you entertained yourself.'

Smiling, I answered her. 'Yes, I have been well-taken care of. I see Marta wasted no time in introducing herself to you.'

'Well, Marta mentioned Albert has been saying nothing but wonderful things about me and I have yet to meet the man.'

'Well once you meet him for the first time, you will not forget him. He normally comes here once or twice a week and Marta said he closed the place last night so I doubt you will see him tonight.'

As if to make me into a liar, here walks up to the table Albert with Gabriella and Mandy hanging from his arms. He looks like he just got out of bed.

'Danny cariño, so good to see you. Is this the delicious Alessia whom I am yet to meet?' Taking her hand, he gives her a quick peck on the cheek before Alessia can react.

Gesturing to his left and then right Albert continues speaking. 'This is Gabriella and Mandy, my dearest of friends beside darling Danny here.'

A quick hello is exchanged and Albert continues in his grandiose persona to let us know that he and the girls will not be joining us at our table because they will just grab a quick drink at the bar and then head into the city so Gabriella and Mandy can start their cabaret show at midnight.

'Ta, sweethearts. A pleasure to meet you, Alessia. I believe you are the one! Oh, Danny, don't forget,' as he looks at Alessia and blows us both a kiss.

As we watch them go towards the bar Alessia questions me; 'The one? The one what Danny? Don't forget what?'

'Oh, the one that loves to buy and collect books. The one that loves me. I told him all about your collection of books and how you work at the library. That is all.'

'Ah, that did not sound like it was what he meant. What have you said about me, Danny? Come on. Be honest with me.'

'Well of course I said you were really nice, intelligent, gentle, and smart, very smart.'

'Geez Danny, you describe me as if I was a puppy.'

'No, I did not mean it that way. I meant it all truthfully. He knows what I mean.'

'Yes, Danny, I know what he means, and I know what you mean as well. It seems I will have to have a conversation with Albert one day on my own. Now, what are we going to have for dinner?'

'Well, let us see what is on the menu tonight, shall we?'

Alessia looks over the menu. As always *Petite Maison* has their regular menu but Timothée loves to come up with several creations as specials and tonight two of them pop to my attention.

'Danny, how about we order the Bouillabaisse and the ratatouille? They sound delicious.'

'Yes, I agree. Timothée makes the Bouillabaisse with various fish and shellfish. The menu says that Timothée has added tomatoes, aromatics from the South of France, mustard, and egg yolks. It comes with bread and potatoes. The ratatouille will be an excellent accompaniment to the Bouillabaisse. Count me in.' I gleefully answer.

Gesturing to Marta to bring the wine menu I asked without looking at it; 'We decided on both the Bouillabaisse and the ratatouille. Do not make me go through the wine menu. I know you have something nice to suggest.'

'Well, I would recommend a 2019 Coteaux Varois: Chateau La Calisse Patricia Ortelli White which is a lighter white wine from the Sauvignon Blanc grape because it has a good acidity level and adds some personality to complement the fish in the Bouillabaisse. It is quite nice, and it is a reasonably priced bottle.'

Looking at Alessia who nods to me I say: 'Well Marta you twisted our arms We will go with your suggestions.'

'Great. I will send the server with your bottle and remove the beer glass.'

Knowing that tonight was going to be an amazing night I wait until Marta leaves then I ask Alessia: 'So what is new in your life?'

'Danny, I have been so busy these past few days. First, I scheduled several author visits and book signings. Followed that up with several community classes that I had to organise. Then I had to attend several offsite meetings since we are going to offer new technical services. Twice I had run story times because the person who was scheduled called in sick. I spent one entire afternoon helping a local writing group write up a grant requesting funds to create an audiobook of their stories. So that has been what is new for last week and of course one more thing.'

'What is that?'

'You sweetie. You are the one more thing in my life? Am I the new thing in yours?'

Oh my, are we getting mushy!

'You are Alessia. We have been spending so much time together and yet I cannot seem to get enough of you.'

Laughing so much she lets out a snort and I crack up. Everyone in the place is looking at us. Let them look all they want for I know I am in love.

Oh my, I am in love.

'What are you thinking sweetie, you look so far away at this moment?'

'Alessia, I am thinking I have never said I love you.'

'Oh silly, you have said it.'

'When did I say those words?'

'First in the beginning of our friendship you did not come out and said the words. As we spent more and more time together, you showed me with actions, not words. Finally, I said it first to you that morning in your store, remember Albert was there, and that is when you said it back to me as well.'

'Wow, I must be losing my brain cells. Yes, I do remember now but let me say right now Alessia Vassallo, officially again so I can indeed remember, I love you!'

'I love you too Daniel Monk' and reaches out and takes my hand.

I think to myself that the time is now perfect to let Alessia know why she is here. I start the conversation and go into a complete detail description of Albert's plan. The target, the timing, the execution, the disguises, the process of acquiring the necklaces and the sale of the necklaces and our reward which we will share equally amongst us three. Everything is laid out for her. I finish and I hear her answer.

'Yes, darling, sweet Danny. I will go into this 'acquisition' as you call it for, I love you deeply.'

I know I am in love because I hear tingling bells all around me and...

'Mister, are you OK?'

As if something has startled me from my daydream. I realise I am in my store and I look around and see a young man standing in front of my counter. 'Yes, can I help you?' I ask.

'Man, you looked like you were far, far away. I just came in to see if you sell used uni books.'

'No, I do not. Just best sellers and general interest books.'

'Oh. I am studying Aboriginal culture and just wondered if you had any used books I could use for a report.'

'Ok. Come with me,' and I lead the young man to the back of the store. I open the glass bookcase and take out *Sydney's Aboriginal Past. Investigating the Archaeological and Historical Records* by Val Attenbrow and explain to the young man: 'This second edition draws on the latest historical, archaeological, geological, environmental and linguistic research, as well as oral evidence of present-day Aboriginal people revealing the diversity of Aboriginal life in the Sydney region before and during the first thirty years of British settlement. It is $35. Are you interested?'

'Yes, that sounds cool.'

So, we walked back. I ring the sale up and I am brought back to reality.

Goodness I seldom daydream but I surely did this moment. I looked at the wall clock and saw it was 5:49 PM, almost closing time and time for me to get ready for my dinner date with Alessia. So, I just realised that not only that was my first sale of the day, but I conclude that I will tell Alessia, again, that I love her tonight at dinner.

I wish my mother were still with us so I could say to her; 'Mum, your Danny is in love!'

CONVINCING ALESSIA

'N ow that we have ordered our dinner and drinks, Danny please tell me where in the world were you when I walked in. It looked like you were off with the pixies,' a smiling Alessia says.

'Yes, I know. I must have been for I did not even see you or Marta approach the table. I must have looked like a zombie or something worse when you walk up to the table.' I answered because I was really in daydreaming mode. My conversation with Alessia in the daydream at the store went so well. Let's hope it goes as well in this reality.

'I am concerned about you Danny. First this impromptu dinner and the mystery behind those two words: important and controversial. It all sounded enigmatic.'

Oh boy, oh boy, oh boy, I thought.

My first thought is not now. Now is not the time, but she looked so beautiful. Her face was so anxious as she waited for an answer, that I decided I would trust my gut feeling and tell her how I felt about her.

'Alessia, there are two things I need, no, that I want to tell you and then I will ask you the controversial part. Please be patient as I share with you something which I hope is something you know already. First, I love you with all my heart. I loved you from the moment you stepped into my bookstore and walked into my life. I do not know what I would do without you in my life,' and with that statement, I get up and go to her, take her hand and help her get up and give Alessia the longest kiss in time. I mean it felt longer than that kiss on the movie credits for the 2005 movie *Kids in America*.

It must have been quite a spectacle because after a while we heard small clapping from some of the patrons of *Petite Maison* approving of my action. Not at all embarrassed, we both sat down.

'Oh Danny, you do not know what this means to me. I have the same feelings for you and I share them with you that morning in your store and you also told me how you felt. I have been in a cloud since then. All I do is think about you at work, all day long. I am so ecstatic that you told me how you felt. As soon as I walked in and saw how spiff you are dressed, I figured this was going to be an incredibly special evening.'

Before I can continue speaking a server appears with our bottle of wine and two glasses. He opens it, pours some into the glass and allows me to sniff it and taste it. Nodding my approval, he poured the wine into Alessia's glass and finished topping my glass off. I could have done with a beer but tonight is special I thought. Darn, I daydreamed that already.

I have to admit I am nervous. I am not sure how to start the conversation. Do I gently go into the story behind Danny Monk or just plunge right in? Oh well, I look at Alessia and start.

'Now how about we enjoy our wine and revel in our meal first and then I can speak my mind about what concerns me?'

'Of course, Danny, if that is what you want to do, I can wait. I am all yours tonight and forever.'

Marta approaches with our salad. 'Alessia, Danny, Timothée presents you with his version of a Niçoise salad. He has placed a mix of lettuce, fresh tomatoes, boiled eggs, tuna, green beans, Niçoise Cailletier olives, but no anchovies, since Timothée knows Danny does not like them. I will bring you mains shortly.'

'Thank you, Marta. They look just yummy.' Alessia says as she picks up her fork to enjoy what looked like an incredibly special salad indeed.

'Yes, Marta. They look delicious. Cannot wait for the mains.' I added.

Alessia and I enjoyed the salad. We looked like ballet dancers as we interchanged the fork and knife for a sip of our wine. Marta has suggested a bottle of Dopff Pinot Gris from the famous Alsace region because of its supple and full-bodied body. The wine showed off its charming palate with its soft, delicious flavours of banana, honey, and camomile. A pale-yellow colour made it look splendidly on the white tablecloth. Marta selected well I thought.

It did not take long for us to devour the salad and finish the first bottle of wine. Good, I thought I needed the alcohol to heighten my courage before I spoke to Alessia. So, I motioned to the server to get us a second bottle.

'Danny, another bottle. Are you trying to seduce me Mr Monk?'

Gosh, she is adorable.

'Yes, of course, I am.' As the server approaches with the second bottle, opens it and pours the wine into two fresh glasses.

Having just poured the wine, Marta walked up with our mains. The aromas she brings are to kill for, I thought.

'Tonight, Timothée prepared a confit de canard. Timothée has marinated the duck meat in salt, garlic, and thyme for thirty-six hours and then slow cooked in its own fat at low temperatures. It comes with confit roasted potatoes and garlic on the side for dessert. He has a desert surprise for you both. Please let me know if you need anything else.' With a big smile, Marta leaves us to enjoy our dinner.

'Danny, can this evening be even better? I cannot wait to finish this wonderful meal and spend the rest of the evening with you!'

'Yeah, me too. Now let's eat,' it is getting time for the courage to kick in as I gulp down my glass of wine before pouring more into my glass.

'Whoa, Danny. You are really drinking tonight. That is not you. You are a one-to two-glass man. You must be feeling great,' my Alessia said as she nibbled into the savoury and juicy duck meat. When Albert and I partnered up with Timothée and Marta and encouraged them to open their restaurant in Northport, we knew it was going to be good, but this meal has turned out even more spectacular than I imagined.

'The wine tonight is exceptional. I am OK.' Yes, my courage is indeed building. I can sense it going through my veins. Maybe another bottle will finish the treatment, so I gesture to the server for the third one.

'Another bottle Danny. Remember the night is a young sweetie. We have all the time in the world. If I have to play hooky from the library tomorrow I can but you still have a store to open,' said Alessia laughing.

The third bottle of wine arrives with fresh glasses. Alessia gestures she does not want anymore but I nod in approval so more liquid courage goes into the fresh wine glass.

As we both finish the confit de canard, I realise it is time for my conversation to start so I muster my courage with one big gulp of vino and I start.

'Alessia, there is another reason I asked you to join me tonight. I must share with you an element of my life that I have not commented on in all these months we have been together. You know one aspect of me, the small bookstore and office supply shop proprietor who works six days a week and lives above his store in a building he bought years ago. What you do not know is how I came about getting the building or have maintained it, the store and my lifestyle all of these years.'

'Danny, my love, I am not sure where you are leading with this talk, but I know you have been in your store every day working hard. For the last eight months, we have spent many evenings and weekends together talking, sharing tales of our families and friends. We spoke about our emotions, our hobbies, our common pursuits so I am pondering what you have not told me. What is it Danny that troubles you? Tell me please.'

'Alessia, what you have said is all correct. These past eight months have been the finest in my life. I have never found a soul I could share so much of my personal life with and be truly safe and relaxed with.'

Alessia laughs. 'So, I become something like your second Albert? Which by the way, I must call him to thank him for the magnificent Hermes bag he got you to give me. I have yet to use it. I guess we will have to find another occasion where I can use it,' as she continues giggling.

'Yes. Albert would like to hear from you but as you know it might be tricky since he now sold his business and is preparing to go overseas. To where I do not even think, he has decided.' I am sure my face went into a depressing look when I spoke about Albert, I thought.

'Oh, Danny you look so sad saying that. I am sure Albert will always keep in touch with you and you will visit him in the future. I am sure of that.'

'I am glad you said that. I am sure I will. Now let me share with you what I need to tell you.'

Alessia put on her best thoughtful face and I began.

'Several years ago, Albert brought up a chance for both of us to have a nice increase in our income, and specifically for me, the potential to buy the building where the *Village Books & Stuff* is. This opportunity was to break into a car parked in our car park while the proprietor was in Albert's beauty salon and the perp of the break-in was me. I figured out swiftly how to circumvent the security system in the car, open the boot and I walked away with a precious small square chunk of white marble worth $1,250,000 to each of us. With my share, I paid off the building mortgage and had a little left over to put in an overseas bank account in Nives.'

Alessia was reserved for a few moments and then she said, 'Well, that is something I never would have believed you, or Albert would ever get into. This I hope was a one-off thing.'

In for a penny, in for a pound, I thought.

'No, this was just the start of many more opportunities, Alessia. I do not know how to describe it other than besides the cash being good it was exciting, pleasurable, thrilling and with Albert's connections our 'acquisitions,' that is what Albert said we were in the 'acquisition business.' The 'acquisitions' kept coming up and over the years we both pulled off more than a few more break-ins and added several million to our overseas bank account. We even help a local detective unravel a murder a while back even though this officer has always been leery of both Albert and me and has alluded on many an occasion that he believes we are nothing but a duo of dirty rotten scoundrels masquerading as 'respectable business owners.'

'Oh, I see. All these robberies.'

'Acquisitions,' I inject.

'OK, 'acquisitions' have earned you what?' Asks Alessia.

'Currently, I have $10.3 million in an overseas account.' Nervously I respond.

'Okay. Now you told me everything, right? You are done with this stupidity, correct?'

'Not exactly Alessia. Albert has contracted us out to 'acquire' some priceless diamond necklaces that would make us each $5,000,000 thus growing our overseas accounts to over $15 million give or take a few thousand. But there is a tiny hiccup to this last venture.'

'What is it?'

'We need to bring in a third party and this third party has to be of the female persuasion.'

Alessia sat there and then not only did the penny drop, but it also seemed to drop like a tonne of bricks.

'You want me to help you and Albert in this senseless act?'

'Yeah, we do.'

'How is this criminal act supposed to go down, anyway?'

So, I explain to Alessia the entire thought process that Albert this time had devised and how after some careful consideration I thought it would work.

Before Alessia can answer, Marta walks up and asks; 'Are we ready for dessert?'

Alessia turns to face Marta and with the meanest look I have ever seen come over her face she almost yells at Marta: 'Not now Marta, not now,' which makes Marta quite embarrassed and she retreats from our table.

Looking back to me Alessia says, 'Go on,'

Continuing I explain to Alessia that the $5 million I mention was for each of us, including her. We each would have $5 million and with that kind of money she and I could plan out a future together.

Alessia waits for what seems to be an eternity but it could not be more than forty-five seconds and begins a litany of questions:

'How can you even think I would consider taking part in such an activity?' 'I thought you knew me, but you do not, Danny. I do not have the larcenous heart you apparently have. You just professed your love for me and now I wonder did you do it so I could join you and Albert in stealing these necklaces? What kind of monster are you? Playing with my heart in this way? First, you tell me you love me so what, you can butter me up and then you ask me these questions? What am I supposed to do? Melt in your arms and say, oh yes, Danny of course I will become a criminal. Anything for you! Goodness I feel bad when I forget to return a book to the library and I work at the library,' she almost screams.

'Calm down Alessia, please. Let me explain,' and I let Alessia know more details of her involvement. I let her know how I would pick Mr Carmichael's pocket and get the key and then I would pass it to her. I specifically explain how she would wear a beautiful black wig, some fantastic makeover and that she would look so different when she retrieves the necklaces. She would simply show up at lunchtime when there were new customer service personnel at Protector Vaults relieving the morning individuals for lunch. How she would then go into a private room after opening the door that contains the safe deposit box, extract the three necklaces, place them in her bag, close the safe deposit box, place the box back and close the lock and then simply walk out the front door.

Once she is done, she would return to Albert who then would cut, dye, and style her hair so completely different not even her mother would recognise her. Afterwards Albert would take the necklaces and play his part of the 'acquisition' by contacting our 'distributor' to start the sale to the necklaces.

After explaining all this I paused and waited for a reaction.

I got one all right.

Alessia placed her napkin on the table, leans across the table and said, 'No Danny, I will not join you and Albert in this madcap adventure of yours. I cannot believe you even consider asking me here tonight to ask me to commit a crime. A serious crime at that and expect me to sit here after hearing the secret you have kept from me for all these months we have dated. Then you dare to think I will join you in this endeavour. You explain my part in this madcap action and you do not even mention that if we get caught, we could land in jail for many years. You do not care for me at all - that is the way I see it. I have no more words to share with you. I am leaving now. Do not try to stop me or speak to me in the future. Do not contact me in any way, shape, or form for I will not respond. When I am ready, and if I am ever ready, I will call you but at this moment the furthest thing in my mind is Daniel Monk and his pal Albert. I want to think about the criminal activities you have done in the past. I want to think of the nefarious activity you expected me to take part in. Mostly I want to think about how I failed to see all of this before and worst, how you thought you could even approach me to consider this escapade. Goodbye, Danny.' Alessia turned and left me with my mouth wide open.

Tonight, basically sucked!

I preferred the daydream version better.

A NEW START

It has been more than four months since I have spoken, seen, or heard from Alessia. My attempts at contacting her have been fruitless in the weeks after she stormed out of the restaurant. My phone calls go directly to her voice mail. Not wanting to be pushy, I waited over a month before I headed to the library to see her and try to see if we could talk about what had happened. To my surprise, I was told she had resigned from her position about a month ago and no one has heard from her. Astonished about this, I waited until the next day and went to her home where I found a realtor's 'For Sale' sign with a 'Sold' sticker splattered over it. Flabbergasted at this, I called the real estate agent who said the house was put on the market a little over one month ago and it sold quickly since the house was empty when sold, which made it easier to sell because *'an empty home is a canvas for the prospective buyer.'* Was I interested in buying? I hung up on him.

These actions told me Alessia had decided to be out of my life but to such an extreme? Did I hurt her that much? Or was it an insult that I thought she cares for me so much to go into a life of crime with me and Albert?

So, these past months I have concentrated on the business and given up on the 'acquisition' of the necklaces. Albert has come to me frequently hoping that I changed my mind but to no avail, for I no longer had the interest, the passion. The excitement seemed to have evaporated the moment Alessia walked out of the restaurant that evening.

So, my days have been routine. Get up, get ready, open the store, receive deliveries, inventory the deliveries, stock up the shelves and serve the customers, close up and head back upstairs to my lair and lick my wounded heart.

This Monday morning, I expected my day to be like the many past days but Albert walked into my store, nearly tearing my front door off its hinges, and making my little bell swing wildly and loudly. He approaches me while I sit behind my counter and slaps the newspaper on my counter. 'Look at this headline Danny, look!'

I grab the newspaper and read the headline. OK, that is news but who cares.

'Come on, Danny, you need to snap out of it. Alessia has made her decision. It has been over four and a half months since you last saw her. You tried calling, and she has not answered your calls. You tried the library to no avail. You even went by her home and she sold the house. It seems to me you need a fresh start, Danny; I think you do. Who knew our idea of bringing her in on our 'acquisition team' would upset her so much but after this morning's paper, it does not matter because someone beat us to the prize!'

Albert is right. Someone beat us to it. A crime was reported to the police by Miss Wang Xiu Ying and Mr Barry Carmichael of *River City Diamonds* that three 'beautiful and expensive necklaces' were stolen while they were in the possession of the Protector Vaults. Protector Vaults has provided the New South Wales police CCTV video, and the police has supplied said video to all the national network channels to get the public to assist with the identification of the solitary woman that is seen going in and out of the Protector Vaults premises. The insurance company, General

Insurance Ltd has even offered a $2.9 million finder's fee, no questions asked, for the necklaces but there have been no takers.

I look up at Albert. He had been so infuriated at losing this 'acquisition' that he did not even do his normal routine of flipping my sign to the close position and lock the door and do you know what, I did not care.

'Now Danny, please snap out of this zombie mode you have been in. These things happen. Love is a fickle thing, and it hurts everyone at one point or another. I hate seeing you like this darling. It is quite a downer.'

'Yeah, I agree,' I think. 'It is quite a bummer, but then how do I snap out of it?' It's not like I can just forget her. For Alessia like Albert said a while back, is, was the one. Now I have nothing but memories of her voice, her smile, her face, her feelings for me. I do not think I will find another woman like her.

'Well, Danny I see I cannot be of any good to you today so I will leave you with your thoughts. Please if you need me, call me and I will rush over. Any time. Day or night. Any time! OK?' Then Albert comes to me and gives me a big, long hug which I can tell you I needed very much.

'Thanks, Albert. You are the best.'

'I know darling. I know.' He walked out leaving my little bell tingling.

I hear my rear doorbell ring which means I have a delivery, so I go to see what is coming in today. As I opened the door, I found Aarif, my usual delivery guy smiling. 'Good morning, Mr Monk. Here are this week's books from *Northport Booksellers*. Do you want me to leave them in the stockroom or take them to the front of the store?'

'Front of the store is fine. I am not too busy today.' I followed him with the four boxes of books being pushed in a trolley. Dropping the four boxes by the counter I sign the delivery slip, walk Aarif back to the rear door where we both say our goodbyes for the day, and I lock the door. Until next week, I think.

As I approached the front door, I saw Mr Ewan Carmichael and the same young man I saw with him at the *Northport Sunrise Centre Ball* a few months ago. The young man seems to be carrying an odd-looking briefcase with him.

'Hello, Mr Monk. How are you today?'

You really do not want to know I think; 'Fine Mr Carmichael. How can I help you today? Is there a book you need? Please do not tell me you need the Northport newspaper because you know I do not sell said newspaper or any newspaper for that matter.'

'No Mr Monk. I remember because you have told me so on many occasions. Have I ever introduced you to my grandson, Mikey Carmichael?'

'No Mr Carmichael, you have not.' I shook the young man's firm handshake.

'Mr Monk, have I ever mentioned to you my connection to *River City Diamonds*?'

'No sir, you have not,' I wonder where this conversation is going.

'Barry is my oldest and Mikey here is his son.'

'Oh, now that you mentioned it, there is a slight resemblance, yes, I see it now.'

'I have a proposition for you, Mr Monk,' as he nods to Mikey who places the odd-looking briefcase on my counter, opens it, takes out a bunch of papers and closes the briefcase and hands me the paperwork and goes and stands by his grandfather.

'What is this Mr Carmichael?'

'That is a contract to buy your store, building, stock. Everything. Lock stock and barrel-like Sir Walter Scott said.'

I take a quick look at the paperwork and look quickly for any mention of figures and such and find all I needed to see in the middle of the first page in big and clear numbers.

'Mr Carmichael, why the interest in purchasing my business?'

'It is a long story Mr Monk, but I will give the condensed version. Mikey here has been running several stores for his dad on the northern beaches, four stores to be exact. Over the past few years these same stores have been broken into and while some items have been stolen, just a few, as if the thief just wanted a few, each time the break-in occurs netting the thief $40,000 to $50,000 in items. Never more, never less as if the thief did not want to hurt us too badly, but hurt he did for it has impacted my grandson's mental health.'

'Oh grandad, don't go into that with Mr Monk.'

'It is okay Mikey. The more Mr Monk knows of our intention the less he will be a concern for his business exchanging hands.'

'Go on Mr Carmichael,' I say but Mikey takes over.

'Let me speak Grandad. Mr Monk, it is not mental stress or anything like that is more of a family issue. My dad cannot seem to understand what is happening and on more than one occasion I have told him that the jewellery business is not the retail business I would like to be in. So, while the break-ins have been a pressure point, it is not the point of our meeting here today. I simply have no passion for this trade, retail overall yes, but not this trade. As my grandad said, it just seems that the thief enjoys breaking into the stores I manage, and by the way, other local jewellers were also 'hit' - for the police have mentioned this to me - so I am not alone, and they also had small amounts of items stolen, again in the same vicinity of $40,000 to $50,000 each time. Strange. So long story short I spoke to my Granddad about it and we came up with this solution.'

'I see. How come the police have had no success in apprehending the burglar or burglars?'

'I cannot speak for the other stores but with my four stores the individual has been very crafty by passing our security system. Just hacking it enough to divert both audio and video for enough time for him to pick the locks to our doors, enter, get what he wants. Then he leaves and resets the alarms as if nothing ever happens. It is just when my assistant managers come in the next day and start setting up for the day that they notice the vaults have been broken into and the articles, again small ones, taken. It baffles the police at the expertise of the individual and wonder why they just don't take more. Quite a strange situation. Why do you ask Mr Monk?' said Mikey.

'Just curiosity on my part. Now answer me this. Your solution to your dilemma is buying my store. How come?'

Mikey continues. 'Mr Monk, my grandad has studied your store over the past few months and sees the care you have put into the store. How you treat your customers. The clientele base that this customer service has brought into the store and the quality of said clientele. My grandad believes that if he were to buy the store, as a personal investment, that over time I could in turn, by running it for him, work into an ownership status as well.'

'Mr Carmichael, Mikey, thanks for coming in today and making this proposition. I am not ready to give you an answer today because I need to get this paperwork to both my attorney and accountant. Please leave it with me and I will get back to you Mr Carmichael as soon as possible. Does that seem fair?'

'Indeed, it does, Mr Monk. By the way, Mr Monk, I am an old-fashioned type of businessperson. I do not haggle. I did my research and have provided you with the best price. It is a take-it-or-leave-it proposition. Do you understand me?' as he shakes my hand and I shake Mikey's afterwards and nod showing my understanding of this proposition. An honourable way to do business I thought. As they leave the bell tingles, this time softer as if the little doorbell knows the end of our relationship is near.

Taking the sales agreement to the backroom, I made two copies of it. I place the copies into two separate envelopes. I then place a call to *Northport Rapid Couriers* and request for a driver to pick up both envelopes and deliver them. One to my attorney and the other to my accountant. While I waited for the courier driver to arrive, I wrote two short and different notes to each accountant and attorney and then I placed the note inside with the sales agreement. I then place two calls to said professionals and inform them what has happened and to be on the lookout for the delivery of said envelope and said note at their respective offices. I told them I kept the original document.

About seventeen minutes later a courier vehicle stops in front of my store. Was he lucky to get a spot I thought or is it a premonition? The driver comes in, introduces himself, makes me sign a receipt of pickup and presents me with an invoice. I take out my wallet, take out enough to cover the invoice and a small tip, OK, I am in a generous mood, moody but generous. The courier promptly gives me another receipt for the cash received and walks out the front door. Now all I have to do is wait for the two package recipients to call me back acknowledge receipt and wait for their analysis based on my notes to them.

After the driver pulls out of the parking space, I pick up my landline phone again and wait for the answer.

'Danny sweetie, are you OK? What do you need? How can I help? Are you OK?'

'Calm down, Albert. All is well. I was wondering if you would come to a Friday night dinner at Petite Maison. Just you and me. Say 7 PM. I need to talk with you.'

'Of course, my love. I will be there. By the way, your voice sounds intriguing. Did you hear from Alessia?'

'No Albert I have not. You are a good friend. Thanks for asking, I will see you then.'

As I hang up the phone, I sit behind my counter and think of everything that has transpired and yes maybe this opportunity might just be a way for a new start.

ONE LONG NIGHT

The rest of the week went quickly with more of the same each day and most of my thoughts were concentrated on Alessia wondering if I will ever see her again and of course Mr Ewan Carmichael's proposal for buying my business and letting his grandson Mikey run it with the hope Mikey will eventually buy it from his grandfather or inherit it.

Promptly at 6 PM, I closed my store and headed up to my unit to get ready for my dinner meeting with Albert at *Petite Maison*. Yesterday I received written recommendations from both my attorney and accountant. The bottom-line recommendation from these professionals was that Mr Carmichael's proposal was solid. Not solid but generous was the word both of them used in their recommendation. The financial aspects were robust and generous and they recommended that if I were ready, all I needed to do was to sign the original document I kept, forward it to Mr Carmichael's attorney and that they would handle the rest of the paperwork. The total time for all the transactions to complete was about one month. One month I thought as I was getting dressed and my entire life in this place would finish. Everything I worked for. Everything I devoted my time to would be gone. My legacy gone. What legacy? I thought without Alessia there would be no legacy to pass on. Alessia and I never spoke of children, but she is seven years younger than me and is still in that 'goldilocks time' for a woman to produce children. Would she have been open to a little Alessia or a little Danny? I guess I will never find out.

Taking a quick look in the mirror just to make sure I was, at a minimum, presentable to go out which I was or so I thought I picked up my keys and walked out the door of my place and walked to *Petite Maison*.

My reason for meeting with Albert was multipurpose. First, I may mention to him Mr Carmichael's proposal. Then to let him know what I thought we could or should do with all our current business activities in the area; *Petite Maison,* and *Ophelia's Pink Petals Flower Shop* since he is thinking of leaving the country. I really wanted his input in these areas for I have to admit I have not been thinking straight since Alessia left and I need to decide my future from this moment on. Albert has decided on this already. He has sold *Cut Me Crazy* and has maybe three months left in his contract with the crowd that bought him out and then he might move overseas with Gabriella and Mandy and I would have no one to bounce ideas with so I needed to make sure my time with Albert is well spent.

Arriving at *Petite Maison* I am welcomed by Marta; 'Good evening, Danny. So nice to see you again. I have no two-seat table available for you and Albert, but I hope you do not mind a larger table over by the big window overlooking the back garden. Please follow me.'

'No Marta. Not a problem I understand,' I said, following her to the table and Marta placed two menus on the table. I grabbed a menu and wondered what to drink. Being quite indecisive these past few months I ask Marta for a suggestion. She retorted, 'Well Danny I am sure you will like a new blend that is making the rounds all over Sydney and which we have also adopted here at

Petite Maison. It is called the Eucalyptus Martini. I tried it and while this drink might not be for everyone, it might be worth giving it a shot and surprising your taste buds. It did to me when I tried it. Can I interest you in one?'

'What is in it?'

'It is a simple drink. It contains gin, syrup, lime, egg and one leaf of eucalyptus.' 'It looks sort of foamy, but it is not. Quite a delight.'

'Okay, Marta I will try one. By the time you return, I should have my menu order ready.'

'Excellent Danny. Take your time. No rush.'

Marta turned and headed to the bar to order my drink and I noticed Michelle from the *Royal @ Bondi* is behind the bar. Well, it seems Marta and Timothée pinched Michelle from their old establishment. Good. She pours a mean brandy if I remember correctly. Glancing at the menu I was not sure what to have and since Albert will join me in a few minutes, as I glanced at my watch, unless he is late, which is normal for him, we might order different things and then sample each other's plates. I did it many times with Alessia and now I am doing it with Albert. What a turn of events.

'Danny my love. You are here already. Nice. I thought I was going to beat you for once but alas it was not to be,' said Albert as he sat. Before sitting down, I could not help but look at his outfit for the evening. Albert must spend a fortune on his clothes since I have yet to see him wear the same outfit twice so either he has the world's largest closet or he simply buys inexpensive clothes, wears them once and throws them away. With his short arms and long pockets, I believe he has a large closet. Tonight, is no different for he has a solid soft linen pink two-piece suit with one button and an open collar white shirt and would you believe he has complemented the outfit with a pair of Yuki authentic comfy cushion shoes with the SpongeBob motif and no socks. Only Albert can get away with this.

'Darling, I am here at your bequest, so I am all yours this evening. Tell me what is on your mind?'

Just then Michelle walks to the table holding my drink: 'Mr Monk, here is your drink.'

'That looks yummy Danny.'

'Well, it seems that this drink, the Eucalyptus Martini, is the latest rage in all of Sydney. It has…'

'Oh, I do not care what it has. It looks just delicious. I will also have one, please.'

Nodding Michelle went back to the bar to create another masterpiece - this time for Albert.

'So come on darling tell me. Why have you inviting me to dinner?'

'Albert, what makes you think that only an issue has prompted this dinner? Is it not possible that I wanted to see you and spend some quality time with my best friend?'

'Of course, sweetness, of course, is just you have been so down lately that I thought something was the matter, that's all.'

'Well, I want some quality time and yes I do want to discuss a few topics but it can all wait until after dinner. Oh look, here comes Michelle with your drink.'

A smiling Michelle walked up to us and placed the drink in front of Albert who took it and offered me a toast. We knocked glasses and drank. Damn, it is good for the taste buds as Marta stated.

'Oh my, oh my. This drink looks not only yummy, but it is! Please two more,' said Albert. It is going to be a long night.

Michelle nods and departs to work on our second order of drinks.

'So, Danny, has Marta come over and told you of any specials we should know or do we go with Timothée's excellent menu dishes.' He says as he passes me the menu on the table.

'Let's see what is on the menu and if we do not find something that we like, we can call Marta over to see if there is a special that Timothée has created for the evening.'

We both started looking at the menu and I realise I am hungry, so I look over the entrees available and decided that the Potage Parmentier, which is a hot soup with potatoes and leeks. I know that Timothée's adds onions to it, which are cooked then puréed until they develop a smooth, delicate consistency, thus making this dish his recipe. I had it before and that sold me. For a main, I decided that the Basque-style fish with green peppers and Manila clams presented on a deep serving platter with the scattering of various mild green peppers such as Anaheim, poblano, bell and shishito with the fish and clams on top. Timothée dispels any notion that this dish is dry by stating that he will personally spoon the remaining broth over the fish and garnish it with chopped parsley and Espelette pepper. Quite a splendid menu I thought. I am not sure I will have dessert after this but there is always a possibility. I put my menu down and look at Albert.

'Well Albert, what have you decided?'

'I cannot make my mind up. What are you going with, darling?'

I take a moment to tell Albert my selections and he seconds my recommendation and go for the same, so I motion to Marta who comes over and takes the order. 'Would you like a wine with that Danny?' she asks. And before I can answer Albert blurts out; 'No, we are staying with the martinis. They are sumptuous Marta. Could you bring us another two?'

So, again I think it is going to be one of those nights. We have almost finished our second round and Albert is ordering the third. Should be an interesting night.

'Danny, when you asked me here tonight, I thought you had heard from Alessia and you wanted to talk about it. did she call sweetness?'

'No, Albert, she did not, and I want to cover some ground on several topics tonight. We can start now and continue as we eat. Is that okay with you?'

'Of course, precioso, I am all ears! Shoot.'

'My first question concerns you. When are you leaving Australia?'

'Well, I have three months left in my transitional agreement with Tommy Wynn and his company and I cannot wait since the woman I have been,' and Albert does the air quote sign here, 'training' is hopeless. I think she is going to ruin all the work I built over the years. It is quite disheartening to see what will probably happen when I leave. I hate to even think of it.'

'A second question Albert. Are you sorry you sold the business then?'

Albert takes a couple of sips from his martini and takes a moment to answer. 'Yes, Danny I believe I do regret selling *Cut Me Crazy* to the Wynn mob. Why do you ask?'

'Just thinking Albert. Just thinking aloud here. Got energy for one more question before the food arrives?'

'Yes, I do darling. This is almost like a scavenger hunt, you ask questions and leading me to a glorious plan. I can just feel it! Where is Marta with our drinks?' He gulped the last bit down from round number two and if as summoned by the alcoholic gods, Michelle shows up with two more Eucalyptus Martinis and takes the old glasses back.

'Albert. Can you clarify when you plan to leave the country?'

Here Albert becomes a bit more solemn and absorbs almost half of the martini before answering me: 'Darling both Gabriela and Mandy are having second thoughts about leaving. They were offered a two-year contract extension at the *Little Parrot* which they are thinking about. They love their careers but also wish to be with me. So, they are torn between two choices now. I feel their anguish as well since the last thing I want to do is to stress them.'

'I see.' And now it is my turn to savour the martini before I continue my questions but here comes Marta with the Potage Parmentier and the bowls are steaming. 'Danny, Albert, these are really hot. I will bring you a couple of baguettes to soak up the soup while you wait for it to cool down a bit. Are you ready for another martini?'

Albert nods with a big smile on his face and I agree with him. Marta smiles and waits while we take the last drops of the elixir and then takes the empty glasses with her. Round four coming up!

We dig into the hot soup, but Marta quickly returns with plenty of warm baguettes and we each grab one and start breaking the baguette into smaller pieces and dropping the pieces of bread into the soup bowl and let the bread soak up our wonderful choice of an entrée. Michelle arrives with our drinks and we just about finish the soup when Marta returns to check on us.

'How is the soup, gentlemen?' Marta asks.

'Excellent,' we both said in unison. 'Good. I see that you almost finished with the soups and the martinis. Would like another round?'

I look at Albert who smiles and nods and I have to agree, they are delicious so I nod to Marta. Yes, round five on its way.

'Excellent. Let take the soup bowls with me and Michelle will be here shortly with your drinks.'

As soon as Marta departs, I continue with my questions. 'Albert, did the sales agreement contain a non-compete clause in it or a non-solicitation clause that you remember reading?'

'I had my attorney read over it and he mentioned nothing and to be honest, I do not remember reading anything on this matter. I will call him in the morning and ask him to double-check on your question. Why do you ask, Danny?'

'Your attorney works on Saturdays?'

'Well, you open your store on Saturday and so do I. Why would an attorney not open on a Saturday?'

'Touché Albert, touché indeed. So, if you are not sure you should have sold *Cut Me Crazy*, and both Gabriela and Mandy are torn about leaving their careers and you are not sure about leaving Australia for overseas without them, why don't you and I start a new salon together and that way you do not have to leave Australia and both girls do not have to decide between their careers and you, they can have both! Are you interested?'

Albert's entire face lit up! It was like a sun rose over the horizon to a brand-new day!

'Oh Danny, can we do this and not get sued? Are you sure? I do not want to go into a long legal battle with the Tommy Wynn mob. Are you sure?'

'Guys, here are your martinis. Glad you are enjoying them,' and Michelle turns and takes the empty glasses away.

I looked at Michelle leaving and then at Albert.

'Let's see what your attorney has to say tomorrow when you call him and ask him the question so for tonight let's drink up Albert. We will have our meal shortly and maybe a couple more martinis for there are many points I wish to discuss with you and start a strategy plan. I feel it is going to be one long night!'

WELL...

The rest of the evening went quickly with our delicious Basque-style fish tasting delicious as promised and I must tell Marta that Michelle really kills it with the Eucalyptus Martinis for I lost count on how many we had. Albert and I planned everything we wanted to do, and it all hinged on Albert calling his attorney on Saturday and confirming what we hoped was a lack of a non-compete clause and a non-solicitation clause. It would make our plans so much easier to implement.

During my conversation with Albert, I did not mention Mr Carmichael's purchase proposal for I wanted to hear the answers to the non-compete and non-solicitation clauses first so a couple of more days of waiting should not be a big thing although I have a gut feeling that Mr Carmichael wants to move fast on this proposal.

At exactly 10 AM, I came downstairs, no rush I felt. Whatever shape the store might be in from Friday it cannot be bad. So, after turning off the security alarm, turning on all the lights, I walked to the front door, unlocked it, and flipped my little sign to the 'We Are Open' position and now waited for the first Saturday customer.

That first customer turns out to be none other than another business partner to both Albert and me for here enters Allison Standerton of *Ophelia's Pink Petals Flower Shop* and girlfriend of Marcelo Gutierrez also a fellow partner in the flower shop.

'Good morning, Danny. I need to rush in and out and get a couple reams of printer paper and some magenta ink for our inkjet printer. Our order has not arrived.'

'Take your time Allison. Let me know what you get and I will put it on your tab and invoice you at the end of the month as usual.'

'Great, thanks Danny,' replied Allison as she went looking for her supplies.

Now you may wonder why if Allison and Marcello are partners in the flower business with us, why would they get their office supplies from the big box company and not from us. That is an excellent question, I might add, but the reason is that while we are partners, Albert and I are silent partners and the occasional purchase from the *Village Books & Stuff* will go fairly unnoticed if there is ever an investigation. Cannot be too careful with Detective Cassell always on the lookout for any reason to investigate us. Besides many times I cannot beat their prices, match them yes, but not beat them.

'Danny, I got three reams of paper and one magenta ink and just in case a black one as well. Thanks, and see you around,' and Allison blew me a quick kiss as she headed out the door leaving my little doorbell tingling away. I make a quick note of the supplies in my notebook and grabbed my current book of interest. Not sure why but I took a liking to the title and now I cannot put the book down.

Asgard: Legends, Myths and Truths by Witham C. Hudson. This is a mint copy first edition with a pristine dust jacket as well. The book has illustrations in black and white and photographs and drawings. Signed by the author it covers everything: religion, mythology, sex, unexplained phenomena, archaeology, anthropology, movies, Atlantis, witchcraft, arithmetic, language, genealogy, even aircraft design. You name it and if there is something weird out there, it has a very good chance that it is recorded in this book or there is some commentary about it. I picked it up and cannot put it down. As I sit behind my counter, I gingerly continue reading the book until I hear my little bell tingle again, I glance at my wall clock; 11 05 AM, well at least the day seems to move fast and there comes Albert with the flashiest outfit I have seen today and a smile to complement the outfit.

As normal for Albert, he performs his routine which at times is ballerina-like. He pirouettes and locks the front door and switches the 'We Are Open' sign to the 'We Are Closed' position and motions me to follow him to one of the lounges. I place my bookmark on the page I am reading and head over and sit next to him. Walking up to the lounge, I think to myself that he is radiant this morning. Albert has on a double-breasted purple striped two-piece suit with a violet tailored shirt button up and as if he meant to be obnoxious, he has a western belt with a roll edging in grey with a huge gold 'A' emblazoned on the buckle. Topping this he had a beautiful R. M. Williams burnt ginger burnished leather boots on, which gave him a few extra centimetres in height.

'Okay, Albert you have one humongous smile on you. What gives?'

'Well, cariño I just got off the phone with my attorney and he tells me the sales agreement has neither a non-compete or a non-solicitation clause. He said he found it very strange when he first read it but found nothing wrong so that is why he said nothing about it and that is why he recommended I take the offer because not only was the financial offer generous, but this meant if I wanted to get back into the 'hair business,' as you call it I could. By the way, don't you go thinking I do not know that you got me down on your phone listed as 'Hair Man.' Quite insulting by the way.' He huddled into me and continued, 'Danny, I say we start that partnership we spoke about last night and do it on the up and up now that we have all the facts. What do you say, my boy?'

Before I can answer, there is a knock on the door, and I see this striking blonde lady with a cute short haircut motioning that she wants to come in.

'Albert, I need to get this. Just hang in there while I see how I can help this customer.'

'Sure, sweetie I will sit here in silence like I am in a monastery but before that, I am going to make myself a coffee upstairs. Is that all right?'

'What Albert, no Venti from *Java Hutt* today?'

'Not in the mood darling, not today. See you in a jiffy.'

So as Albert went upstairs, I unlocked the door and looked straight into the lady's eye. I froze. 'Alessia, it is you, right?'

Alessia comes in and repeats Albert's pirouette and locks the door behind her and plants a long and sweet kiss on me before I can react. This was not how I thought I would see her again, but who cares. Alessia is back, at least for now.

'Alessia, where have you been? How come you look like you do? How come you sold your house? Why did you quit your job?' I had probably a few more questions, and all she did was place her index finger on my lips and she took my hands and took me back to the same lounge in which I had been sitting with Albert a few minutes ago.

'Oh Danny, I have been a fool in the way I treated you and a dishonest fool at that!'

'What do you mean Alessia, how do you mean dishonest?'

'I saw Albert go to the back. Is he coming back? I want him to hear what I have to say as well.'

'Yes, he went to the back. He went upstairs to make himself a cup of coffee. I will get him to come downstairs,' so I take my mobile out from my pocket and when he answers all I say: 'Albert. Downstairs now, pronto,' and I hang up.

What sounds like a herd of elephants stomping upstairs we see Albert running down the stairs and towards the lounge where Alessia and I are sitting and he suddenly stops.

'Alessia! You came back darling!' and pulls her onto her feet and gives her a bear hug and kisses both of her cheeks but then, he steps back; 'Wait, why should I be happy to see you. You destroyed my best friend's heart when you left!'

'Albert! How did you recognise me?'

'I did not recognise you. I recognised the Hermès magnolia Togo leather Birkin bag with unique palladium hardware that I gave you, darling, which by the way, looks marvellous on your arm.'

'I see the change does makes me look quite different. Let me explain why the change and the reasons I came back to see you both, first to apologise and explain why. May I?'

We both nod and Albert crosses around the coffee table and takes the second lounge across and facing us and Alessia starts her story.

'I told Danny that I had been dishonest with him and I am here to explain and to apologise. When Danny asked me to join you in the 'acquisition' of the necklaces and he explained the plan I looked and acted as if it outraged me but in reality, it was an act, a dishonest act at that.'

Looking from me to Albert, Alessia continues to speak. 'You see, I also kept from Danny a secret which I did not divulge that evening like he did when he mentions the extracurricular activities you both have been in. I too have had extracurricular activities of my own. These activities are a simple means to provide me with funds to buy and expand my book collection. I am a petty thief. A common break and entry burglar of the modest kind. I only break into stores to get items I could sell or hock but in lesser amounts. Enough to help me in my purchase of collectable books but never in the magnitude that you both have done. I mostly steal from jewellery stores and in small quantities of items up in the north shore part of the city. Sometimes one or two items would net me between $40,000 to $50,000 enough to make it worthwhile for me and hopefully just little enough that after a while the police would slowly stop looking especially after the insurance companies would pay the jewellery store their compensation.'

'Why Alessia, why did you not share this with me that night at *Petite Maison*. I would have understood. Honestly, I would have - and I would never, never would have - judged you. And by the way, from experience, I can tell you the police do not forget a break-in. It might take them forever, but they do not stop looking at suspects.'

'Okay, that is good to know,' said Alessia. 'For a silly reason. I thought if I was going to spend the rest of my life with you, I needed to be in the same class of an 'acquisition expert' as you both are. So, I pretended to be insulted and stormed out of the restaurant to steal the necklaces myself using the plan that you said Albert had devised.'

'You used my plan?' Asks Albert and before Alessia can answer he adds; 'Did it work?'

At this moment Alessia opens her Hermes bag and withdraws a large Tiffany blue box and slides it over to Albert who gradually takes the top off and his eyes bulge out and then he slowly turns the box around so I can see its contents and, yes I can emphatically state that Alessia has now reached the 'big leagues' in the burglary trade.

Looking at Alessia I simply ask: 'How.'

'I merely followed the plan you explained to me with just a few minor adjustments as to the tactic of obtaining the key but overall, I followed step by step what you had explained to me. The only thing I cannot do is dispose of the necklaces so now that I have become the proverbial third wheel in this partnership, I thought I would come, apologise, and deliver the goods to the professionals.'

I take a moment to think of what Alessia just said and look over to Albert who seems to drool over the necklaces for yes, they are stunning, but I am still hurt, terribly hurt, and yet seeing Alessia the hurt seems to be less.

'Alessia, I can only say that I am still hurt. These past months have been horrendous for me. I felt lost, alone, worthless is probably the best word to describe my self-worth and now you walk in, tell us you are sorry, drop the necklaces in front of us like a token of an apology and expect what? What do you expect Alessia? Answer me that?'

I see a few tears roll on Alessia's eyes and, my goodness, from Albert as well and before Alessia can answer me Albert almost shouted, 'Oh you dummy. Do you not see that she loves you? Look into your heart to forgive her. I have. Her actions cemented her relationship with you, Danny. Can't you see that? She felt that only doing a big score would create the level of trust that is required to be in this type of 'acquisition business' we have been for years and we trust each other, do we not? Again, Danny, I understand where Alessia is coming from and accept what she did. Will you do the same?'

I look at Albert across the coffee table and see the sincerity in his face and the tone of his words then I turn and look at Alessia sitting next to me waiting for an answer that would either state that I accept or reject her. Which is it to be? In what had to seem like an eternity I looked straight at Alessia, took a big breath, and confronted her with my answer.

'Alessia. Will you marry me?'

Before Alessia could answer, Albert jumped out of his lounge and started whooping it up, jumping and crying, yes a lot of crying and a lot of short bursts of words like: 'Wonderful. So bloody splendid, A wedding, a wedding. What am I going to wear? Who are we going to invite? Where are we going to have it? When? What is the best month for a wedding, anyway? What are the girls going to wear? So much to do! So much to plan!'

Great I think and it is not even his wedding. What is he going to be like when it is his turn? I wonder and I turn to Alessia who still has tears in her eyes but a smile beaming as well and as I wait for her answer, the front door rattles.

Looking at my watch, I see it is almost 1 PM and I wonder how many customers I lost today because I had my closed sign up. It did not matter but time flew and during our conversation, it seemed to stand still. So, I nod to both Alessia and Albert to let them know I am going to see who is at the door and as I approach, I see it is Mr Carmichael.

While I opened the door to him, he came in, looked at Alessia and Albert and then said, 'Am I interrupting something? I can come back later if you wish.'

'No Mr Carmichael that is OK. How can I help you?'

'I need to ask you something privately. Can we go to the back of the store?'

Pointing toward the lounge where Alessia and Albert are sitting I say, 'Come Mr Carmichael and sit next to my friends. What you have to say you can say in front of them. I have no secrets from them.' I notice that Albert carefully hides the Tiffany box behind him and leaned back to obscure it from Mr Carmichael. Alessia also got up and sat next to Albert.

'Secrets? What secrets Danny?' asks Albert.

I do a quick introduction of Mr Carmichael and then tell him to raise his questions as we sit in the empty lounge across from Alessia and Albert.

'Well then, Mr Monk, have you thought about my proposal about the store?'

'Danny, what proposal is Mr Carmichael speaking of?' Enquires Alessia.

'Well, Alessia, Albert. Mr Carmichael has made me a very generous proposal to purchase the store, the building, and the entire stock. Everything.'

'What? When did this happen? How come I know nothing about it? Danny, were you going to tell me this at some point?' a very unhappy Albert blurted while Alessia just sat in silence. Watching and listening.

'Mr Monk, is this man your business partner? My record shows that you are the sole proprietor and owner of the *Village Books & Stuff*. Care to explain what is going on?' A quite indignant Mr Carmichael speaks.

'I am his spiritual partner Sir, not his business partner. Until now I am the one who has taken care of him, but I will pass the baton shortly,' nodding at Alessia who smiles at that statement.

'I do not understand Mr Monk. Have you made your decision, Sir?'

'Yes, Mr Carmichael. Your offer is extremely generous, but I will decline it. *Village Books & Stuff* is not for sale.'

As always, Albert started clapping and making funny faces at Mr Carmichael, which was uncalled for and I sternly looked at him and he stopped. Alessia got up, gave me a quick peck on the cheek and softly whispered in my ear: 'good for you' before she sat back down next to Albert.

'Well, that is that. As I mentioned, I do not haggle, and I thank you for your decision. Good day sir.' Mr Carmichael rose and turned to leave, and I walked him to the door. I asked him as he started out the door, 'Mr Carmichael, where are you going to make any changes to the store if I had said yes to the purchase?'

'Yes. I was. I was going to sell the Northport newspaper in the store and save having to walk all the way to the newsagent.' He shook my hand and left me with a smile on my face. I locked the door again and returned to my comrades.

'You were going to tell me, right Danny,' said Albert.

'Yes, I was going to tell you Albert but after your attorney clarified the question, there is no reason for me to sell and if I get the right answer from Alessia, well, that also sort of cements the answer.'

'So Alessia, what is your answer? Will you become Mrs Daniel Monk?'

Alessia looked at Albert, then at me and then said, 'Well…'

ABOUT THE AUTHOR

The Cuban revolution in 1959 presented José with one of his many life challenges. José was born in La Habana; Cuba and the Cuban revolution saw him get on a plane alone at eleven years of age and arrive at an orphanage in the small town of Washington, Georgia. He did not get to see his parents again until he was eighteen years old and had graduated from high school in Atlanta, Georgia.

He studied Business Administration at Georgia State University. From university, he headed into the finance world working for the First National Bank of Atlanta (now Wells Fargo) and then moved into the financial consulting world working as a project manager, travelling to many assignments in the United States, Europe, and Australia.

José began his writing his debut novel after getting his feet wet in creative writing at a writers' group in Camden New South Wales, Australia. This gave him 'the bug' as he calls it and soon his mind created his first major character, Danny Monk.

Currently, José is working on an anthology of short stories based on his escapades at the orphanage and other funny life experiences.

When José is not writing you can find him sitting at the local shopping centre mall watching people and getting inspirations for his future characters.

When not in front of his computer working away, José is reading or spending time with his wife in long, leisurely walks around the Camden area.

Visit www.jfnodar.com.au or www.northportbooksellers.com.au for more information.

If you have any comments you wish to share about this book or any of my books, please email me at; info@jfnodar.com.au I will respond to you in 24 hours.

Thank you for your purchase!

José F. Nodar © 2022

www.ingramcontent.com/pod-product-compliance
Lightning Source LLC
Chambersburg PA
CBHW070056120726
47909CB00002B/409